To Catch an Actress

TO CATCH AN ACTRESS

and other mystery stories

Elizabeth Elwood

To Lee,
Best Wishes,
Elizabeth Elwood.

iUniverse, Inc.
New York Lincoln Shanghai

To Catch an Actress
and other mystery stories

Copyright © 2005 by Elizabeth Elwood

iUniverse books may be ordered through booksellers or by contacting:

iUniverse
2021 Pine Lake Road, Suite 100
Lincoln, NE 68512
www.iuniverse.com
1-800-Authors (1-800-288-4677)

ISBN-13: 978-0-595-34409-3 (pbk)
ISBN-13: 978-0-595-79168-2 (ebk)
ISBN-10: 0-595-34409-7 (pbk)
ISBN-10: 0-595-79168-9 (ebk)

Printed in the United States of America

CONTENTS

▼

To Catch an Actress

▼

When Aunt Maud was found bludgeoned to death in her apartment, Steven and I were the obvious suspects. Although we had what is commonly referred to as cast-iron alibis, the sergeant in charge of the case was determined to prove our guilt. In the eyes of this particular minion of the law, an actress like myself and a bureaucrat like my brother were, by virtue of our professions, skilled in the art of deception, and therefore not to be trusted. And, of course, Aunt Maud had lived frugally in spite of her wealth, and it was amazing, even to us, what the old darling had stashed away. Steven and I both inherited a lot of money. One could hardly blame the law for wanting to cast us as first and second murderers.

I could understand the bee in Sergeant Wilson's battered trilby, though I certainly couldn't comprehend his appalling outdated fashion sense—how could any self-respecting modern policeman go around looking like a refugee from *A Touch of Frost*—but I found his preoccupation very wearing. The man was like a spider. Every time a thread in his web broke, he would patiently commence weaving again. By the time the investigation had dragged into its fifth month, I was having nightmares about tarantulas in trench coats.

Throughout the ordeal, Steven was my fortress and my psychoanalyst. Just as he had removed the spiders that frightened me as a child, he removed the imaginary spiders now. He made me see that my fears were groundless, and in time he was proved right. However much he might have wanted to, Sergeant Wilson could not invent evidence. After months of harassment, the pressure eased.

Steven and I claimed our inheritance and started enjoying a considerably improved lifestyle. Aunt Maud's death appeared to have been just one more tragic example of random urban violence.

Steven left his job at city hall, and he used the knowledge acquired there and the capital from his inheritance to speculate in real estate and various other ventures. I, on the other hand, invested in an elegant new wardrobe, a red BMW, and a stylish townhouse. Steven might know how to make money, but I knew how to spend it. Thrifty Aunt Maud, bless her, had gone without a great deal during the course of her lifetime, but much as I was grateful for her restraint, I had no intention of emulating it.

Life was looking up professionally too. I had finished a run in a particularly slick production of *The Norman Conquests,* and, on the strength of my performance, had been granted an audition for a Noel Coward revival planned for the upcoming season. Blonde I may be, but I had always known I would be perfect for the role of Amanda in *Private Lives.* Steven says I have exactly the right breezy, self-centered personality for Amanda.

Steven and I saw very little of each other, not that we had seen a great deal of each other before the change in our circumstances. We got together for the annual exchange of Christmas and birthday presents, and now and then he would bring a girlfriend to see me on stage. Otherwise, we went our separate and busy ways. However, one day when there was no special occasion in the offing, I was surprised to receive a call from him.

I could tell he was anxious. Steven has a variety of voices acquired over his years in public service. This was the tone he used on nervous politicians. I dropped the script I had been studying and shifted the telephone receiver from my shoulder into my hand.

"What's happened?"

"I've had a visit from Councillor Beary."

Councillor Beary prided himself on his poll-defying durability. Steven loathed him.

"He brought his niece with him," Steven continued. "Her name is Adrian Wright. She's a journalism student, and she wants to do a story on Aunt Maud."

My heart sank. "Why didn't you send them packing?"

"I couldn't. I daren't put Beary's back up because I have a property due for rezoning. I gave them half an hour. You can do the same."

"I don't want to see them. I hate talking about the murder. Life has returned to normal. I want to keep it that way."

Steven's voice assumed the tone of icy calm he used to use on nervous senior planners.

"Half an hour, Angela. Set your watch, and stick by it. Then send them on their way and put them out of your mind."

Within the hour, my buzzer signalled the presence of someone at the door. Resigned, I opened it and found myself staring at a large, red-faced gentleman with a bushy moustache and untidy grey hair. Beside him stood a dowdy girl with beige hair and jeans that looked as if they had never been washed, but as Councillor Beary was renowned for his *bas couture,* I supposed being a slob ran in the family. Miss Wright blinked at my purple spandex pants and pink halter top. Then the watery blue eyes laboriously worked their way up to my platinum ponytail.

Her uncle barked a question.

"Angela Benson?"

My brother might be intimidated by elected officials, but I had no intention of letting this coffee-stained foghorn put me down. I put on my Lady Bracknell voice.

"You can have exactly half an hour of my time," I responded. "I'm working to a deadline."

I led them into the living-room and managed not to flinch as Miss Wright lowered her filthy jeans onto my cream chesterfield with the border of pale pink roses. I sat down and made a showy gesture of peering at my wristwatch. Miss Wright appeared unoffended. She eyed my script.

"*Private Lives*? That's a Noel Coward, isn't it? Are you playing in it?"

"I'm preparing an audition."

Councillor Beary's piggy eyes squinted at me.

"Your accent's wrong," he harrumphed. "Though if you're any good, you'll be able to change it. You're trying for Sybil, I suppose."

"Amanda, actually," I said shortly. I considered Sybil a wimpy and thoroughly second-rate part.

"Then you look wrong too," stated the councillor flatly.

I took a deep breath. "Mr. Beary," I said firmly, "I told you a moment ago, my time is limited."

Adrian Wright cut in tactfully. "Then let's begin. I'm interested in your own memories of the day of the murder."

"My memories would hardly interest you," I said civilly. "I was between acting assignments and was working at my back-up job at Holt Renfrew. I spent the entire day selling designer clothing. Everything I know about the murder is merely information I received later from Steven and Sergeant Wilson."

Miss Wright looked confused. She glanced at her uncle, but he appeared to have settled in for a nap. I recalled that Councillor Beary had a reputation for sleeping through the municipal manager's report.

"All right," Miss Wright said nervously, realizing that she was on her own. "Let's begin with your aunt. How long had she lived in that apartment?"

"Aunt Maud moved into the high-rise six months before her death. Her house in Toronto was too cumbersome, and she wanted a smaller place. Steven and I were the only family she had, and she wanted to join us in Vancouver. When an apartment in Steven's building became vacant, he rented it for her. He was always helpful and accommodating. He even bought furnishings and appliances so it would be ready for her to move in."

"Did she like it once she got here?"

"I was away on tour when she first arrived, but when I got back she seemed happy."

"Which company were you touring with?" Miss Wright asked, the watery eyes showing some animation. The girl was obviously stage-struck.

"Do you want to know about my theatrical career, or are you interested in the murder?" I demanded. "I really don't have time to chat."

It was always fun to deliver a rebuff. Adrian wilted, and feeling more cheerful, I carried on.

"As I was telling you, my aunt was independent. She enjoyed having Steven nearby, but she didn't breathe down his neck. She made friends with an elderly lady two floors down. They'd team up for lunch once a week, and they went on bus tours together."

"The police report indicates that your Aunt's habits were very regular," said Miss Wright, reading from her notes. "Up at 8:30. A leisurely breakfast while she read the newspaper. Showered and dressed at 9:45. Out and about by 10:00. Mondays and Thursdays—shopping. Wednesdays and Saturdays—laundry, followed by lunch with Mrs. March."

Miss Wright looked up from her papers.

"Did your aunt really do her own shopping and laundry?" she asked incredulously. "Surely she could have afforded household help?"

"She could have, but she didn't. She had a girl in to clean every Tuesday. Otherwise, she did for herself."

Miss Wright, who looked as if she had never made contact with a washing machine in her life, shook her head in amazement. Then she continued reading her notes.

"On Sundays, your aunt attended church. Tuesdays and Fridays were reserved for outings, but she was always home for dinner. Every evening she watched TV until ten o'clock."

"Are you sure you're Beary's niece?" I interjected, staring at her sheaves of notes. "Steven says your uncle has never read a report in his entire spell in office."

The councillor's heavy breathing remained steady. Miss Wright ignored the diversion.

"How could anyone pin down the exact time your aunt used to shower?" she asked curiously.

"High-rise apartments have thin walls. The couple in the next apartment said they could set their watches by Aunt Maud's banging pipes and Jerome Kern lyrics."

"Yet in spite of the thin walls, no one heard sounds of a struggle?"

"The next-door neighbours were shopping, the girl in the apartment below was away for the weekend, and the man upstairs was out jogging. They were the only ones who would have been likely to hear thuds or screams."

Miss Wright glanced at her notes again.

"Was your aunt on bad terms with anyone in the building?"

"Good heavens, no. She had very little to do with the other tenants, except for Mrs. March, and they got along extremely well."

"Did you ever meet any of her neighbours?" Miss Wright asked. "I had hoped to speak with them, but, except for Mrs. March, they'd all moved away."

"Mrs. March is the only one I really knew, though I did meet the young man in the suite above my aunt's. He was very interested in the case. He and Steven teamed up to talk with residents and compare notes, but neither came up with anything. The two old dears next door were devastated by the murder and were bent on moving away as soon as possible, and the girl in the suite below was one of those robust Anglo-Saxon types, always off hiking or skiing. I never met her, but I believe Steven talked with her after she'd been questioned by the police, though I suspect his interest was not so much the murder as getting an introduction. Steven has a weakness for attractive brunettes."

"Did she tell him anything?"

"No. It sounds as if she knew nothing and cared less. She moved soon after the murder, but not because of it. She was the transient type. She'd only been there a few months. Every avenue Steven followed turned into a dead end."

Miss Wright pondered the dog-eared papers balanced on her grubby knees. With alarm, I noticed a greasy stain on her pant leg. Every time she bent over, the stain inched closer to my pale pink rose petals.

Oblivious to my distress, Miss Wright continued her questions.

"Your brother was the last person known to have seen your aunt alive?"

"Yes. The night before she died. He dropped in for a short visit on his way home from shopping."

"So no one actually saw your aunt on the day of the murder?"

"That's correct."

Adrian Wright read from her notes again.

"Your aunt was killed on Saturday morning between 10:15 and 12:30. The next-door neighbours heard her shower at 9:45. Her washing was found later in the laundry room. It had gone through the wash cycle, but had not been transferred to the dryer."

"That's right. Aunt Maud was in the habit of leaving her front door open while she bobbed up and down to see to the laundry. The murderer must have gone into the apartment and been waiting for her when she came back from putting the load in the washer."

"Your brother's alibi depends on a single witness, is that correct?"

"Steven was working with a member of the museum committee at the time—a Mrs. Phoebe Partridge. She's a lady of the highest integrity and she wouldn't lie to protect my brother."

The councillor stirred.

"I know Phoebe Partridge," he mused. "Irritating old bat, but scrupulously honest."

He nodded, closed his eyes, and leaned back, causing my Queen Anne chair to creak ominously. Adrian Wright continued with her questions.

"Why was your brother working on a Saturday?"

"He was a volunteer with the Village Museum. He and Mrs. Partridge had arranged to spend two or three hours on the weekend to complete a report for the board. Mrs. Partridge agreed to work at Steven's apartment because he had the computer there."

"What time did she arrive?"

"Around ten, I believe. Just after Steven got back from the pool."

"The pool?"

"Steven always swam at nine o'clock on Saturdays. There were two or three regulars, and they all saw him at the pool. After his swim, he returned to his apartment, changed, and went back to the lobby to meet Mrs. Partridge."

"Why didn't he just buzz her in?"

Councillor Beary came to life with a loud snort and made both of us jump.

"I know the answer to that," he boomed. "Phoebe Partridge hates high-rises, right? I bet she was terrified of riding up and down in the elevator by herself."

"If you know all the answers," I said tartly, "then why are we conducting this interview?"

Beary was impervious to sarcasm. Steven used to say he had a rhino hide to deal with the public and a rhino horn to deal with the civil service.

"I'm actually amazed," he went on, "that your brother could persuade Phoebe Partridge to ride in an elevator to the fourteenth floor of a high-rise. Phoebe the Phobic. It's inconceivable."

"Well, he did. It's all on record."

"Astounding," reiterated Beary. "Benson could never persuade me to do anything in council."

"Steven can be extremely charming and convincing when he wants to be," I said. "Besides, Mrs. Partridge trusts him."

"Ah, well, there you are. I never found him charming or convincing, but then, I never trusted him either."

I ignored this flagrant rudeness and continued my story.

"Soon after Mrs. Partridge and Steven got back to his apartment, the phone rang. Aunt Maud wanted Steven to return a cookbook he'd borrowed as she was making something special for Mrs. March's lunch. Steven was downloading files on the computer, so he sent the book down with Mrs. Partridge."

"Now, here's a discrepancy," said Beary. "Mrs. Partridge wouldn't have gone in the elevator alone. Even your charming brother couldn't have been that persuasive."

"Steven directed her down the stairs," I said coldly. He nodded and the piggy eyes closed once more. Miss Wright continued her questions.

"Your aunt's apartment was directly below your brother's?"

"Not quite. Steven's apartment was 1401. Aunt Maud's was 1101. But they were both tucked at the end of the hall opposite the stairwell door. And you know what those apartment towers are like—very short flights of stairs. It was easy to go back and forth between the suites."

"But when Mrs. Partridge got to 1101, your aunt had already left to do the laundry?"

"Yes."

"Is there any chance that Mrs. Partridge went to the wrong apartment?"

"None whatsoever. There was a note on the door saying the suite was unlocked and to leave the book on the kitchen counter."

I noticed a glimmer of Miss Marple-like enthusiasm on Adrian's dog-like face. I took pleasure in crushing it.

"No," I said. "The note wasn't a forgery. Handwriting experts said it was written by my aunt. Besides, the police took Mrs. Partridge down to the apartment after the murder. In spite of the blood and disarray, Mrs. Partridge recognized the place. She even recognized the paperweight that had been used to kill my aunt. It was lying beside the body, but it had been on the hall table earlier on."

"So when Mrs. Partridge delivered the book, no one was in sight and the place was neat and orderly."

"Yes. She set the book on the counter, and returned to Steven's apartment. Then she and Steven worked steadily until 12:30, when the building manager called to tell Steven what had happened."

"Who discovered the body?"

"Mrs. March, when she arrived for her lunch date with Aunt Maud. You know," I added, looking at my watch, "I really don't know what you hope to achieve. The police were incredibly thorough. If they came up with nothing, you won't find anything new, especially following a cold trail."

Miss Wright frowned.

"I don't think there is anything new to come up with," she said. "The facts are before us and the solution is there, but nobody has analyzed the information correctly."

"The information has been analyzed to death," I said coldly, allowing my polite veneer to slip momentarily. "Personally, I'm sick of going over it."

Councillor Beary's eyes opened. They glinted like two shiny black beetles.

"People with perfect motives and perfect alibis should be wary of stifling further detective work," he barked. "That kind of attitude makes people suspicious."

I looked him straight in the eye and delivered one of Amanda's better lines.

"That was very rude. I think you had better go away somewhere."

Their half-hour was up anyway.

*   *   *   *

Three months later, I had forgotten Miss Wright and her tedious uncle. I had won my leading role, my co-stars were dynamite, my director was a dream, and the producer was not only efficient, but also incredibly good-natured. It was a production made in Heaven. Even my understudy was a bonus. Steven's latest girlfriend was a pretty English brunette, and at his urging, I had wangled her a job understudying the two female roles. She followed me about like a little dog, pandering to my every whim and listening with adoration to my theatrical anecdotes. I had never had a pet slave before, and Susan's presence greatly enhanced the run of the show.

By closing night, I was floating miles above cloud nine. The play had gone perfectly and the future looked rosy. Flocks of admirers had promenaded through my dressing-room and finally, the last stragglers were shepherded out. A deeply satisfying peace descended.

Then came the knock at the door. It was Sergeant Wilson, and I could tell he had not come to praise my performance.

He wasted no time on preliminaries.

"I have some bad news for you, Miss Benson," he said quietly. "Your brother has been arrested."

My soul plummeted through cloud nine and rocketed to earth, and all my earlier feelings for Sergeant Wilson rushed to the surface. The resulting collision made my head swim. Finally, I found my voice.

"I don't understand. Why?"

"Instead of being content at getting away with murder, your brother has been finding a variety of ways, not all legal, to increase his inheritance. A policewoman who was working on a drug case made a breakthrough when she followed a lead to several stores where your brother does business. A pattern emerged that connected your brother and a dark-haired English girl who had made identical purchases at the same stores."

Sergeant Wilson fixed me with a singularly unpleasant stare.

"No," I gasped. "There must be some mistake."

How many times had I delivered that line in predictable mystery dramas, and yet suddenly the words were not trite anymore. Genuine distress removed the staleness from the most hackneyed script.

Sergeant Wilson continued as if I had not spoken.

"Premeditation on a grand scale," he said. "Your brother bought furnishings and accessories for your aunt's apartment, and passed on an inventory to his accomplice so that she could go out and purchase identical items to furnish the suite directly below. He only had to allow a couple of days to alter the look of the suite after your aunt's death, and prior to the girl downstairs giving notice. It wouldn't have done for the manager to have noticed the resemblance when she was bringing prospective renters to see the suite."

Sergeant Wilson droned on. My ears were ringing, yet I heard every word with deadly clarity.

"Once we realized there were two identical apartments, it was easy to break your brother's alibi."

"I don't understand. His alibi still depends on Mrs. Partridge, and she wouldn't lie."

"Mrs. Partridge didn't lie. Your brother murdered your aunt before Mrs. Partridge arrived. When he visited your aunt the previous night, he slipped the contents of her laundry basket into his shopping bag and closed the lid of the basket so she wouldn't notice. Then, the next morning, he put her washing on. The laundry room is in the basement, right next to the pool. He left the pool by 9:40, but instead of going back to his own place, he went to your aunt's apartment. He must have invented some kind of emergency, something that would make your aunt change her routine and dress hurriedly."

Suddenly galvanized by the force of the sergeant's attack, I interjected with force.

"This is ridiculous. Steven couldn't have killed Aunt Maud. There was blood everywhere. He'd have got it on his robe. And his fingerprints would have been found on the paperweight."

"Your brother had gloves in the pocket of his robe," said Sergeant Wilson. "When your aunt's back was turned, he slipped off his robe and thongs before he struck the first blow."

I put my hands over my ears. I didn't want to hear the details of what Steven had done. As a child, I had never watched when he got rid of spiders. I had always had the feeling he enjoyed disposing of them. I had never minded Steven's results, but I didn't want to hear about his methods. But Sergeant Wilson's voice penetrated no matter how hard I tried to block it out.

"Your brother cold-bloodedly beat your aunt to death and created the signs of a struggle. Then he showered in her bathroom and gave a horribly appropriate falsetto rendition of *Smoke Gets in Your Eyes*. He must share something of your histrionic talent. As he left the apartment, he put the note on the door, making sure it covered the door number."

"But the note was authentic. Your experts said so."

"Yes. It had been written by your aunt on an earlier occasion. Your brother kept it stashed away until he needed it. He also copied it, as he needed a duplicate to cover the number on suite 1001. Once he'd set the notes in place, he hurried back to his own apartment and got dressed just before Mrs. Partridge arrived. His wet hair would have been explained by the fact that he'd been swimming. And the phone call about the cookbook was in actual fact a call from your brother's accomplice."

Transfixed, I gazed into Sergeant Wilson's steely blue eyes. As I stared at him, I suddenly realized who his mysterious undercover policewoman was.

"The journalism student! Adrian Wright. She isn't Councillor Beary's niece at all. She's working for you."

"Actually she is the councillor's niece," said Sergeant Wilson, "but she also happens to be a policewoman. A very good one too. She figured out how the murder was done, and she also established the identity of the girl downstairs. She suggested that if I came here tonight I would see the dark-haired English girl I'd interviewed after the murder."

"There's only one dark-haired English girl working on this production," I said, "and she only got the job because she was Steven's girlfriend..." I paused, the significance of the words striking me with the force of a thunderbolt. I rose to my feet and clutched my forehead in my hands. Sergeant Wilson looked up, startled at my stricken expression.

"Susan!" I gasped. "They only pretended to meet after the murder. They must have known each other all along. They must have planned the whole thing."

I sank down again. I felt dizzy, and my heart was pounding. There was no response from Sergeant Wilson, and suddenly frightened by his silence, I glanced up at him. He looked almost amused.

"Ever the actress," he said. Mesmerized, I noticed the shadows cast by the lights of my make-up mirror hitting the rim of the sergeant's hat and the point of his collar. It was as if a giant black spider was hanging on the wall.

"No, Miss Benson," Sergeant Wilson continued. "Your understudy is not a suspect in this case."

His steely blue eyes took in the dark wig standing on the counter beside the sticks of Tan No. 2.

"You gave an admirable performance tonight, Miss Benson," he said. "You make a stunning brunette, and you do an impeccable English accent."

"Wigs and dialects are an actress's stock in trade."

"Exactly," he said smoothly. "The minute you came on stage, I knew I'd seen you somewhere before. When I heard the voice, I knew immediately. *You* were the girl downstairs. You really deserve an Oscar. It's quite an achievement to sustain a performance on and off over a period of over six months."

"This is beyond belief. You're simply theorizing."

"Not at all, Miss Benson. When Miss Wright and her uncle came to see you, you didn't tell them anything new about the murder," said Sergeant Wilson, "but you did give them several useful pieces of information. They noticed that you talked with a great deal of familiarity about the girl downstairs, even though you were supposed never to have met her, and you also revealed the fact that the girl downstairs moved in around the same time as your aunt and left within weeks of her death. You created a neat diversion when Miss Wright asked you about the tour you were on at the time your aunt moved into the tower. And before your visitors left, you delivered a line in a perfect English accent. Councillor Beary had a sudden hunch, and he suggested that his niece follow it up. That's why she started inquiring about your brother's purchases for your aunt's apartment."

"How does any of this prove I was the girl downstairs?"

"It doesn't prove it."

"Then it's all speculation. Over the years, Steven has had a whole string of girlfriends with English accents. Susan is the latest, but she follows a predictable pattern. She, or any of the rest of them could have been the girl downstairs."

"Believe me, Miss Benson, I have talked extensively with Susan. She isn't the girl downstairs. However, she's full of interesting information."

I have never liked understudies. I glowered at the sergeant and he dug the knife a little deeper.

"You'd be amazed the things you told Susan," he said. "You gave her consumer tips which helped us follow up your brother's purchases, but you also told her about your touring experience. All your tours have been with the Market Square Players, yet when we checked with the troupe, it turned out you were not working with them when your aunt moved to Vancouver. We soon realized your play-acting was closer to home. You were spending the month getting established as the resident of the lower suite."

I felt sick. The beautiful clothes, the car, the townhouse, and my theatrical success all appeared to be sliding away from me. It had been such a wonderful plan. How dare this horrible man ruin everything for us!

I noticed the sergeant's sly smile, and suddenly I realized how he had trapped us.

"Susan!" I said. "She made friends with Steven deliberately. She's another of your plants!"

"Not exactly," said Sergeant Wilson. "That comment you made about wigs and dialects being an actress's stock in trade is very true. You see Adrian Wright and Susan are one and the same person. We set an actress to catch an actress. Personally, I found all the performances remarkable."

Fury gave me strength. I glared at the sergeant and issued one last challenge.

"It's a clever theory," I snarled, "but how could we possibly have fooled a smart lady like Mrs. Partridge? Even with notes over the door numbers and identical suites, the woman could count. How could Steven have tricked her into going down an extra flight of stairs?"

"Your brother selected Mrs. Partridge for a very special reason, Miss Benson. Remember her aversion to apartment towers. That's what finally tipped me off. A person who doesn't frequent high-rises wouldn't be aware of the fact that in the interests of renting all the suites, developers always cater to people who might be superstitious."

I looked at him blankly. I'd never understood the intricacies of Steven's plan. I'd simply played my role as the girl in #1001, and placed the necessary phone call on the day of the murder.

Sergeant Wilson looked more spider-like than ever.

"When numbering the rooms on each floor," he said smugly, "the builders always skip floor number 13."

FUGUE FOR TWO FERRARIS

▼

Philippa Beary was bored. She looked across the table at her companion's handsome face and wondered if his mouth would ever stop moving. Conrad Waverley was telling her something about his car, or rather something else about his car. Philippa found it hard to believe she had not heard everything there was to say about Conrad's red Ferrari on the drive to Seattle, but evidently there must be more, for Conrad was still gesticulating and uttering something about carburetors.

Still, thought Philippa, car talk was preferable to Conrad's only other topic of interest. He appeared to have given up trying to turn their day trip to the Seattle Opera into a dirty weekend, having ruined an enchanting matinée of *Madama Butterfly* with heavy breathing and creeping hands. Conrad and Pinkerton had a lot in common, Philippa decided. However, it was her own fault for accepting a date with someone she barely knew just because he had devastating good looks and drove a spectacular car.

On the plus side, Conrad was good-natured. He seemed unoffended by the tongue-lashing he had received at the end of the opera, and had amiably offered to buy Philippa dinner *en route* to the border. Philippa had been a little nervous at Conrad's choice for a post-opera meal, for once out of Seattle, he had wheeled off the highway and pulled up at the Holiday Inn. However, the Inn turned out to have a luxurious dining-room and throughout the meal Conrad had managed to avoid a single reference to sex, so she assumed her resistance had finally sunk in.

Conrad burbled on. Smiling and nodding whenever he paused for breath, Philippa leaned back in her huge rattan chair and entertained herself by studying the decor. The wall directly opposite her ran the width of the restaurant and sported a mural of golden sands, a turquoise ocean, and an unblemished expanse of sky in a brilliant shade of blue that never formed part of the scenery of the Northwest Coast. *If I decide to pursue a career in opera,* Philippa mused, *this is probably as close to a Hawaiian holiday as I'll ever get.* Beside her was a rock pool surrounded by palm trees and edged with exotic flowers. A waterfall splashed into the far end, its steady drone providing a complementary background for Conrad's monologue.

Their waitress, who had flirted outrageously with Conrad throughout the meal, approached with coffee. Ignoring Philippa, she gave Conrad a dazzling smile.

"Coffee, Pippy?" Conrad asked Philippa.

Philippa shuddered.

"It's Philippa," she said tartly. "I'm not a grapefruit. And I really think we should get going. We have a three hour drive ahead of us."

Conrad leered.

"You're really bent on heading back? The Inn is a great place to spend a weekend."

"No, Conrad."

"If I promise to behave myself?"

"No, Conrad."

"Scout's honour?"

"No, Conrad. And since when were you a boy scout?"

"Does that mean you'd like your bill?" chirped the waitress. Philippa gave a glacial nod. The waitress shrugged, raised her eyebrows at Conrad, and removed her coffee pot. Philippa picked up her purse and pulled out a twenty-dollar bill. She had no desire to increase her obligation to Conrad. But he waved the money away and pulled out his own wallet. Seeing that he was determined to pay, Philippa slipped away to the washroom.

The restrooms were in a corridor adjacent to the lobby, and as Philippa returned, she rounded the corner and almost collided with a well-dressed man carrying a suitcase. He was short and slight, barely taller than she was, but very good-looking. However, the effect was ruined by the lascivious expression on his face as they dodged around each other.

"Too bad we didn't make contact when I checked in last night," he said lecherously, giving her an outrageous wink as he moved towards the exit.

Philippa stormed back to the table, grabbed her coat, and glowered at Conrad. He blinked, looked bewildered, and sheepishly followed her out of the hotel.

When they emerged into the brilliant sunlight of the parking lot, Conrad suddenly perked up and pointed toward the exit. A gleaming, silver-grey Ferrari with B.C. licence plates was pulling onto the road. It was driven by the lecher from the lobby, now wearing a jazzy motoring cap and dark glasses.

"Nice rig," said Conrad.

"Do you think so? He looks like something out of the post-war British movies that my grandparents used to watch."

Seeing Philippa standing by Conrad's red Ferrari, the driver tooted a fanfare on his horn and waved cheerily.

"I meant the car," said Conrad. "It's a beauty," he enthused, as he held the passenger door open for Philippa. "And there's nothing wrong with the driver having a classic look. You'd hardly expect him to wear a T-shirt and a backwards baseball cap. It's a question of status."

"Must be hard for him to maintain his lofty status when he's such a shrimp," said Philippa acerbically.

"Napoleon was a shrimp," Conrad pointed out. "Anyway," he added, leering, "you know what they say about small men."

"I don't know, and I don't want to. Do shut up, Conrad."

"I was merely trying to point out that there's something very special about Ferraris, and," he preened, "the people who drive them."

"There sure is," snapped Philippa, and plopped herself into the passenger seat.

*   *   *   *

Conrad talked non-stop as they flew up Interstate 5. The combination of technical jargon spewing from the driver and the medley of great soprano arias pouring forth from the CD player was particularly irritating, especially as Conrad seemed to be dominating the duet, in pace as well as volume. Sutherland's high-speed coloratura was nothing compared to the tempo Conrad was setting. Philippa gritted her teeth as he passed every car in sight, zooming in and out of the left-hand lane with a cavalier abandon that made her weak at the knees. It was probably Conrad's theory of seduction, she decided, to reduce a girl to a condition of nervous vulnerability, so that at the end of a drive, she would be in no state to resist his advances.

A sign announcing that Vancouver, British Columbia, was 120 tortuous miles away whipped by with the speed of light. Feeling her neck muscles going into spasm, Philippa forced herself to unclench her fists and eased her head carefully back against the headrest. Out of the corner of her eye, she noticed a single-engine Cessna taking off from a small airstrip that bisected the fields to the right of the road.

"Don't they patrol the freeway with helicopters?" she asked hopefully.

"Only in California," said Conrad, stepping on the gas and cutting in front of a Winnebago. Don't you love the feeling of speed," he crowed. "It makes one feel tremendously dashing. Almost piratical. I should have definitely been a buccaneer if I'd lived in the old days."

Philippa refrained from comment.

As they closed in on the bumper of a Ford Expedition, Philippa braced herself. With two inches to spare, Conrad slid the Ferrari into the passing lane and roared by the SUV. Philippa closed her eyes, but they flipped open again at a whoop from Conrad.

"Look, there he is, up ahead!"

Philippa saw the silver-grey Ferrari a few car-lengths ahead. Conrad stepped on the gas and the car lunged forward. Within seconds they had pulled level with the other car. Conrad blasted his horn, waved, and pulled ahead.

The next quarter hour was a nightmare of blaring horns and the blur of coloured metal. Philippa would not have repeated it for a million dollars. Everett came and went in seconds, the boats in Puget Sound racing backwards and disappearing from view in a flash. Philippa found herself starting to pray.

The traffic became heavier after the Snohomish River crossing, and Conrad was momentarily becalmed behind an ancient Dodge Station Wagon, loaded to capacity with two parents, four children, and a large German Shepherd wedged in the rear compartment between a pile of suitcases and an ice cooler. A Nissan occupied the right-hand lane, and both cars remained aggravatingly parallel. Muttering epithets about rust buckets, Conrad tailgated the wagon, and Philippa found herself eye to eye with the dog that stared balefully at them through the rear window. The tips of its pointed ears were bent against the car roof, and as Conrad continued to ride the rear bumper, the dog began to puff.

Seeing the silver-grey Ferrari hovering in his rear view mirror, Conrad leaned on the horn. The German Shepherd erupted into barks, distracting him for an instant, and he missed taking advantage of the space that materialized in the right lane as the Nissan exited the freeway. In the second he delayed, the silver-grey

Ferrari darted ahead, passing on the right, and cut back into the center lane to avoid a transport trailer in the curb lane.

Conrad's eyes narrowed and he tightened his grip on the steering wheel.

"Hold on," he said.

The transport trailer loomed beside them. Philippa gripped the armrests, clenched her teeth and intensified her pleas to the Almighty. Conrad switched lanes, manoeuvring the Ferrari through a one-car-width gap between the trailer and the station wagon; then he shot up the right lane, catching his opponent at the next overpass.

Philippa's prayers were not answered until they approached Lakewood, where to her immense relief, the silver-grey Ferrari veered into the exit lane and zoomed down the ramp. Philippa added an addendum to her prayer, that the driver be stopping for food, and not merely gas. She suddenly found that her legs were aching badly. She had been braking far more often than Conrad during the past fifteen minutes.

Having lost the challenge of his automotive peer, Conrad slowed to a mere 75 mph. In spite of the fact that they were still gliding by adjacent motorists, the car felt almost at a standstill. Philippa leaned back and began to relax. Even Conrad's running commentary on the operations of his machine had ceased to irritate her. She selectively tuned her ear to mute his monologue and focused on the sounds coming from the dashboard. The glorious tones of Renee Fleming singing Rusalka's *Song to the Moon,* combined with the bright summer weather, was exhilarating, and if one managed to reach a state of suspended indifference, the drive might almost be enjoyable. She gazed benevolently at a cluster of cows lying on the grass, enjoying the late-afternoon sun. Their field was bordered by a row of alder trees and a fast-running creek that raced toward the highway and disappeared, presumably into a culvert, at the edge of the road. In the adjacent field, two horses stood, swishing their tails, in front of a red barn, while a pair of collies frolicked, forming a whirling donut as they nipped at each other's hindquarters. In the distance, Mount Baker gleamed golden and majestic.

Rural tranquility. Bliss, thought Philippa.

Her peace lasted exactly sixteen minutes. As they passed the Mount Vernon exit, she was admiring the soaring legato line of Leontyne Price's *Aida,* when suddenly *Ritorna Vincitor* acquired an extra trumpet obbligato. Groaning inwardly, for she recognized the familiar fanfare, Philippa looked up to see the silver-grey Ferrari pull alongside. The driver's grin was even wider than before, and it was easy to see why. He had acquired a companion. A flashy blonde sat in the passenger seat. Philippa caught a glimpse of a round face with a California tan, a short punk hairdo, long earrings, and bright lipstick covering a pouty mouth. She had time to notice that the girl wore a black leather jacket. Madonna before she discovered Motherhood, Philippa decided. Then the car pulled ahead and her view was gone.

"Wow!" said Conrad, approvingly. "How did he manage that?"

"Maybe she came with the gas coupons," Philippa said sourly.

"Now, Pippy, don't pout. Let's face it, a good-looking guy with a fast car has a pretty easy time finding girls. After all, you hardly knew me, but you agreed to come on this date."

"One lives and learns," said Philippa.

Conrad stepped on the gas and pulled into the passing lane. Philippa closed her eyes and recommenced her prayers.

However, the next time they passed the grey Ferrari, there was very little reaction from the driver of the other vehicle. He seemed more preoccupied with his passenger. Without the stimulus of competition, Conrad pulled ahead and slid back into the right lane. He glanced in the rear view mirror and smiled.

"He's doing OK, lucky devil. Friendly girl he's picked up."

"How can he change gears with her sitting there?" mused Philippa, genuinely curious.

Conrad's smile became lecherous.

"It can be done," he said. "Want me to demonstrate?"

"Thank you, no," snapped Philippa, and looked straight ahead.

Conrad kept ahead of the grey Ferrari and periodically checked his rear view mirror. Philippa did not like the smile on his face, or the fact that he had started to hum.

Conrad took another glance in the mirror.

"I'd say someone is getting raunchy," he chuckled.

More like some-two, thought Philippa. She glued her knees together and leaned toward the passenger door. She stared resolutely at the rural panorama of mountains and streams. It was still very light, but dramatic shadows were beginning to form dark green stripes on the mountainsides. As they roared up a steep incline, Philippa noticed a rest stop on the right hand side. It was a particularly picturesque spot, with a picnic area set beside a sparkling creek, and a small green surrounded by a grove of cedar trees. There were very few cars in the parking area, although one family was eating at a picnic bench while a dog loped about the table.

Conrad crowed.

"I knew it. There they go. Lucky beggar."

Philippa looked through the rear window and saw the grey Ferrari glide off the freeway into the rest stop. Then, before she could blink, the freeway curved and the car was lost to view.

"Maybe she needed to use the washroom," said Philippa.

"Be reasonable, Pippy," said Conrad. "He only picked her up forty-five minutes ago. You know as well as I do what they've stopped for."

"Drive, Conrad," said Philippa. "Put your mind out of gear, and drive."

Obediently, Conrad concentrated on his driving. Peace descended for a while, but as they neared Bellingham, Conrad started to look reflective again.

"I tell you what," he said suddenly. "Why don't we detour into Bellingham for an hour. It's a beautiful evening and it's early yet. Seems a waste not to look around a bit while we're across the border. You might even want to do some shopping."

"I suppose there are some nice motels in Bellingham," Philippa said reflectively.

Conrad looked hopeful.

"There certainly are," he said. "Shall we turn off? The exit is coming up just ahead."

"Absolutely not," snapped Philippa.

"Oh, come on, Pippy. You're enough to try a saint. Couldn't you even go for dessert and coffee?"

Philippa weakened. Having refused coffee after dinner she was beginning to feel a craving for caffeine and chocolate.

"I tell you what," she said suddenly, "there's a steakhouse on the other side of Bellingham, and it's right by the freeway. You can't miss it. There's a McDonald's and an Exxon Station, and the restaurant is directly opposite." She refrained from adding that there were no overnight accommodations within miles of the restaurant. "Why don't we stop there for coffee," she suggested. "That would be a nice break before the rest of the drive."

Conrad beamed.

"You're on," he said and roared past the Bellingham exit.

Fifteen minutes later, they were ensconced in a dark glass booth. The tables in the restaurant were made of heavy wood and surrounded by black leather-upholstered benches, but the back of each seat abutted a smoked plexiglass divider, so the overall effect was of a separate room for each diner. Wrought iron lanterns hung from the ceiling of each enclosure, but as they emitted more of a gentle glow than actual light, Philippa had to hold her menu at eye level in order to be able to read it.

"This is very cozy," Conrad said approvingly, sliding round the bench so that he could sit beside Philippa. He transferred his cutlery to his new location, moved the square ornamental candle so the light glimmered on their water glasses, and sighed contentedly. The humour of the situation struck Philippa suddenly, and she started to laugh. Conrad beamed hopefully, and before long, they had given their order to a motherly waitress, who very quickly dispatched two gigantic sundaes to their table and watched with approval as they tucked in enthusiastically. Between mouthfuls, Conrad talked about cars, but Philippa was by now immune, and she waded through her dessert with genuine enjoyment. When the last mouthful of chocolate sauce and the last drop of coffee were gone, she looked at her watch and was amazed to see it was close to eight o'clock. They had been at the restaurant for almost an hour.

Leaving Conrad to settle the bill, Philippa went to wait outside. The evening was still bright and the fresh air was exhilarating. Sunlight glinted on the mountaintops, rising far in the distance above the McDonald's golden arches, and in the foreground, a tall row of stately birches lined the entrance road. As Philippa watched the procession of cars moving in and out of the parking area, the station wagon that had almost proved Conrad's nemesis at the Snohomish River pulled into a space at the far end of the lot. The doors flew open and the family members piled out of the car and trooped into McDonald's, not even turning to spare a glance for the German Shepherd, who looked even more baleful at being abandoned. Philippa hoped that some remnants of hamburger buns and McNuggets would find their way back to the car when his people returned.

Vehicles continued to move in and out of the lot, and suddenly, with a start, Philippa recognized a familiar car pulling alongside the gas pumps at the far end of the complex. She also recognized the figure in the motoring cap that hopped out of the car and loped into the gas station.

He came out a moment later and returned to his car. The Ferrari purred toward the steakhouse and Philippa cringed against the wall, but she need not have worried. The driver seemed preoccupied and he did not look at her. Philippa noticed he was opening a package of gum, presumably the reason for the stop. She was surprised to see that he was now alone in the car. The Ferrari headed for the freeway entrance and Philippa hoped fervently that it would get so far ahead that Conrad would not be able to catch it.

A moment later, Conrad reappeared, and soon they were gliding along the freeway in the direction of the Canada/U.S. border. The evening was still light and the sun very bright in patches. With the Pacific Ocean to their left, the mountains of British Columbia beckoning in front of them, Leona Mitchell singing *Rondine,* and the sense of repletion that came with a full stomach, Philippa felt tranquil, contented and proof against any irritant Conrad could offer.

A green road sign flashed by indicating that Blaine was ten miles ahead, and as they passed it they saw the grey Ferrari ahead of them in the curb lane. It was moving swiftly, but not with the manic speed of the early afternoon. Conrad pulled alongside, blasted his horn and waved. The driver raised his hand and gave an answering toot, but the gesture lacked exuberance. Philippa presumed the driver was subdued because his passenger was no longer with him.

"Obviously not going for a second round," said Conrad, pulling back once he realized the driver was not to be goaded into another race. "Pouting because he's lost his dolly."

Philippa frowned.

"Don't you think it's odd?" she said suddenly.

"Why odd?" said Conrad. "Maybe they didn't hit it off."

"He only picked her up in Everett, and she must have been hitching a ride somewhere. Why would she let herself get ditched at a rest stop miles from anywhere?"

"Perhaps he dropped her at Bellingham."

"He didn't have time to drive into Bellingham, and besides, I'm sure he didn't stop at any towns since we last saw him."

"How can you possibly know that?"

"Because I saw him outside the steakhouse. He whipped off the freeway to buy a pack of gum. If he stopped anywhere else to drop the girl, he'd have bought his gum there."

Conrad wrinkled his nose in distaste.

"Gum!" he said. "Very classless. No wonder he didn't make it with the girl."

"She wasn't exactly a classy girl," said Philippa. "And we don't know that he didn't make it. I'd say the time they stayed at that rest stop would suggest they had ample time to 'make it'."

"So they had a fight and she hitched a ride with someone else."

"It's possible," said Philippa. "But it's not that easy to get people to give you rides from a family rest stop."

"What are you suggesting?" said Conrad.

"I'm suggesting that any girl who lets herself be picked up on Interstate 5 and takes off for the border with a complete stranger is asking for trouble."

"You're not suggesting she's lying in the woods, raped and murdered, are you?" Conrad sounded shocked. "Ferrari drivers don't do that sort of thing."

"The wealthy classes have their share of homicidal sex maniacs," Philippa said tartly.

"I have been a model of self-control today," Conrad said with dignity.

Philippa grinned.

"Yes, you have," she agreed. "Conrad, a thought occurs to me. Could you fall back somehow and get level with that car again?"

Conrad frowned.

"I don't want to get arrested for blocking the passing lane," he said.

"Conrad, if you haven't been arrested today for every other highway infraction in the book, then you're not likely to be arrested for that. Please. Just for a moment."

Obligingly Conrad slowed down, and soon other cars began to pull out and pass him. Conrad looked mortified, but dutifully he watched the needle and held the car at 55 mph. Before long, he looked in his mirror and nodded.

"There he is," he said.

He waited until two more cars had passed him. Then, when the grey Ferrari was on his tail, he pulled into the left lane and slowed until the car was alongside. Philippa peered at the car and driver, trying to see some evidence of the girl or sign of disarray in the car. Nothing appeared abnormal. The driver of the grey Ferrari suddenly noticed them, and he waved and gave a friendly toot.

"OK?" Conrad asked Philippa.

Philippa nodded.

Conrad heaved a sigh of relief. He blasted the horn, waved back at the other driver, and trod on the gas. The red Ferrari leapt forward, and within seconds, the other car was a diminishing speck in the rear window. Conrad did not reduce speed until the gleaming white Peace Arch loomed before them, whereupon he allowed the car to crawl sedately through the park and come to a halt in the shortest line at Canadian Customs.

"This doesn't look too bad," said Conrad. "As long as we don't get stuck behind any suspected terrorists, we should move fairly quickly."

"Nothing moves quickly at the border these days."

"At least the current exchange rate has reduced the cross-border shoppers," Conrad said sanctimoniously. "Unpatriotic lot."

"Everyone doesn't have your money, Conrad," said Philippa. "Besides, a Ferrari isn't exactly your average Canadian model."

"All right, I get your point. Now, here we go. Smile sweetly at the officer and we'll be through in a jiffy."

"Conrad, we've only been to the opera. We're hardly likely to be hauled in and strip-searched."

An impassive face topped by a blue cap loomed in the driver's window and fixed them both with a draconian stare. Conrad answered the terse questions with a friendly smile and the customs officer, having ascertained that Philippa was not traveling under duress, visibly thawed. He was about to wave them ahead, when suddenly Philippa sat up straight.

"Just a minute," she burst out. "Conrad, pull in over there. I'll be back in a moment."

She leapt out of the car and ran into the customs building. Conrad sat, bemused. Five minutes later, Philippa had still not returned. Several more minutes slipped by. Then Conrad glanced in his rear view mirror and suddenly noticed a flurry of action behind him. The grey Ferrari had been pulled over, and the driver was being led, suitcase in hand, into the customs building.

*   *   *   *

Ten minutes later, Philippa reappeared. She walked briskly along the sidewalk that adjoined the brick building; then darted across the lanes of traffic to reach the Ferrari. She hopped into the car and nodded to Conrad to proceed.

"What was that all about?" Conrad asked her as they joined the line of traffic heading for Vancouver.

"Something that often occurs at the border," said Philippa. "A drug bust."

Conrad turned and stared at her.

"Drugs!"

"Cocaine, to be precise. In the suitcase."

"Good God! Who was he?"

"A man called David Morton, according to his driver's licence. And I'm afraid the police *are* going to find a body in the woods when they get back to the rest stop."

Conrad gulped.

"You mean he murdered her?"

"Not quite," said Philippa. "She murdered him."

Conrad paled and looked very upset.

"That pretty girl murdered the driver of that beautiful car!"

"Yes. Probably after they'd gone in the woods to 'make it', as you so charmingly put it. What a convenient way to get him to take off his clothes. Then once she'd killed him, she scrubbed her face clean, put on his clothes, and with that cap and dark glasses, became a quite reasonable facsimile of David Morton for the purposes she needed, which was to get herself and the cocaine across the border. Once in Canada, she'd have changed into her own things, abandoned the car, and David Morton would have disappeared without a trace."

"But to kill him! Why kill him?"

"I suppose he wasn't willing to take her across the border. Perhaps he was suspicious of her reasons for going to Vancouver. So she killed him and took his car."

"But that's...that's..."

"Piratical?" Philippa smiled at Conrad's expression. "I imagine there's quite a few modern day privateers that hang around Interstate 5," she continued, "waiting to find someone with a B.C. licence plate who is easy to pick up."

Conrad shuddered.

"You may not believe it, but I've picked up girls in the past."

Philippa grinned.

"Oh, I believe it," she said.

Conrad got a grip on himself, and pulled into the passing lane. After a few minutes of concentrating on his beloved car, he started to look more like himself.

"But how did you guess?" he asked suddenly. "Whatever made you suspicious?"

"Think, Conrad."

"Ah! The gum. Quite out of character."

"Yes, but it was more than that. It suddenly occurred to me that there was a fundamental difference in the behaviour of the Ferrari's driver after he had stopped at the rest area."

"He didn't drive as fast?"

"No. That didn't bother me. There are lots of reasons why people slow down. He could have been tired, or he might have got a ticket...or he might have simply been fed up after a fight with the girl."

"Then what was the difference you noticed?"

"Lechery, Conrad. Simple lechery. Or rather, the lack of it."

"I can't imagine what you mean," said Conrad.

Philippa raised her eyes heavenward.

"Didn't you notice?" she said.

"Notice what?"

Philippa smiled.

"For the last part of the journey," she said, "the driver was waving at you, not me."

THE DEATH OF TURANDOT

▼

Philippa Beary made her professional opera debut at the age of twenty. When the curtain rose, she was downstage centre, but as she was a mere Chinese peasant grovelling at the steps of the Imperial Palace, even her own mother was unable to recognize the aspect she presented to the audience. Still, a professional debut is a professional debut, even in the chorus of a minor-league company, and therefore she considered the production memorable.

The production was memorable for one other reason, for it marked the final performance of the most exciting soprano of the decade. Of course, a great number of people had threatened to murder Lisa Metz over the years, but no one had ever taken the threats seriously. Therefore, everyone was stunned and shocked when five minutes after Lisa took her final bow, she was found stabbed to death in her dressing room.

Lisa Metz, like Callas, became a legend in her own time. She had the glamorous blonde beauty of a Gabor, the histrionic talents of a Garbo, and the promotional flair of Madonna. She also possessed a dramatic voice that was capable of finding its way around a spectacular variety of roles in the soprano repertoire. Unfortunately, although intelligent, she was also flamboyant and impatient, and her rapid ascent to stardom was made at the expense of technical training.

As a young singer born on the wrong side of the Berlin Wall—for Lisa was a cut-throat capitalist if there ever was one—she snatched her opportunity when she met a peripatetic millionaire from New York. Without a qualm, she detached him from his wife and family, and in so doing acquired both a rich husband and an American visa. His money and connections, combined with her own impressive talents, soon won her an early debut at the Met, and in 1985, she took New York by storm with her Violetta. Once the major opera houses started to clamour for her services, the millionaire became expendable, so she shed him to marry a Hollywood idol, thus enlarging her fame and her fee per performance. During this period, she socialized a great deal, neglected her voice, made a movie, and began to have bouts of temperament that brought even more attention from the popular press. By the mid-nineties her name was a household word, but the major opera houses were becoming nervous about engaging her. Sensibly, Lisa disposed of her movie star, who had been something of an indulgence anyway, and ensnared Otto Schmidt, the dynamic young conductor who was almost as much of a legend as she was.

With the acquisition of Schmidt, her career took off again. The press had a field day and the duo became the most powerful drawing card since Fonteyn and Nureyev. No one cared that the years of neglect had weakened Lisa's high notes or that her voice lacked its original luster. Her stage presence was still magnetic and her lower registers rich and beautiful, so audiences forgave her the occasional scream on top, especially when she stood side by side with her husband for the final bow—much to the chagrin of the tenor who had been elbowed off stage— and exchanged roses and kisses with perfectly-timed tenderness. This display always ensured a standing ovation, no matter how mediocre the performance had been.

But in reality, although Lisa and Otto were extremely fond of each other, their partnership was one of prestige and convenience. Lisa closed her eyes to the fact that Otto, a former navy man, considered it his right to have a girl in every chorus, and Otto benevolently smiled on Lisa's handsome young admirers. The marriage was harmonious in every respect. However, after a while a sour note crept into the relationship—or more accurately, several sour notes. By the turn of the century, Lisa's abuse of her voice became more apparent and her high notes started to sound strident. As she felt less secure, she grew more temperamental, and to her husband's embarrassment she became erratic in her behaviour and prone to furious rages.

But to young Philippa, who had a deep reverence for famous prima donnas, nothing could diminish her excitement when she heard she would be singing on the same stage as Lisa Metz. Being of a happy temperament, Philippa was especially pleased that the piece was *Turandot*, one of the rare operas where the leading soprano survived to rejoice at the final curtain. Luckily for her peace of mind, she could not foresee that this production would dispense with the usual happy ending for Princess Turandot. She would have been even more nervous had she known that a member of the chorus was also going to die when the murderer made a horrible mistake. But blissfully ignorant of the tragedies to come, she anticipated the show with unadulterated pleasure.

Her disillusionment began slowly. During the chorus rehearsals, she continued to think the world of opera welcoming and exciting. As her presence was singularly unthreatening—her voice being so light that even with years of study, the right contacts and several lucky breaks, the highest goal she could attain would be an Adele with a second-string company—the ladies of the chorus welcomed her warmly. Also, as Lisa Metz and Otto Schmidt had never been to Vancouver before, the members of the company were in a festive mood.

It was only as the staging rehearsals approached that the atmosphere started to change. One day Philippa overheard Christopher Bell talking to the chorus master. The stage manager was a cynical young man, and his assessment of the situation jerked Philippa off her cloud.

"Well, of course Turandot is one of her great roles," Christopher said. "She doesn't have to sing a note in Act I, so if she rests up for a couple of days before the show, all she has to do is scream her way through *In Questa Reggia,* negotiate the final duet and she's home free. She even has the chorus to beef out the hit tune and get the audience's adrenalin up before the final curtain. Just like a bloody musical comedy," he added morosely. "Let's face it, *Turandot* is a short role for a leading soprano. It's a natural for someone like Metz who's all show and no stamina."

The chorus master was an optimistic, good-natured man.

"I don't care what she's singing," he said cheerfully. "I can't wait to see her. She's a great star."

"Vancouver never gets the superstars at their peak," said Christopher gloomily. "We see them either on their way up or on their way down. Metz is definitely descending."

"It's still a tremendous thing for us to have her here," insisted the chorus master.

"Sure," said Christopher. "We'll sell out. But if you want my advice, I'd make certain the understudy is well rehearsed."

Philippa returned home feeling subdued.

*   *   *   *

But in spite of Christopher's words, on the evening of Metz's arrival, Philippa felt a quiver of excitement as she entered the rehearsal hall. However, to her disappointment, Lisa Metz was nowhere to be seen. Then a moment later, with a flutter of her heart, Philippa noticed Andrew Sharpe, the stage director, in consultation with three other men. One was a god-like creature, fair and breathtakingly handsome, and the other, short and balding, had a face like a frog. Between Beauty and the Beast, Otto Schmidt was holding court.

As Philippa stood transfixed, Christopher Bell hurried by.

"Impressed, Pippa Squeak?" he asked.

Christopher had given her this label at the first rehearsal. As long as it referred only to her stature—Philippa could just manage five feet if she took a deep breath—and not to the noises she made when she opened her mouth, she was prepared to ignore it.

"Yes, terribly," she said. "Who's the man beside him?"

"The tenor," said Christopher.

"Really? How marvellous."

"Not him. The other one. Toad of Toad Hall."

"Oh dear."

Christopher grinned.

"Not to worry," he said. "Once we wig and beard him, stuff him in padded tights, plop a turban on his head and perch him on elevator shoes, you won't know him. He won't be able to walk, but at least he'll manage to look Lisa in the eye."

"Is he any good?" asked Philippa.

"The caricature of the Italian tenor," said Christopher judiciously. "He struts. His voice isn't particularly beautiful, but he can reach the high notes and hold them indefinitely. He sings as if the audience weren't interested in anything below a B-flat."

"Who's the Greek God?"

"Pang. Jimmy Forbes. But you'd better get that infatuated look out of your eyes. He's Andrew's boyfriend."

"Andrew! Not…"

"Andrew Sharpe. That's right. The director."

Grinning at Philippa's shattered expression, Christopher moved on. He made a beeline for two chorus girls, Turandot's handmaidens, who had minuscule solo parts in the first act. One of them, Anne Marie Lesier, was Christopher's girl-friend. Anne Marie was an exquisitely pretty brunette with violet eyes. She had a big mezzo voice, limited in range and projection, but with enough weight to bal-ance Robin Tremayne, the second handmaiden who was also Turandot's under-study. As Philippa watched, Anne Marie and Christopher merged into an intimate huddle and Robin tactfully turned to chat with a dowdy woman who was knitting in the corner. When Christopher emerged from his huddle with Anne Marie, he called the chorus together and introduced the Maestro. Otto Schmidt nodded courteously to the gentlemen, then carefully scrutinized the three rows of ladies. His eyes rested for a moment on Philippa, who with her curly auburn hair and pert face was very pretty, but then he inspected the alto section and his roving glance stopped dead when he reached Anne Marie. Chris-topher's perpetual smile of amusement vanished as if he had been struck. Oblivi-ous to the agonized expression on the stage manager's face, Otto leaned back on his stool, tapped his music stand, and leered like Don Giovanni. Philippa's spirits sank another notch.

However, her respect for the Maestro returned during the next hour. Schmidt insisted on a musical rehearsal of the first act, and under his expert tutelage, the piece came vibrantly alive. Magically, he melded the odd assortment of humanity into a tightly unified ensemble. The transformation of individuals was fascinat-ing, and the resulting sound was magnificent. Philippa was especially thrilled by the dowdy knitter who turned out to be Liu.

"That's Doreen Flagg," hissed Robin Tremayne, who was sitting next to Phil-ippa. "Nice. She's also one of the few sopranos of any renown who'll work with Metz."

Philippa nodded, automatically respecting any information passed on by Robin, whom she admired greatly. Everyone knew that Robin Tremayne was destined for glory. At twenty-seven, she had a huge soprano voice, eerily reminis-cent of Metz's own voice, but unlike the diva, Robin had worked carefully and meticulously until her technique was perfected and she had the bright sound, projection and placement that usually went with much lighter voices. She could sing for hours and her voice would still soar effortlessly into the stratosphere. So far she had attempted nothing more strenuous than a Micaela, but she had pre-pared a phenomenal variety of arias for the Met auditions and was now ready, as Christopher Bell put it, 'to knock their socks off in New York'. Robin was also a good actress, and though not particularly pretty at close range, had red-gold hair and the strong bones and beautiful eyes that made for the best kind of beauty on stage. All through the first act, Philippa was conscious of the glorious sound emanating from the girl on her left.

When the break was called, Lisa Metz still had not arrived, but the members of the company, exhilarated by the thrilling perfection of the past hour, milled around in happy confusion, eagerly anticipating further excitement in the evening ahead.

Then suddenly silence descended. Philippa glanced up and saw a gorgeous creature in a brick-red suit standing near the entrance of the hall. With a startled jolt, irrational in the circumstances, she realized that this was Lisa Metz. Equally irrationally, she felt a sense of loss. The feeling of cohesion achieved during the early part of the rehearsal had evaporated.

For a moment, Philippa wondered if she had imagined the disquieting change in atmosphere, but when the diva spoke, her worst fears were realized. Smiling like the Queen of the Night, Lisa waved a graceful hand towards Doreen Flagg and uttered a cruelly humourless witticism about Madame Defarge. A ripple of uneasiness flowed across the hall, but the other soprano proved the aptness of Lisa's metaphor by displaying great composure of manner, briefly acknowledging the diva's presence while her large hand steadily continued to count stitches.

Having failed to rile Doreen Flagg, Lisa went to work on the rest of her colleagues. She quickly singled out David Benson, the brilliant Australian newcomer singing Timur. Lisa always tried to undermine the confidence of potential crowd-pleasers, and by disguising belittling criticisms as well-meant advice, she mercilessly harassed the young bass. Andrew Sharpe suffered more open abuse. She dictated to him, downgraded every one of his suggestions, then rendered him apoplectic by flirting with Pang. Pong and Ping fared slightly better, for she simply ignored them. However, Pong, who was a nervous, extremely fat man, was sweating profusely after ten minutes in Lisa's presence, and the dour, puritanical Dutchman playing Ping started to eye her with the same kind of glances that John Knox must have cast on Mary Queen of Scots. With the tenor, whom she knew well, Lisa was outright nasty.

"Carlo," she spat, "if you draw out the C-sharp for as much as one sixteenth of a second, I'll have your head on those spikes along with the Prince of Persia."

To Philippa, when she remembered the promise of the early evening, the descent into darkness achieved Miltonian proportions.

✳   ✳   ✳   ✳

By the weekend the situation deteriorated. Christopher Bell roamed about looking thunderous and Andrew Sharpe's clipped British accent became as staccato as gunfire, for Otto Schmidt made predictable headway with Anne Marie, and Lisa Metz drew a surprisingly warm response from Jimmy Forbes, who appeared to have abandoned his usual proclivities. Carlo Gatti was sulking and strutted less arrogantly than usual, Ping looked thunderous, Pong continued to sweat, and David Benson's voice started to sound strained. Only Doreen Flagg seemed unaffected by the atmosphere, and she continued to knit serenely in her corner whenever her presence was not required.

Soon Lisa found a new victim. Anxiety about her voice was making her tetchy, and having convinced herself that she was incubating a cold, she insisted her understudy sing on Sunday afternoon. As Lisa had not yet seen Act One, she appeared early and sat down to watch. She eyed the opening line-up and frowned as she noticed Anne Marie standing alone. While Lisa never objected to her husband's liaisons, she expected his girls to remain unobtrusive.

"Why is that girl not with the rest of the chorus?" she asked.

"She's one of your handmaidens, Miss Metz," said Christopher.

Lisa knew the score in detail.

"As I recall," she said acidly, "nine voices are required for the *Silenzio.*"

"We have nine girls, but we can't spare them all from the opening chorus, so the seven who don't sing the solo parts will exit right, throw cloaks over their peasant costumes, and re-enter left."

"And what is to stop the other two girls doing the same?"

"They couldn't make it in time," explained Christopher. "They have to get to the top of the set, whereas the others are simply going to bob through the door onto the palace steps."

Lisa looked genuinely affronted. "But that's ridiculous," she said. "They're supposed to be coming from Turandot's apartments. They wouldn't go down to the palace steps."

Christopher looked uncomfortable.

"We have a problem with the set," he admitted. "There's a railing that creates the illusion of a balcony, but the actual standing room is the size of a postage stamp. You'll manage to get out for your wave, Miss Metz, but we'll never fit nine girls on it. We can't even squeeze Robin and Anne Marie up there together, so we're putting Robin on the ramparts."

"That will look silly," said Lisa.

"Not really. The set is bathed in moonlight and the figures will be in shadow. The audience will barely notice them. The focus is still on the principals, even though the girls are singing. I'm afraid it's the best we can do, Miss Metz."

Christopher waited for an explosion, but Lisa merely arched an eyebrow.

"How provincial," she said.

Relieved, Christopher started to move away, but suddenly Lisa's eyes narrowed and she called him back.

"Wait a minute," she said, eyeing Anne Marie. "You mean that girl will be the only one on the balcony with me?"

"You won't be there together, Miss Metz…"

"The handmaidens come on after me. She would be waiting on the stairway when I exited."

"Yes, but…"

"I don't want that girl hanging around me off stage," Lisa snapped. "Switch her with the other girl, the one on the ramparts."

"Here we go," said the peasant next to Philippa. "Open warfare."

"The balance is better this way," said Christopher bravely. "Robin sings the higher part, so she has the projection to cope with the distance from the ramparts."

"So change the voice parts too," snapped Lisa.

Christopher sighed and looked at Andrew Sharpe. Wearily the director ordered Robin and Anne Marie to change places, but as the run through began, Lisa's eyes glittered dangerously. Philippa had envied Robin Tremayne her chance to shine, but now she felt sorry for her. The understudy would be an irresistible target for the diva's malice.

As the second act approached, Robin looked apprehensive, but when the time came, she began her aria so splendidly that Otto Schmidt jerked his head up from his score and started to watch her closely. His wife's reaction was predictable. After a few bars, she found an excuse to interrupt, and for the next hour the rehearsal inched forward while Lisa lacerated every move Robin made. Robin gritted her teeth and bravely continued, but by the end of the scene she was visibly shaken. When, like the referee in a prizefight, Christopher Bell called for a fifteen-minute break, Robin darted into the washroom, and a few minutes later Philippa discovered her there in a flood of tears.

"Rotten jealous bitch," sobbed Robin miserably. "I'd like to kill her."

However, when they returned to the hall, Otto Schmidt was eyeing Robin with interest and respect. He took her aside and spent the rest of the break politely discussing her potential. As the anguished look on Robin's face abated, Philippa's respect for Schmidt returned, though the effect was marred when, at the end of the break, he beckoned to Anne Marie, smiled lasciviously, and invited her out to dinner.

*   *   *   *

Philippa was relieved when the rehearsals were transferred to the theatre. At least there, separated by dressing-rooms, labyrinthine corridors and massive flats, the company was fragmented and the friction became less apparent. However, there were still the disruptions caused by the odd prima donna in the ladies chorus. The worst offender was Anne Marie. At first her major complaint was boredom, for she hated being "alone" downstairs during the first act. She spoke as if Robin did not exist. But soon she had a worse grievance. Although pleased with her pale blue dress, she was enraged that she had to cover her gleaming black hair with one of the standard-issue felt wigs, stitched into vaguely oriental knobs, that all the handmaidens were required to wear. Even when the dresser, a giant of a woman named Ethel March, arrived with an armful of white flowers to decorate the offending wigs, Anne Marie was not mollified, and she muttered viciously as she made herself up. To Philippa, who was condemned to make her debut in sackcloth and coolie hat, Anne Marie's discontent seemed incomprehensible, until she saw how the girl looked in full costume and make-up. The severe wig and oriental eyebrows obliterated Anne Marie's chocolate-box prettiness and she looked rather silly. To make matters worse, Robin, in the same outfit, became beautiful.

Anne Marie was close to tears.

"You'll look fine from the audience," said Ethel.

"It's not the audience I'm worried about," Anne Marie replied pathetically. "How can I let *him* see me like this?"

"If that's what's worrying you, you're a silly fool," Ethel snapped. "That man doesn't care what you look like on stage, and what's more, he'll drop you flat once the show ends."

Ethel clumped out of the room and Anne Marie's tears started in earnest. However, the deluge ceased abruptly when a note written on expensive stationery was delivered to the dressing-room. Anne Marie brightened as soon as she read it, and smiling enigmatically, she tucked it inside her robe.

Bored, Philippa wandered into the hall, where she saw Ethel March holding a huge arrangement of dahlias. Ethel had no respect for union rules.

"Can you run these upstairs," she ordered. "They're for Miss Metz."

Looking like a tree with bound feet, Philippa hobbled down the hall and negotiated the stairs that led to the principals' dressing-rooms. Once at the top, she peered through the dahlias and saw a set of double doors in front of her. She started towards them, but stopped when she heard a sharp voice behind her.

"Not through there. You'll end up in the wings."

Turning her head, Philippa saw a shrivelled crone sewing a purple cape. She was seated beside the stairwell. "For Lisa?" she asked. "Through there and down to the end of the hall. Room on the left." She nodded towards a narrow hallway on her right.

Philippa passed several doors as she went down the hall, but most were closed. However, through one that was slightly ajar, she caught a glimpse of an outsize oriental wearing horn-rimmed spectacles. The steadily clicking knitting needles revealed the lady's identity.

As Philippa reached Lisa's dressing-room, her heart sank, for although the door was closed, the voices inside the room were clearly audible. Lisa was having a battle royal with Andrew Sharpe who had abandoned his BBC-home-service voice and was screaming hysterically. Petrified, Philippa stood outside the door. As she wondered what to do, the door of the next room opened and another massive oriental appeared. This one was an ancient man, complete with flowing robes and a long, grey beard, but when he spoke, his vigorous voice had a cheerful Australian twang.

"Hey you! Don't go in there," said David Benson. "If we don't interrupt them, the Pommie Pansy might kill her. Good Lord," he added, scrutinizing Philippa carefully, "are you the cute little redhead? They must have really worked hard to make you look that awful."

Philippa was saved from responding by Andrew Sharpe who hurtled out of Lisa's room, narrowly missing the white dahlias, and stormed down the hall. Nervously, Philippa inched into the doorway. Lisa was coolly drawing an elongated eyebrow. When Philippa knocked, she looked up and flashed a dazzling smile.

"For me," she trilled. "So sweet! Just set them on the counter."

Philippa looked desperately for an inch of counter space, for the room already resembled a florist's shop, and between the floral arrangements the counters were littered with make-up, magazines and an odd assortment of paraphernalia that she took to be mementos of Lisa's career. Curiously, Philippa's eyes lit upon an elaborately decorated tube about two feet long. Lisa followed her glance. Picking up the tube, she pulled it apart and revealed a lethal-looking blade.

"Exotic, isn't it?" she said. "And authentic. Otto has one just like it. One of our dearest friends gave us a matched set when we did our first *Butterfly* together." She set the dagger down without returning it to its sheath, then made a space on the counter and nodded towards it. "Put them there, dear," she said.

Philippa set down the dahlias and turned to go, but Lisa stopped her. "Could you run a note to Jimmy Forbes?" she asked sweetly. "He's four doors down on the other side of the hall. It won't take me a moment to write it," she added, opening a pale blue box of stationery. "Now who's been using my notepaper?" she said peevishly, staring at the torn ribbon. "This was a brand new box." Her elegant, expressive hands, which she used so effectively on stage, rippled quickly through the envelopes. "Yes, only eleven," she snapped.

With a start, Philippa recognized the stationery. Anne Marie's note had been written on identical paper. Blithely unaware of Philippa's consternation, Lisa pulled a sheet of paper from the box and started to write. But before she could finish the note, there was a knock and James Forbes appeared in the doorway. He seemed less godlike costumed as Pang, but Lisa greeted him with a dazzling smile and tore up the note she had been writing.

Feeling redundant, Philippa left. By now David Benson had disappeared, but Doreen Flagg could be heard vocalizing in her own room. Her bright soprano echoed eerily down the hall. "*Tu che di gel sei cinta,*" she sang. How apt, thought Philippa, and momentarily distracted, she turned the wrong way and went through the door at the end of the hall. She found herself on a square landing with a stairwell to her right and double doors on her left. Peeking through the doors, she saw the back of a massive flat and realized she was on the upstage corner of the left wing. That means, she thought slowly, that the doors I passed earlier must lead to the downstage corner of the same wing. Having calculated her position, she went down the stairs, reached the hall that adjoined the chorus dressing-rooms, and found she had made a complete circle. As she approached the dressing-rooms, the doors opened and a steady stream of peasants and soldiers emerged. Act One was about to start.

*   *   *   *

Four long hours later, Otto Schmidt cornered Andrew Sharpe.

"Andrew, *mein Freund,*" he said pleasantly, "just a few *kleinen Probleme.* You simply have to rearrange Ping, Pang and Pong. No, my dear fellow, it's not any particular section. Every one of their appearances is a disaster. Yes, I know they're badly mismatched sizes...I don't expect the Three Tenors...but there must be something you can do to make them look better—especially Herr Pong. *Ein Katastrophe.* You must speak to wardrobe. All that jiggling flab must be visible from the back of the balcony. Very distracting. Now, we have trouble with the handmaidens too. They cannot be so far down on the revolve when it is in motion. They were wobbling like my wife's tremolo when they came into view. Also, the *Silenzio* in Act One is no good. The girls on the palace steps cannot see me. You must move the principals stage right so the girls have a clear view. And Anne Marie and Robin must be changed again. As they are now, the balance is all wrong. Anne Marie will be heard better from the balcony. Now don't argue, it has to be done. Another thing, Lisa has a problem in the third act. Her position is very poor for the torture scene. This must be changed. No, that isn't everything. You must do some work with Carlo. Those shoes. He must learn to move with more ease. The man will be a laughing stock, and this reflects on Lisa. Yes. But how should I know when? You must arrange something before the final dress. *Gut.* What else? Ah, yes, the head of the Prince of Persia. There must be blood…"

And so it went on. Andrew Sharpe went home that night with a splitting headache.

By seven o'clock on the evening of the dress rehearsal, his headache had not abated. Exhausted, in pain, and miserable—for he had had another fight with Pang—Andrew drifted into the lower hall and watched the auxiliary ladies setting out long tables for the sandwich buffet they traditionally served at the final rehearsal. The guild president, a wealthy lady in her sixties, looked at him sympathetically.

"Trouble?" she asked.

Andrew nodded unhappily.

"Yes," said Mrs. Beale, "there would be. That Lisa Metz is a nasty piece of goods. Cruel, ruthless and amoral. But never mind, dear. It'll all be over soon."

Mrs. Beale returned to her tablecloths and Andrew, slightly comforted, went out to the lobby and smoked several cigarettes. Having regained his equilibrium, he braved the auditorium.

Miraculously, the first act went without a hitch. The last minute adjustments fell smoothly into place and improved the overall effect immensely. Andrew felt much happier when he returned to the rehearsal hall for the break and waded into the auxiliary ladies' sandwiches. Not only were all the principals present, they were even being civil to each other, and they mingled cheerfully with the guild ladies, instrumentalists, supers and chorus singers.

The only people conspicuous by their absence were Otto Schmidt and Anne Marie. Andrew also noticed that Robin Tremayne was missing. The festive mood continued until Christopher Bell's voice crackled over the public address system and called the second act beginners. Feeling considerably more relaxed, Andrew returned to the front of house.

The members of the company gradually drifted into their positions and Philippa took her place on stage with the other peasants. As they positioned themselves by the upstage backdrop, they heard an unusual sound.

"Good Lord," said the Mandarin. "Lisa must be practicing her C-sharp. I didn't know she could hit that many in succession."

Then abruptly silence fell. The singers remained motionless, although those at stage right were faintly conscious of movement in the stage manager's corner.

Fifteen minutes later, when the curtain still had not risen, Philippa realized something was seriously wrong.

∗   ∗   ∗   ∗

The death of a girl from the opera chorus was a relatively minor matter to the RCMP, whose senior officers were run off their feet coping with drug peddlers and vice rings. However, a mere staff sergeant could not possibly be sent to interrogate the famous Lisa Metz, so Richard Beary, the youngest detective inspector in the local detachment, was speedily dispatched to the theatre. Four hours after his arrival, he looked wearily at the sergeant who had accompanied him and lit a much-needed cigarette.

"What now, sir?" asked Sergeant Martin.

"What indeed. We've got statements from all the chief witnesses, but none are contradictory. There were no fingerprints on the murder weapon. There was also very little blood. Nothing tangible to help us at all."

"Yes, I see," said Sergeant Martin slowly. His vowels were as interminable as a CPR freight train.

Martin was a British expatriate and the closest thing to Constable Plod that Richard had ever seen this side of the Atlantic. Richard could never decide whether the music hall mannerisms were cultivated or came naturally—not that it mattered for they were extremely useful during interrogations. People were so fascinated by the sergeant that they tended to relax and fall off-guard. Many a criminal had felt a deeply personal sense of disillusionment when he discovered that Martin, under his comic exterior, was as tough as Elliot Ness.

"Sounds to me like the Lesier female was asking for it," he said finally. "With a name like that she was probably French," he added disapprovingly.

"From Montreal," said Richard. "She was certainly carrying on blatantly with the conductor, but it's the circumstances surrounding her death that puzzle me. For some unknown reason, she went to Lisa Metz's dressing-room and tried on Turandot's train and crown—a massive, exotic affair that covers the whole head. The stage manager, who was Lesier's boyfriend, says the girl was the type who would have been tempted by the sight of the cloak and headpiece in an empty room. Then, while she was standing with her back to the door, someone came into the room, picked up an oriental dagger, one of the diva's souvenirs, and stabbed her from behind. She was killed instantly. The killer then, as if performing some bizarre funeral ritual, shredded the floral arrangements in the room and scattered the flowers over the body."

"What was the girl doing up in the principals' corridor?" asked Martin.

"A note from the conductor was found on the girl's body. Schmidt had invited her to visit with him during the breaks between acts, also to make use of his room when she wasn't on stage. He had the room opposite his wife's. I gather this was one of the arrangements they insisted on whenever he conducted—a sort of private green room and dressing-area. The girl may or may not have made use of his invitation throughout the first act. No one seems to know. The principals' dressing-rooms are accessible from both ends of the upper corridor, and virtually anyone could have been in and out without being noticed. However, Lesier was last seen when she sang a small solo part about eight minutes before the first act ended, so it's almost certain that she went directly to Schmidt's room when she left the stage. From there she got sidetracked into Lisa Metz's room where she was killed. And there you have it. Any suggestions, Martin?"

"You haven't drawn any conclusions, sir?"

"Only one. That the general manager doesn't care whom we arrest as long as it's neither Lisa Metz nor Otto Schmidt. Anyone else will be inconvenient, but he can manage replacements. And if we do have to incarcerate his stars, could we please hold off until the final curtain on closing night."

Sergeant Martin sniffed.

"I bet *she* did it," he said. "The jealous wife is usually the one to pop off the husband's mistress."

"Not in this case. Schmidt makes a practice of having affairs with chorus girls, and this one doesn't sound any different from the others. Metz considers these girls inconsequential fluffs. She makes the occasional comment when she's in a bad mood, but usually she's venting her spleen because she's annoyed about something else. I also get the impression that her own love life isn't exactly static. The two of them seem to operate pretty much the same way."

"Maybe this time Schmidt got too serious."

"I don't think so. The girl was the standard type he goes for. Extremely pretty, but short on brains and character. Short on talent too. It sounds as if she had lots of lovely dark tone in her voice, but insufficient technique to ever go anywhere. There are lots of singers like that. They can belt out a bit part and sound fantastic, but they're usually sprinters—metaphorically speaking. They don't have the stamina to go the half-mile, let alone the marathon, and believe me, singing opera is a marathon. No, Schmidt was only interested in one thing about this girl, and he'd have dropped her without a qualm when he left the city. Metz knew that. She's never been jealous of his girls before so why should she start now? Besides, she has an alibi. After she made her balcony appearance in Act One, she watched the performance from the rear of the platform. The ASM had a clear view of the stairway leading to the platform and she saw Lisa come down at the end of the act."

"Was there any other access to the platform?"

"None. There's no doubt that Lisa remained there for the last half of Act One. And when she came down, she was joined by her dresser, who accompanied her to the lower hall so they could make an early start on the buffet. Metz was in the hall during the break. She was in full view of the entire company, and when she finally returned to her room, her dresser went with her. Besides, when Metz saw the body, she went berserk, and she's been bordering on hysteria ever since."

"Because she assumes she was the intended victim."

"Exactly."

"Well, if the killer was after Lisa Metz, then the husband is the logical suspect."

"The opera manager would crucify you if he heard you. Anyway, Schmidt has an alibi too. As Act One concluded, he invited the first violinist back to meet Lesier—something to do with a show the man was directing—and they returned to the room together. Schmidt was surprised Lesier wasn't there, but he didn't bother to go looking for her as he assumed she'd show up. The two men started talking music, and before they knew it, the break was over. Schmidt didn't leave the room the entire time. Besides, why should he want to get rid of his wife? She accepts his foibles with no more than a token snarl, and they make millions together all over the world. It's the combined names that draw the crowds. Why kill the goose that lays the golden egg?"

Sergeant Martin looked closely at his superior officer.

"You know a lot about these people," he said. "I don't remember any of this in the interviews. Where do you get your inside information?"

"I have a personal source. She's a midget-sized soprano with a mind as sharp as the murder weapon."

"Pity we don't have her here."

"Oh, but we do. She's in the chorus. As a matter of fact, I sent for her five minutes ago. Ah, here she is now. Sergeant, I'd like you to meet my kid sister. Philippa, this is Sergeant Martin."

✳   ✳   ✳   ✳

Philippa listened attentively while her brother told her the facts that had come to light.

"So both Schmidt and Metz are in the clear," said Richard. "We can account for their movements every minute of the crucial time. The director also has an alibi, because he was in the auditorium during Act I and he spent the break socializing in the lower hall. The same can be said for the other principals, with the exception of Carlo Gatti, Doreen Flagg and David Benson, all of whom came upstairs at various times during the break."

"Which one was Benson, sir?" asked Sergeant Martin, peering at his notes. "Ah," he nodded, answering his own question. "The pathetic old blind man."

Philippa looked thoughtful.

"You say Anne Marie was last seen when she sang her solo," she said. "Did the people backstage see her, or just the ones out front?"

"What difference does it make?"

"She was tucked away on the balcony. She wouldn't have been seen that clearly from the audience."

"What sort of solo was it?"

"A very short one. Three or four bars. She was telling the people on stage to be quiet."

"In an opera? How optimistic," said Sergeant Martin.

Richard was checking his notes.

"No," he said. "There's no funny business there. Two people saw her backstage. Lisa Metz was one. The other was a stagehand."

"Oh yes," said Philippa. "Lisa would have seen her on the platform. I bet some acid words were exchanged."

"She didn't say that. She just told us she saw Lesier in position for her solo. Mind you, Metz was in a state when she talked to us, but she was coherent and quite definite on that point. I'm quite sure she was telling the truth. I have a pretty good instinct about these things."

"What about the stagehand? Would he know Anne Marie well enough to recognize her?"

"He had a chat with her the preceding night just before she went on. He didn't talk to her tonight, but he came through the upstage doors as she was going to her position. He saw her walking up the stairway."

Philippa frowned, but her concentration was broken by a knock on the door. Sergeant Martin went to see who was there. One of the downstairs dressers stood in the doorway.

The woman moved shyly into the room.

"Excuse me, Inspector," she began. "I understand you want to know when Anne Marie went to Miss Metz's room?"

Richard nodded.

"We certainly do," he said. "If you can give us any idea of the approximate time, we'll be exceedingly grateful."

"It was five past eight, sir."

"How do you know that?"

"Because I saw her go into the dressing-room."

"You what!" exclaimed Richard.

"Yes, sir. I was talking to Mrs. Beale, and I was facing the corridor. I glanced at my watch to check the time, and as I looked up I saw Anne Marie disappearing into the room at the end of the corridor."

"Did you see her close up?"

"No, of course not. How could I? She didn't go past us. She must have gone across the hall from Schmidt's room."

"You're sure it was her?"

"Of course I am. Who else could it have been? The only other person with an outfit like that is Robin Tremayne, and it wasn't her because she was sick as a dog tonight and she spent the entire break in the chorus dressing-room."

"How do you know?"

"I saw her there."

"When?"

"At the beginning of the break, and after I returned downstairs. When I left the room she was pale and looked miserable, and when I returned fifteen minutes later, she was in the bathroom. I could hear her. Stomach flu, poor thing. When she came out, she was white and shivering. She should have been home in bed."

When the dresser had left, Richard looked quizzically at his sister.

"You look perplexed," he said.

"I am. Something isn't quite right, but I can't decide what."

"Think," urged Richard. "You're familiar with these people and with the production. You may be able to pick out something that we'd overlook."

"I'll try," said Philippa. "In the meantime, there's one thing you could do to help. Let me have a quick look in Lisa's room."

"What do you expect to see there?"

"I don't know, but I want to count the envelopes in her box of stationery."

✳   ✳   ✳   ✳

On opening night, Philippa realized how the murder had been done. However, when the solution came to her, startling in its simplicity and shattering in its implications, the performance was in session and Richard was in the audience. She was unsure what to do, but after some thought, and a short, but revealing conversation with Robin Tremayne, she made a decision. She had to talk to Lisa Metz. However, a guard had been mounted at each end of the corridor and only the principals and their dressers were allowed through. Finally, in desperation, she took advantage of David Benson, who had become her friendly shadow, and sent her warning with him in the form of a note. Then, having made a move, she forced herself to concentrate on the performance, and soon, in spite of her anxious state, she became totally absorbed in the drama of *Turandot*.

Lisa Metz triumphed that night. The enchantment she wove made it hard to remember the neurotic, temperamental woman who had wreaked havoc during rehearsals. Miraculously her voice brightened and remained in control, and once more she became the Prima Donna of legend. When the final curtain fell, the audience went wild.

Exhilarated, the chorus and supers filed off the stage while the principals remained to take their individual bows. Otto Schmidt came bounding through, hurling congratulations and trying hard to disguise his amazement. He joined his wife at the centre of the curtain, and as they disappeared together into the cavernous grey folds, the crowd roared and the applause became thunderous. With a sinking heart, Philippa left the stage and made her way to the general manager's office.

The door was open and she could see him volubly lecturing Richard and Sergeant Martin. She looked speculatively at the manager and wondered if he were the type to kill the messenger who brought bad news. At present he was euphoric from the after effects of the performance, with bravos ringing in his ears and dollar signs flashing in his eyes. Philippa sighed. She had the feeling that her debut was going to be her farewell performance.

The manager looked up impatiently when Philippa knocked, but Richard correctly interpreted the expression on her face and ushered her into the room.

"You know something, don't you?" he said quickly. "Out with it."

Philippa nodded.

"Yes," she said. "We were right that Anne Marie's death was a case of mistaken identity. Having accepted Schmidt's invitation to make use of his room, she got bored. No one was about and the door of Lisa's room was ajar, so the temptation of the jewelled robe and crown must have been irresistible. If only she hadn't stood with her back to the door when she tried them on."

"We know all that," said the manager irritably. "It's the reason for the killing that's important. That's what we need to find out."

"The reason is obvious if you consider the relationship between Lisa Metz and Otto Schmidt. That's where the motive for murder lies. You see," said Philippa, "we've all been labouring under a misconception. We've assumed that Otto Schmidt likes being married to Lisa Metz."

"Well, of course he does," snapped the manager. "Lisa's a big star. They're a great team."

"They were a great team, but not any more. Lisa has become a handicap. Otto Schmidt is a fine musician, but in combination with his wife, he's become half of a circus act. Their marriage is a lucrative business because their names have drawing power, but Lisa can't deliver the goods any more."

"Nonsense," said the manager. "Look at tonight's performance. She was brilliant."

"Yes," Philippa agreed, "but tonight was exceptional. Tuesday she might fall apart completely, or even cancel. Working with Lisa is like playing Russian Roulette. A person can't sustain a career that way. Otto Schmidt has reached the point where he should be expanding his horizons and taking on new challenges, but look what's happening to him. His repertoire is becoming more and more restricted because of his wife's limitations, and there are fewer good performers willing to work with him because of Lisa's rages and temperaments. Artistically, his career has become stagnant."

"Otto Schmidt is one of the most renowned conductors on the circuit," insisted the manager. He glowered ominously at Philippa, but bravely she continued.

"I know," she said, "but he'll be out of the top league in a couple of years, unless he manages to get rid of Lisa. Yet he can hardly divorce her, because Lisa isn't a woman to be easily dismissed. It's not just her marriage that's at stake; it's her career. If she loses Schmidt, she'll be on the scrap heap in no time, so she'll fight to the bitter end rather than give him up. And Otto knows it. The man is trapped. I imagine the situation has been fermenting for some years. It could have boiled over at any time."

The general manager looked apoplectic.

"But why did it have to boil over here?"

"Because we provided the catalyst."

"The catalyst?"

"Yes. Robin Tremayne. We all know how special she is. Naturally Schmidt spotted her right away. Haven't you noticed how he works with her and encourages her?"

"All I noticed was the way he carried on with Anne Marie. With Robin he's been very businesslike. Nothing like his usual goings-on."

"That's what caused the trouble. Otto is serious about Robin. She isn't one of his 'fluffs'. In her he can see the potential for a spectacular new partnership, and Lisa is determined to prevent it. She may tolerate her husband's light-hearted affairs, but she couldn't stand his interest in Robin. There's your motive for murder."

"This is lunacy," said the manager. "You're suggesting that Otto Schmidt tried to murder his wife, and ended up killing his mistress, all because of another female. It just isn't possible."

"It isn't possible, Pip," Richard said thoughtfully. "Schmidt couldn't be the killer because he was never alone during the break."

"Anne Marie wasn't killed during the break," said Philippa.

The manager stared at her as if she had lost her mind.

"The dresser," he said icily, "saw Anne Marie enter Lisa's room several minutes after the break started."

"No," said Philippa. "The dresser saw Robin Tremayne."

Before she could elaborate, the office door opened. In came the policewoman who had been posted to guard Lisa Metz. She looked apprehensive.

"Miss Metz insisted I leave," she said. "She said she was expecting her husband any minute and she wanted to talk to him alone."

"She's alone with Otto Schmidt?" Richard howled.

"Yes. I came down right away. She won't listen to reason."

The manager made a strangled sound and leapt to his feet, but Richard was even faster. He darted forward and hurried out the door. Philippa tried to stop him, but she was pushed back by Martin and the manager, who jostled past her and paraded down the hall after her brother. Biting her lip nervously, Philippa followed them.

As Richard turned into the corridor of the principals' dressing-rooms, the end door flew open and Otto Schmidt staggered into the hall. His face was white and his hands were shaking violently. Richard accelerated down the hall, but Otto seemed barely aware of his presence. Listlessly he leaned against the wall and let Richard pass.

Philippa was the last person to reach the prima donna's dressing-room. Her heart was pounding but she steeled herself to look into the room. At first, her view was obstructed by the bulky form of Sergeant Martin, but as he stepped forward, Philippa saw her brother kneeling by the body of the soprano. Lisa had slid down beside the armchair. Her beautiful, expressive hands were still pathetically clutching the hilt of the oriental dagger that protruded from between her ribs.

*   *   *   *

In spite of the diva's death, the remaining performances went well, for the audiences were overwhelmed by the special magic of Robin Tremayne. Instinctively, they realized they were seeing a future star at the beginning of her career.

However, after the final performance, Robin was troubled. When Richard Beary took Sergeant Martin backstage to congratulate her, he could see she was under a strain. When Robin became aware of Richard's presence, she cleared the crowds of well-wishers from her dressing-room—tactfully the general manager had given her a room at the other end of the corridor—and asked the policemen to sit down.

"Philippa won't tell me a thing," she said plaintively, "but I have to know the truth for my own peace of mind. It was Lisa, wasn't it? She killed Anne Marie."

"Yes," said Richard. "But of course, she didn't mean to. You were the one she wanted to get rid of."

"That's what I've been thinking all week," said Robin. "It's been awful. You see, she sent me a note during the dress rehearsal. Philippa guessed, though I don't know how."

"She'd seen a box of notepaper in Lisa's room. She knew one envelope had been used for Otto's note to Anne Marie, but when she checked later, two envelopes were missing."

"Lisa sent the note just after the first act began," said Robin. "She wanted me to come to her dressing-room, but I didn't go. I was terrified of her. She'd been nasty to me during rehearsals and I knew if I saw her she'd say something to undermine my confidence. But I worried about not going too. In fact, I worked myself up into such a state that I felt sick all evening. One of the dressers actually commented on the way I was moping around, but I told her I had a touch of flu. Finally, during the break, I decided I'd better go up in case there were worse repercussions because I'd ignored the note."

"So you went up the back stairway just after eight o'clock."

"Yes. No one was around, and Lisa's door appeared to be closed. However, when I knocked, it swung open, and then I saw the body. I thought it was Lisa. It was horrible. She was hunched over, and the folds of the cloak hung away from the hilt of the dagger as if the knife had pinned it into place. I started to feel faint and I rushed out. I shut the door, and raced back to the dressing-room where I was violently sick. Later I was scared to say anything because I was afraid people would think I'd killed her."

"Very irresponsible," said Richard. "Your movements completely misled us. The dresser saw you go into Lisa's room, but she didn't notice you come back out. From the rear, you and Anne Marie were as alike as the Bobsy twins, and as the dresser was the same lady who thought you were ill, she was positive she'd seen Anne Marie upstairs. Especially as she returned to the chorus dressing-room and found you being sick. Naturally she assumed you'd been there the whole time."

"But when did Lisa kill Anne Marie?"

"During the first act. Lisa was in costume early, so she wrote her note to you, wandered down the corridor and gave it to one of the make-up girls to deliver. Then she stopped to chat with Mrs. Beale in the end hall. She didn't realize that Anne Marie was in her husband's room. After a moment, she glanced up, just as Anne Marie crossed the hall into her room, and like the dresser, she was confused by the identical costumes. She assumed you'd responded to her note, come through the end door from the other stairwell and gone into her dressing-room, for that's what she was expecting to happen. So she returned to her room, thinking you were inside."

Robin shuddered.

"She may not have meant to kill you, you know," said Richard gently. "She might have intended to buy you off, or thwart you in some other way. But as she entered the room, she saw what appeared to be her understudy trying on her costume. She was insanely jealous of you, and the dagger lay unsheathed on the counter. When she snatched it up and plunged it into Anne Marie, she was probably consumed by one of her uncontrollable rages. She didn't realize her mistake because Anne Marie sank to her knees and fell forward. But whether the murder was premeditated or not, once Lisa had committed the crime, she was very clever and deliberate in creating an alibi for herself. The rest of the company was on stage during the first act, so she had to make it appear that the murder had occurred much later. That's why she took your place for the handmaiden's solo— or what she thought was your place. She didn't know you and Anne Marie had been switched back again because Andrew Sharpe hadn't had the nerve to tell her about the change. That's why we believed she was speaking the truth when she said she'd seen Anne Marie on stage. She was as bewildered as the rest of us. She'd looked across to the ramparts, seen you standing there, and assumed you were Anne Marie. That's why she became hysterical when she saw the body, for it was only then that she realized she'd killed the wrong person."

"It seems incredible that no one noticed the substitution."

"Not really. Trained voices sound alike if the basic colour is similar, and like you, Anne Marie and Lisa had dark middle voices. In that part of the voice, for three or four bars, no one would notice the difference. Lisa stood well back on the balcony, partially shielded by the gauze curtain and the people in the audience saw what they expected to see—the principals reacting in the center spotlight, the handmaidens on the steps, and you and Anne Marie in the background. Theatrical illusion is very powerful. The handmaidens' dresses were pale blue, whereas Lisa's was white, but as the stage was flooded with blue light, her dress appeared to be blue. Her wig was made of real hair arranged in a long, glossy braid, but the top was smooth so as to fit under her various headpieces. So she pinned the braid into a knot, arranged flowers around it, and her hair looked like the handmaidens' wigs. That's why she destroyed the flowers in her room. She was afraid someone would notice if she picked off four blossoms, but by shredding all the floral arrangements, she was able to take what she needed and no one realized any flowers were missing. There was a largish pocket on the inside of her skirt. In it we found four crushed white flowers and several hairpins."

"And she knew there was no risk of anyone seeing her at close quarters," interjected Robin, "because no one else went onto the balcony."

"Exactly. And we were led astray by the stagehand who told us he'd seen Anne Marie, but as Philippa pointed out, the stagehand wouldn't have known about the last minute switch either. He must have seen *you* going up the steps to the ramparts and thought you were the girl he'd talked to the previous evening. Philippa was able to work everything out because she was familiar with the show."

"Well, she knew about Anne Marie and myself being switched again because we'd discussed it in the dressing-room, but she still must have been guessing a lot. There was no proof. Lisa might have got away with it. Why did she kill herself?"

Richard frowned.

"My sister is young and sentimental," he said. "Even though she'd discovered her idol had feet of clay, she couldn't bear to see her arrested and carted off to prison. So she sent her a note telling her what she knew and warning her that an arrest was imminent."

"So Lisa chose death over dishonour."

"Philippa's exact words," Richard said dryly. "Lisa took the other dagger from her husband's room during the intermission. She was a bitterly unhappy woman and she must have realized that everything was finished for her."

"*Tutto e finito per me,*" Robin said thoughtfully.

"Philippa said that too," said Richard irritably. "I wish you girls would stop spouting phrases from Italian operas at me. Life doesn't imitate art, you know. It's the other way around."

"Not when you're Lisa Metz," said Robin with spirit. "I bet she asked Otto to come to her room after the final curtain. She wanted him to find her. She really should have been singing Butterfly, you know. Turandot is simply not supposed to die."

*   *   *   *

"I told you the Metz woman did it," said Sergeant Martin as he and Richard left Robin's room. "Mind you," he added, "all these opera types give me the pip. You mark my words," he predicted, "that girl will end up as loony as the one she replaced. Especially if she marries the Merry Widower."

"She won't," said Richard. "She's too sensible and much too nice. Besides, she's good. She can make it without him. Otto Schmidt will still be chasing chorus girls when he's as old as Toscanini."

Martin sniffed.

"I still think your sister is the only sane one in the whole bunch."

As the two policemen reached the stage door, Philippa darted up the stairs. She was looking pert and pretty in a shimmering green evening dress and she smiled a friendly greeting.

"You look nice," said Richard. "Where are you off to? Cast party?"

"No," said Philippa, winking at Sergeant Martin as she sailed out the stage door. "I've been invited out to dinner by a pathetic old blind man."

DEATH AND THE
DOOR-KNOCKERS

▼

"Campaigning is bloody murder," growled Bertram Beary, unaware that Poll 24 was about to produce a corpse. Beary was only conscious of the lethal potential of row upon row of steep front steps. He gritted his teeth and wheezed up another flight.

On the welcome mat, he spied a card promoting his unworthy opponent, so he swooped it up and stuffed it into his pocket. He knocked on the door and a volley of barking erupted from inside the house. While he waited for the door to open, he whistled a tune from *Patience*, wrote 'Sorry I missed you' on the top card of the stack in his hand, and waved to his daughter, Juliet, who was pressing along the pavement armed with bundles of his campaign literature. The door of the house remained shut, so he stuffed the card into the letter slot. The barking stopped and the card was ripped from his fingers. He could hear the sound of shredding paper as he plodded down the steps.

Juliet had moved two houses ahead, so Beary, having had the forethought to wear Wellington boots, traversed the wet grass toward the next home. Then he saw the opposition sign in the middle of the lawn, and realizing why Juliet had bypassed the property, he continued across the lot and joined her at the corner.

"Daddy, you really shouldn't walk across people's lawns," she lectured him. "If you put size-twelve craters in people's azalea beds, they'll never put an 'x' by your name."

"Whatever you say, my dear," said Beary. He was very fond of his middle daughter. "Where to now?"

Juliet stood under the street lamp and studied the poll map taped to the bottom of her clipboard.

"Arbroath Street. It's a cul-de-sac."

"Ah yes. The current president of the Chamber of Commerce lives there. Might be good for a quick Glenlivet. I'll do her side of the road."

"Oh no you won't. I'm not having you breathing Scotch on the electorate."

"One cannot stupefy those who are already stupefied," said Beary. "Besides, we won't lose much time because there's a trail at the end of the cul-de-sac so we can cut through to the next street."

"No point," said Juliet. "Philippa and Richard are doing that section."

Richard was Juliet's older brother, and Philippa was her younger sister.

"Are you sure?"

"Yes, Mother has organized the poll into sections. We've all got our assigned streets."

"Your mother could organize Oliver Cromwell's troops to give tea dances for Irish Catholics. She's the bossiest woman I know."

"You're lucky to have her," Juliet pointed out. Having finished with her map, she flipped over the clipboard and turned her attention to the list of electors on the other side. "Mother is the reason you continue to get elected year after year," she continued, checking off the addresses that they had already visited. "She's got the whole family working on your campaign. What's more, if she weren't babysitting all the children tonight, Sylvia and I wouldn't be here to help you."

"True. Speaking of Sylvia and Norton, where has your mother deployed them?"

Sylvia was the oldest of the Beary siblings, and Norton was her husband.

"They're working one block up, along with Mai Ling."

"Ah, Mai Ling," Beary nodded approval. "Nice girl that."

Juliet raised her pretty eyebrows.

"I can't imagine how Sylvia managed to persuade her nanny to help deliver pamphlets."

"I can," said Beary, looking smug. "Mai Ling is Vietnamese. I told her the members of the opposition were Communists."

*   *   *   *

On the far side of the ravine, Richard Beary paused by an impressive multi-gabled residence that was surrounded by a white stucco wall interspersed with red brick columns. He crouched against the wall and tried to angle his clipboard so the light from the lantern on the gatepost beamed onto his poll map. Philippa stared over his shoulder and scowled.

"I can't do all that tonight," she grumbled. "This damp air is terrible for my voice."

"Just a couple more hours," said Richard. "Can't we forge on and finish. This is my only night off this week."

Richard was an RCMP detective inspector.

"It's all very well for you. Policemen are used to being out in all weathers and no one cares if they have hoarse voices. It's different for singers."

Richard smiled down at his sister.

"All right. We'll just do Maynor Street. Then you can call it quits and I'll manage the rest."

"Maynor Street. Is that the crescent with the heritage homes? Box hedges, wrought iron gates and mile-long driveways. Forget it."

"No, I wouldn't do that to you. You're thinking of Manor Street. Maynor is the cul-de-sac that dead-ends by the woods. It won't take long. There are only six houses."

Richard slid the poll map under his pile of pamphlets, and he and Philippa continued round the corner.

Maynor Street looked gloomy and forbidding. The far side of the road abutted a heavily forested ravine, which at this time of night was simply a vast black hole with one mottled dark-green oval where the beam from the streetlight fell against the cedars. The skeletal branches of a large alder tree jutted in front of the solitary lamppost and cast eerie silhouettes onto the road. The houses were dimly lit, with the exception of a palatial mansion that stood somewhat apart at the end of the cul-de-sac. The lot appeared double the size of the adjacent gardens, and the entire front yard was illuminated by coloured floodlights. The red glow did little to reassure Philippa, and she stayed close to her brother as she followed him into the cul-de-sac.

As Philippa and Richard started down the street, a shadowy figure appeared. It walked ahead of them for a short distance; then just as abruptly disappeared again.

"Who's that?" said Philippa.

"I can't see," said Richard, "but whoever he is, he's obviously doing what we are."

"Campaigning?"

"Delivering something. Look. There he is again."

The figure reappeared, and as it passed under the glow of the street lamp, it became recognizable.

"No, he's not doing things political. It's that Sikh we saw earlier. He's delivering the local newspaper. Now come on. Move ahead. You were the one that didn't want to stand about in the night air. I'll do this one. You take the next house."

Philippa shifted the bundle of leaflets to her other arm and checked her watch. It was five twenty-five. Energized by the knowledge that she was nearly through, she forged ahead and dropped the remaining leaflets. As she started toward the driveway of her last house, she saw the Sikh come down the steps of the mansion at the end of the cul-de-sac and disappear into the trail that led to the adjoining street.

*   *   *   *

By the time Beary and Juliet reached the matching cul-de-sac on the other side of the woods, the night air had become bitterly cold. Beary glanced guiltily across the street to see if Juliet was watching him, and seeing her back safely turned, he cut across the grass and puffed up the steps of the next house. He could see the light of a table lamp and the flicker of a television set through the living-room window. He knocked, and as he waited for a response, he heard a movement behind him. He looked round to see a shadowy figure moving across the lawn. It was a bearded Sikh carrying a canvas bag. When he noticed Beary, he nodded and smiled. He was holding a newspaper in his hand and he threw it onto the doorstep; then carried on his way.

Beary waited for a moment longer, but if the occupants were home, they were obviously determined not to come to the door, so he moved off in the other direction and walked toward the last house in the cul-de-sac. This was the home of Jeanne Baird. It was a distinctive building, modern, with clean lines, and none of the imitation turn-of-the-century flourishes that were currently in fashion in the newer homes. The front garden consisted of an open stretch of lawn with two small topiaries on either side of the flag-stoned path. Encouraged, he noticed that

Jeanne Baird's silver Porsche was in the driveway. He climbed the steps and checked his watch in the light of the front porch. He saw that it was six o'clock.

*   *   *   *

Two blocks away, the third section of the campaign team was winding up its route. Sylvia Wyatt finished counting leaflets and called to her husband who was emerging from a fenced yard on the far side of the street.

"Norton, I've only got thirty-five left. That won't be enough to finish the last two streets. How many do you have?"

Norton crossed the road and joined his wife as she reached the driveway of a particularly ugly seventies dwelling that combined yellow vinyl siding, orange brick facing and ornamental stonework.

"Fifteen," he said, flipping through his pile, "and Mai Ling has twelve. That'll be plenty."

"Are you sure?"

"Yes, besides I've had enough." Norton glowered at the stone dragon at the edge of the drive as if it were the cause of his present state of misery. "We've been plodding about in the cold for three hours, and I bet we won't get so much as a thank you from your father."

"Don't be silly," snapped Sylvia. "We want him to get re-elected. It's very useful having a family member on council."

"Well, I'm ready to pack it in. I have an early meeting with a client in the morning and I still have to go over my brief."

Sylvia and Norton were both lawyers.

"It's only seven o'clock. I have to be in court first thing, and I'm not complaining."

"That's because he's *your* father. I haven't noticed Juliet's husband being dragged in to help."

"How can he help when they live out of town? Besides, Juliet is doing more than her bit. She's brought the children down for a whole week so she can work on the campaign. Come on, don't be such a wimp. Let's move on."

Ignoring Norton's aggrieved expression, Sylvia proceeded to march down the sidewalk towards the end of the block. Norton followed mulishly. As they reached the last house, they saw Mai Ling coming down the cross street on the opposite side, so they paused by the box cedar hedge that surrounded the end lot and waited for her to reach them. The windows of the house behind the hedge were blazing with light and a Tchaikovsky symphony floated across the garden, drowning out the sounds on the street.

"Appropriate," muttered Norton. "Napoleon marching into the depths of the Russian winter. I wonder if we'll ever get out."

Sylvia ignored him and continued to watch Mai Ling.

The hedge was high and interlaced with ivy, and it screened the adjacent road from their view, so they were both startled when a Sikh carrying a canvas bag came round the corner and nearly collided with them. He muttered an apology and continued along the street. Mai Ling came hurrying across the road and joined them at the corner.

"I only have three left," said Mai Ling, waving the last of her leaflets.

Sylvia frowned.

"How can that be? I've got all these."

"It's probably because Mai Ling moves at the speed of light and doesn't waste time standing around talking," said Norton.

"Please?" said Mai Ling, with a dazzling smile. Her English was not yet very sound.

"Oh well, here," said Sylvia, thrusting her last pile at Mai Ling. "You can have these. Do that side of the street," she added, pointing at the far corner.

Mai Ling beamed and hurried away again.

"Don't you feel guilty using Mai Ling for this?" said Norton. "After all, she can't possibly understand the first thing about city elections. It's pretty close to exploitation."

"Nonsense," snapped Sylvia. "Mai Ling knows all about oppression, and that's what we'll have if those bloodsuckers get in and start playing around with our property taxes. Besides, if she weren't helping us tonight, she'd be looking after the children, whereas this way, Mother has the children and Mai Ling gets a night off to do something different. How very odd," she added, suddenly staring past Norton's shoulder.

"What's odd?"

"That man delivering papers."

"What about him."

"He hasn't come off the porch of that house. The one with the 'for sale' sign on the lawn," said Sylvia, gesturing toward a grandiose edifice in the middle of the block. The house had a large covered porch completely screened by cypress trees on either side, but the rest of the yard was clear and open.

"Maybe he's tying his shoelace," said Norton.

"For five minutes?"

Norton peered toward the house.

"I wonder if he's casing the place. Perhaps we should walk up and look."

Sylvia and Norton moved along the pavement until they could see into the porch of the house. To their surprise, there was no sign of the paper carrier.

"Well," said Norton. "How mysterious."

"What's mysterious?" boomed a loud voice. Norton looked round to see Beary and Juliet.

Sylvia pointed toward the porch.

"We just saw a newspaper carrier go onto that porch, and he's simply disappeared."

"Perhaps he slipped down a side exit," suggested Norton.

"It doesn't look as though there is one," said Juliet.

"Has it ever occurred to you," said Beary, "that the man might live there. He probably came to the end of his route."

Sylvia sniffed.

"That house must be worth a fortune. Hardly the residence of a paper carrier."

"People will do anything to pay the mortgage these days," said Beary reasonably. "Besides, if he's the same carrier we saw earlier, he has expensive tastes. Didn't you notice his Italian leather shoes?"

Sylvia scowled.

"It's impossible to tell who anyone is these days," she complained.

"Well," said Norton, "whether he's somebody or nobody, he's definitely disappeared."

"There's one way to settle this," said Beary. "I shall go door-knocking."

Beary marched down the driveway and plodded up the steps. He disappeared into the covered porch and rang the doorbell. As he waited, he surveyed the porch carefully. There was no means of exit, other than into the house itself. There was also no newspaper on the front step.

Suddenly the door flew open and he was greeted by a smiling lady with sparkling dark eyes. She wore an elegant sari and she looked familiar to Beary. As soon as she spoke, he recognized her as a volunteer from the Multicultural Society.

"Mr. Beary, how nice to see you. You are on the campaign trail?"

"I certainly am. Can I leave you my card?"

"Of course. And I will tell Ranjit that you called."

"Thank you, dear lady," Beary purred, for he was hopeless at remembering his constituents' names. "Tell me," he added. "Does a member of your household deliver the local newspaper in this area?"

The lady looked surprised.

"No. Why do you ask?"

"We just saw a paper carrier deliver to this house, but we didn't see him leave. We thought perhaps he lived here—that he had finished his route and had come home."

"Oh, no. *The News* did arrive. I just took it in a few moments ago. But the carrier most certainly did not come into the house. You must have missed him in the dark."

"Ah, well, I expect that's it," said Beary. He said his farewells and walked back to the others who were standing expectantly on the pavement.

"Well?" demanded Sylvia, as he approached.

"He didn't go in the house," said Beary. "He came and left. You must have glanced away for a moment and missed seeing him leave."

"I did not," said Sylvia adamantly. "It's most peculiar."

"Could we dispense with the mystery of the missing carrier and get back to the job in hand," Norton pleaded querulously. "We only have a couple more houses to do. Then we can get out of this foul night air and discuss your puzzle in the comfort of a warm house." His faced looked white and pinched and he was starting to shiver.

"Yes," said Beary. "All hands to it. Here, I'll do the three houses at the end. I won't bother to door-knock. I'll just pop the stuff through the mail slots. You three can take the remaining leaflets and do Carleton Street."

Beary barrelled across to the next house and popped a leaflet into the metal box beside the front door. Then, refusing to look at Juliet, he stepped across the low wire fence adjoining the drive and hurried across the lawn.

"Come on," said Norton. "It's pitch black and freezing cold. Let's get this over with."

He put a hand on his wife's shoulder and propelled her along the pavement. Juliet followed, and the trio walked briskly toward the corner. There was no street lighting at the end of the block, and as none of the houses had porch lights on, the night was very dark. Somehow, the inky blackness made the cold seem even more intense. Juliet shivered and pulled her collar up around her neck.

The trio had almost reached the corner when suddenly there was a dreadful shriek that cut the silence of the night and froze them all in their tracks.

"Good Lord, what was that?" said Norton, looking about wildly.

"There's someone flailing about in front of that house," said Juliet. "Look, over there."

Sylvia grabbed her sister's arm and drew in her breath. Then, as the sound of a familiar voice uttering a string of imprecations floated across the night air, she relaxed her grip and raised her eyes heavenward.

"My God," she said. "He's walked into a fish pond!"

*   *   *   *

Edwina's expression was still frosty an hour later after her husband was changed, dry and settled by the fire with a large Glenlivet at his side, Henrietta Plop in his lap and MacPuff at his feet. Sylvia and Norton had gone home, along with their three children and Mai Ling. Philippa, who lived at home, had excused herself and gone to bed, but Richard had stayed to have a drink with his parents. Juliet went upstairs to tuck in her own brood, who appeared quite tired after a long evening of stuffing envelopes under their grandmother's gimlet eye. When she returned, she found the others discussing the mystery of the disappearing Sikh.

"Either we saw two separate carriers, or there's a time discrepancy," said Beary, stroking Henrietta Plop's small head and triggering a tiger-sized purr. "There's more than one local paper, you know. It's quite possible we saw two different people."

"No," insisted Richard. "Our Sikh was the same as yours. I distinctly noticed the expensive shoes."

"Perhaps you made a mistake on the time?"

"No. It was only five-thirty when the carrier cut through the trail. Philippa had just checked her watch."

"Then why didn't he come through to the other street until six o'clock?" said Beary. "The trail is less than a hundred feet long. What was he doing for half an hour?"

Juliet settled by the fire and scratched MacPuff's ears. "Maybe he was having a Glenlivet with Mrs. Baird?" she said facetiously.

"Who is Mrs. Baird?" asked Edwina icily.

"You know Jeanne Baird," grunted Beary. "President of the Chamber. She's a real estate agent."

"Ah," said Edwina. "John Baird's wife. He's in real estate too. He belongs to the local dramatic society. They're separated, you know. She led him quite a dance over the years."

"Does she live at the end of the cul-de-sac?" asked Richard.

"Yes," said Beary. "There are two huge lots back to back with very expensive homes on them. One house faces Maynor Street, and Jeanne Baird's looks out onto Arbroath. The trail between the two cul-de-sacs passes along the edge of both properties, and the ravine abuts the other side of the lots. It's a very private spot."

"Vulnerable for a burglary," mused Richard. "He could have been taking advantage of his route to case the place. It might be worth checking to see if there was a break-in. I wonder if the lady was home."

"No, she wasn't," said Beary. "I knocked. There was no answer, though come to think of it, her car was in the driveway. Perhaps she'd gone to bed early."

"She could have been out with a friend," said Edwina, with a meaningful sniff. "From what I hear of Jeanne Baird, she doesn't lack for escorts."

"It seems to me," said Beary, "that we have two mysteries of the disappearing Sikh. He disappeared for half an hour in the middle of his route, and he disappeared without trace an hour later. I have the feeling that if we could solve the mystery of the first disappearance, we would also solve the second. You know, I'm really beginning to wonder why Mrs. Baird didn't open her door."

It was not until the next morning that Beary received an answer to his question.

Richard telephoned at eleven o'clock, shortly after a report had come in from a hysterical young man who had arrived at Mrs. Baird's house at nine-thirty.

"There *was* a break-in, Dad," said Richard, "but it wasn't a burglary. Somebody got into the house and attacked her while she was in bed. She was strangled to death."

*   *   *   *

Four days later, Richard was still troubled by the details of the case, and he decided to drop in on the Beary household to see what his father could make of the inconsistencies. His mother greeted him at the door. She had just arrived home from work and was looking both weary and irritable.

"He's out back," said Edwina, "in the garage." She eyed Richard's boots critically and frowned. "You'd better go round by the garden gate," she said firmly. "I'd offer you tea, but it's much too close to dinnertime," she added and closed the door. Edwina was never one to pamper her children.

Richard trooped around the house and entered the back garden through the side gate, where MacPuff greeted him exuberantly and made up for his mother's lack of enthusiasm. Beary's workshop, inaccurately called the garage since it never housed any vehicles, abutted the back lane. The sound of a radio floated across the lawn from the garage, and Richard followed the noise across the garden and entered the outbuilding. His father was busy repairing Edwina's hair dryer, which had been broken by one of the visiting grandchildren, but he was perfectly happy to theorize with his son while he worked. He turned off the radio and concentrated on what Richard had to say.

"Mrs. Baird must have been home when you knocked, Dad," Richard insisted. "Perhaps she was in the washroom, or she may have been in bed."

Beary was sceptical.

"In bed at five-thirty in the afternoon!" he said in disbelief. "Was she ill?"

"As a matter of fact," said Richard, "she wasn't feeling well. But this is the puzzling part. Jeanne Baird wasn't killed between five-thirty and six. The man who discovered her was her latest boyfriend." Richard found himself a sawdust-free spot on the workbench and sat down. "And the clincher," he continued, "is that Jeanne Baird left a message on his answering machine at eight o'clock on the night of the murder."

"Answering machines! Those bloody unreliable things," said Beary, pulling a wire free of the dryer and picking up his soldering iron. "How do you know it was eight o'clock?"

"We heard the message. Several people identified her voice. She specified the day and the time on the message. And there were two prior messages on the machine that had definitely been made on the same day, one at four p.m. and one at seven, one hour before Mrs. Baird's call. We've verified the other messages. Mrs. Baird's call couldn't have come through any earlier."

"What did the message say?"

"'This is Jeanne. It's November first, eight p.m. Darling, I'm feeling the pits. Don't come round tonight, and don't call because I'm going to turn in early. Come over in the morning. I'll see you then. Love you.'"

Beary chuckled.

"Edwina was right. She did have friends." He reconnected the last wire and put the casing of the dryer back together. "There, that should do it," he said. "Come on, we'll go in and have a drink." He unplugged the electric heater, turned off the lights, and ushered Richard outside. The winter garden was very pretty at night, with the exterior garage light flooding the evergreen clematis and the lanterns at the side of the patio illuminating the ivy that climbed the wall between the Beary property and the next-door neighbour's house. MacPuff was lying on the deck and he wagged his tail as they came up the stairs.

"What was her young man like?" Beary asked as they reached the back door of the house.

"Young," said Richard, removing his shoes as they entered the kitchen. There was an enticing smell of roast chicken emanating from the oven. "Probably half her age," he added, following his father into the living-room. "Seemed pretty cut up."

"Could he be acting?" Beary went to the liquor cabinet and poured two generous glasses of Scotch. They settled into the armchairs by the fireplace.

"I don't think so. Anyway, he has an alibi. He's a musician. He was in rehearsal all day and went into a lengthy overtime session. He didn't get off until after eleven, and while there's some latitude in the possible time of death, Baird couldn't have been killed that late."

"What about the estranged husband?"

"He has an alibi too. He was holding an open house. It started at seven and continued until after eleven. He had another agent with him, so he's also accounted for."

"Did you say a there was a break-in?"

"Yes. The lock on the back door had been forced. It was one of those flimsy things that wouldn't pass any reputable security test."

"Anyone could have gone into her back yard," said Beary. "That trail is screened from both cul-de-sacs."

"Yes, in theory," said Richard. "But we've had one bit of good fortune. There's a bedridden old lady in the house at the end of Maynor Street. Because her yard is covered in floodlights, she has a clear view of one end of the trail and she amuses herself by watching the comings and goings on the street. She insists that no one went through the trail during the significant time."

"Did she see our disappearing Sikh?"

"Yes, but of course he went through much earlier."

"So whoever killed Mrs. Baird must have entered the trail from the Arbroath Street side?"

The door of the living-room flew open and Edwina came through. She looked annoyed.

"The paper hasn't arrived again," she snapped. "I do wish they'd get reliable carriers."

Beary perked up.

"Which paper?" he demanded.

"The local, of course."

"Which local? There are two."

"*The News.*"

"Ah. I expect you've phoned to complain," said Beary, knowing his wife's efficiency in pointing out other people's deficiencies.

"Of course," said Edwina glacially.

"What's the excuse this time?"

"The most ridiculous one yet," snapped Edwina. "According to the circulation department, the carrier didn't show up for work today. He'd only been on the job fifteen days in total, and when they phoned his home, they found he'd given them a wrong number. It appears the man has disappeared off the face of the earth."

"Well," said Beary. "So we're back to the mystery of the disappearing Sikh."

Richard was not paying attention. His head was turned in the direction of the kitchen where the aroma of chicken was even more potent than it had been when they entered the house.

"Oh, for Heaven's sake," said Edwina, seeing her son's expression and raising her eyes to the ceiling. "You might as well stay and eat. And don't drink any more Scotch," she added to her husband. "I'm ready to serve up."

"You know what I would do if I were you," Beary said to his son as they followed Edwina to the kitchen. "I'd figure out how that answering machine was rigged."

*   *   *   *

The following evening, Richard telephoned his father from his office. His voice sounded tired but triumphant.

"You were right, Dad," he said. "The call was a fake. We played the tape to one of Mrs. Baird's former boyfriends who also happened to be John Baird's business partner. He went quite pale and looked extremely embarrassed. He recognized the message as one that Jeanne Baird had called into his office the previous year."

"Wasn't that rather indiscreet, if he was John Baird's partner?"

"Baird was away on a business trip at the time. What his wife didn't realize was that he returned early and stopped by the office prior to coming home. While there, he listened to all the old messages. Of course, he recognized his wife's voice immediately. He probably took the tape out and kept it with a view to using it as evidence if there was a divorce."

"And later, he decided to use it to murder her."

"Exactly. They separated soon afterward, and before long, Mrs. Baird shed the business partner and took up with the musician. She filed for divorce from her husband, and I guess he decided he'd rather be a widower than be forced to divide their assets. From then on, he kept a close track on all her movements and laid out his plan. He was quite a good amateur actor, and it was easy for him to create the part of the non-existent Sikh. He applied for the carrier job, giving a false name and address, and dutifully did his route twice a week, all the while getting a feel for the area."

"And on his fourth run, he took time out to murder his wife."

"Yes. He delivered the last paper at the end of Maynor, then went through the trail to the side gate of Jeanne Baird's garden and let himself in through the basement door of the house."

"He still had his old key, I suppose."

"Yes. That's how he was able to take his wife by surprise. He murdered her and dressed her in her nightclothes. Then he broke the lock on the back door to make it look as if there had been a forced entry, left the house by the basement door, crept back onto the trail and continued his route."

"Thus the half-hour gap."

"Exactly."

"Later, while at the open house, he slipped into the bedroom to make the phone call that was to create his alibi. He dialled his wife's boyfriend's number, knowing full well that the young man would be at a rehearsal."

"And," said Beary, "he played the old message into the phone when he heard the signal from the answering machine. I suppose he had one of those mini-tape players tucked in his briefcase. Very tricky."

"It certainly was. He knew the message would be as applicable to the new relationship as it was to the old one."

"But surely when you checked with the exchange, you would have found no record of a call from Mrs. Baird's number? Wouldn't that have given him away?"

"Jeanne Baird had all the latest in modern technology," said Richard, "including two cellular phones. Her husband simply took one of them with him and used it to make the call."

"Well, that explains just about everything," said Beary, "except of course, for his disappearance at the end of the evening."

"It's actually so simple it's laughable," said Richard.

"Don't tell me," said Beary. "Let me figure it out." He thought for a moment, casting his mind back and visualizing the scene where the Sikh had disappeared. Suddenly his frown of concentration changed to a look of triumph.

"Aha," he crowed. "The *for sale* sign on the lawn. He ended his route at the location where he was due to hold the open house."

"You've got it," said Richard.

"That voluminous canvas bag must have contained his briefcase," said Beary. "Once hidden inside the porch, he whipped off beard, turban and raincoat, bundled them all into the carrier bag and crammed the lot into his briefcase. And there he was, a respectable real estate agent in a business suit and those telltale leather shoes. Then he knocked on the door, handed the lady of the house her newspaper, which he said he'd found on the step, and was welcomed inside. Naturally the lady of the house told me she hadn't seen the paper carrier. She had no reason to connect him with her real estate agent. Diabolically clever. The mysterious Sikh simply vanished into thin air."

"And," said Richard, "if we hadn't had the entire family out on the campaign trail, he would probably have got away with it."

"Ah well, there you are," said Beary. "Public service is what we are about, whether approving rezonings or apprehending killers. Especially," he added thoughtfully, "those dastardly villains who deprive us of a much needed glass of Scotch while pavement-pounding on a freezing November night."

A Body for Sparafucile

▼

Adam Craig raised his massive head and projected his ringing bass in the direction of Vancouver Island:

"*La tempesta e vicina! Piu scura fia la notte.*"

A startled seagull abandoned its rock and fluttered away to perch on a log that bobbed in the water close to the shoreline. Philippa Beary shook her head and pulled the collar of her jacket high around her neck. It was a sunny February day, but cold, and the view of Georgia Strait was a series of diminishing greys; the sea in the foreground, the Gulf Islands in the distance, and the haze from Nanaimo hovering above Gabriola, blending into turbulent and mountainous storm clouds overhead. A white stripe underlined the islands, marking the only patch of calm water in the inlet.

Another outburst from Adam sent the seagull skittering to a log boom moored further along the bay.

"You're scaring the waterfowl, Adam," she said.

Adam turned landward and stared at the rock face that jutted into the water at the end of the stony beach. The bluff, grey and stark, rose steeply above the log booms and a solitary eagle glided high overhead. Between cliff and sky was a dark strip of green foliage projecting over the edge of the escarpment. Adam's warm, brown eyes glazed over and became as cold as the winter morning. Menacingly, he began to intone:

"*Soglio in cittade uccidere…Oppure nel mio tetto…L'uomo di sera aspetto…*"

With a sudden increase in volume, he lunged forward with a forceful stabbing motion and completed the phrase:

"*Una stoccata…e muor!*"

Philippa watched this display with tolerant amusement.

"Why are you so excited about playing an assassin?" she asked.

A burst of enthusiasm rendered Adam momentarily loquacious.

"Assassination is very fashionable in current times," he said. "Not that the modern day lunatic is a professional like Sparafucile. He was a true hit man…methodical, furtive, and business-like."

Adam fell back into the medium where he was most comfortable. He contorted his features and made his black beard and eyebrows perform a *danse macabre* on his round face.

"*Senza strepito…Comprendo…E questo il mio strumento. Vi serve?*"

Ignoring him, Philippa looked up to the top of the cliff. "Someone's up there," she said suddenly. "The bushes are moving."

"*Fu il vento,*" sang Adam.

"It isn't the wind," said Philippa. "I'm sure there's someone on the path."

Adam bounced jubilantly on his log. "*E strano! Chi e?*" he sang.

"Oh, stop it," said Philippa, turning toward Adam. "I get enough of *Rigoletto* at our rehearsals. I thought we came here for peace and fresh air. If you must sing, get inspired by the West Coast scenery and give me a rendition of the *Indian Love Call.*"

To her amazement, Adam froze, mouth agape, and emitted a prolonged "Oooooo," which bore no resemblance to the music of Rudolf Friml.

Adam stared past Philippa toward the rock face.

Swinging round to follow his gaze, Philippa was just in time to see a figure sailing downward through the air. It landed with a thud against the edge of the floating log boom; then slid into the water. For the third time that morning, the startled seagull flew angrily into the air.

*   *   *   *

"Your sister has found a body," said Sergeant Martin to Richard.

"Another! How does she do it?"

"This one literally fell at her feet," reported the sergeant. "It was hardly her fault. She and a fellow student were on the beach together when a woman fell from the top of the cliff."

"Ah," said Richard, relieved. "An accident."

Sergeant Martin paused.

"It would have seemed that way if there had been no witnesses," he said slowly. "If it hadn't been for the log booms near the shore, the woman would have gone straight into the water. Then, even with an abnormally low tide the body might not have been discovered. The tide would have washed it out to sea."

"Do we know the woman's identity?"

"Yes. Her face suffered some damage when she fell down the side of the cliff, but she was still recognizable. Her clothes and hair were distinctive and the young man with your sister was able to identify her. She was the wife of an associate professor of Geography—a Hugh Graham by name. Mrs. Graham was known as Bobbie—Roberta, I suppose. Her husband is in Edmonton on a conference, but he's been contacted, and he'll be able to confirm the identification when he returns."

"Is the student who identified her reliable?"

"He should be. He's the son of the university dean."

"Robert Craig?"

"Yes."

"Ah! So our witness is young Adam."

"You know him, sir?"

"Slightly. He and Philippa are in the opera workshop together. Craig Junior is said to be exceptionally promising. Philippa is quite fond of him, but he alternates his attentions between her and an erratic mezzo who goes by the unbelievably apt name of Cordelia Trilling. According to Philippa, Adam follows Trilling about like a docile King Kong."

Martin nodded, recalling Adam's bulky and shaggy appearance.

"The boy appears knowledgeable about university life," he said. "Well up on who's who."

"Were there other witnesses besides Philippa and Adam?"

"Not to the fall. When Philippa and Craig reached the top of the cliff, they saw a cyclist, so they flagged him down and sent him to call for help. He's been asked if he saw other people in the area. The only people he saw were on the road…a man jogging on the campus and a middle-aged woman hiking in the direction of the gates. Two cars also passed shortly before your sister and her chum came racing out of the bushes, but the cyclist doesn't have any idea of the makes of the cars, let alone the numbers."

"I've missed something," said Richard. "I still haven't heard anything to indicate the fall wasn't an accident."

"I think you'd better talk to the youngsters," Martin said firmly.

*   *   *   *

Down the hall, Philippa and Adam were arguing.

"The Grahams were devoted to each other," Adam insisted.

"No they weren't," said Philippa. "I took a course from Professor Graham last year, and I heard rumours about him. Everyone said his wife was miserable because he chased girls."

"Ignorant student gossip," snorted Adam. "The stories don't fit the way they behaved."

"How can you be so certain? They'd only been on campus two years. Your family never socialized with the Grahams, so it's impossible for you to assume an understanding of their innermost feelings."

"I'm observant about human behaviour," insisted Adam. "I've trained myself. It's a necessary trait for an artist."

"You can't make a judgment on the Graham's marriage based on the odd 'hello' exchanged in passing on campus."

"My instinct is infallible," said Adam smugly. "It's easy to recognize when people are in love. Look at my father and Katherine."

Philippa gaped.

"Your father and Katherine! Really, Adam! That's a ridiculous notion."

"No it isn't. I intend them to get married."

"You're indulging in wishful thinking. I can understand why you'd love to have Katherine for a stepmother, but she's much too young for your father. He must be well over sixty."

"Sixty-three," said Adam. "It's a bit awkward," he acknowledged. "Dad thinks a man of sixty plus has no business making a play for a woman just turned forty. He doesn't realize how attractive Katherine finds him."

"Your father is devoted to the memory of your mother, not scouting for a replacement."

"My mother died six years ago. Furthermore, she was much too generous a person to begrudge my father happiness with someone else. She'd be appalled at the way he spends his time tied to his desk. The only time he relaxes is around my nephews and nieces."

"Exactly," said Philippa. "His grandchildren. A young widow like Katherine might accept ready-made children, but not grandchildren."

"When my father asked Katherine to take over the workshop, she agreed *prestissimo!*"

"She needed something to challenge her after her own life went downhill. And she's found it—a good working relationship—but not a romance. You are an idiot sometimes, Adam."

"Their working relationship is part of the attraction," Adam insisted. "It's easy to capitalize on that," he added smugly. "I invent lots of little errands and projects to bring them together."

Philippa's blue eyes flashed.

"Really, Adam, you are the limit. You're…" Philippa paused. "Speaking of Katherine," she added suspiciously, "Why did she cancel my coaching session this afternoon?"

Adam's booming laugh rattled the light fixtures and earned him a glare from the clerk processing the traffic reports.

"Dad's flying into Seattle today. He intended to travel to Vancouver on the bus, but I told Katherine I was supposed to drive down to meet him and was feeling too ill to go. I begged her to fill in for me." Adam's tone was jubilant. "A three-hour drive together will be sure to help them make progress, though I may have to resort to more direct methods. They're both ridiculously shy and proper."

"You have no business manipulating them like that."

"Of course I do. My whole life has been manipulation. I have three older brothers. You know what the experts say about the youngest in families—they can't get what they want by force so they learn to manipulate. Studies show that most lawyers are the babies of families. Not that I'm going to be a lawyer, but an opera singer requires the same understanding of human foibles."

"Adam, you're crazy," giggled Philippa, unable to stay annoyed.

"That's why I need a mother," said Adam. "And don't scoff. You'll find my observations are always right. Sparafucile always hits the mark."

"I hope so," said Richard, strolling down the hall toward them, Sergeant Martin following close on his heels. "I hear you have something to tell me about the woman who fell from the cliff on the university lands."

"Yes," said Philippa. "It was murder."

Adam burst into a ringing bass.

"*Senza Strepito!*" he boomed. "*Senza Strepito.*"

"Could we get to the point?" said Richard, observing the frosty gaze from the traffic wicket.

"That is the point. *Senza Strepito! Comprendo!*"

"No, I don't *Comprendo*," said Richard.

Martin interjected quickly.

"He's right, sir. That really is the point."

"'*Senza Strepito*' means, 'without a sound'," said Philippa.

"Pardon my obtuseness," said Richard. "I'm afraid I'm still not with you."

"Don't you see," said Philippa. "She fell without a sound. No scream. No cry. She must have been unconscious when she went over the cliff."

*   *   *   *

Robert Craig stretched his large frame as much as the limited space in the BMW would allow. Rather than watch the panorama of speeding cars and forested embankments of Interstate 5, he concentrated on his driver. Katherine's red hair and serene profile held infinitely more appeal.

"This is very nice of you, Katherine," he said for the third or fourth time, "though really quite unnecessary. I hope you're not putting more pressure on yourself by taking the afternoon off."

Katherine gave him a sunny smile. Robert's formality was part of his charm. "Not a bit," she said, "it's my pleasure. It's lovely to have you back."

Her words were the literal truth. The rest of the world might be enthralled by the bizarre or unorthodox, but Katherine considered this grey-haired man, who wore conservative business suits and was old enough to be her father, to be infinitely more exciting than a jumbo jet full of Pavarotti's."

"I hope you didn't have to wait long."

"I was a bit early," Katherine admitted, "but I had coffee in the lounge and enjoyed people watching. I imagined the human parade was a giant cattle call and I tried casting operas from the different types I saw."

Robert chuckled.

"And did you find the perfect Duke of Mantua?"

"No. But I did see a Maddalena at the baggage counter. She was absolutely striking. Black glossy hair in one of those sculpted styles…dramatic clothes, exotic makeup. Gorgeous figure. Every man in sight was looking her way."

"If they'd had any taste," Robert said gallantly, "they'd have been looking your way."

Katherine smiled, but said nothing. She pulled out into the fast lane and concentrated on passing a logging truck. Afraid he might have embarrassed her, Robert brought the conversation back to a less personal footing.

"Was it hectic at the airport?" he asked.

"Not bad, if you don't mind being surrounded by security guards. Still it's less depressing than it was in the Sixties. I had a gorgeous young aunt who used to take me on trips, and I remember going through Seattle airport with her. It was awful…full of babes with death in their eyes lined up against the walls while they waited for their flight to Saigon. I still remember how indignant she was because the soldiers didn't so much as glance in her direction."

"Trauma, whether it's caused by shock or fear, deadens the spirit. You know that, Katherine. You've been through it yourself."

Katherine thought back to her thirty-third year, when after six blissful years of marriage, a car accident had caused the death of her husband and the loss of the child she had been carrying. The prolonged depression that followed had ended Katherine's highly promising singing career. She could remember the deadness that engulfed her at the time, but she could not recall how it had felt. Working with Robert Craig had sparked her back to life.

"Do you miss your singing career?" Robert asked suddenly.

"No," Katherine said truthfully. "I love music, but I have no desire to go back to the gypsy life and the international circuit. Besides, my career was tied in with my marriage. John and I worked together constantly, and it didn't seem lonely trekking all over the place. If it hadn't been for him, I'd never have made it as far as I did."

"I find that hard to believe," said Robert. His admiration for Katherine stemmed not only from her physical charm, but also from her energy and discipline.

"It's true," Katherine insisted. "He had none of the volatile temperament one associates with musicians. He was very calm and matter of fact…a bit like your Adam. I was nervous, hyperactive, always rushing." Katherine paused, then continued thoughtfully. "I used to go for walks, ostensibly to relax, but I'd always be in such a hurry to get round my prescribed itinerary that even if I got a rock inside my runners, I'd keep moving, even though I was in agony. John taught me to stop to remove the stones from my shoes. Somehow, when I applied that principle to the other aspects of my life, everything fell into place."

Robert was not jealous by nature, and considered Katherine's happiness in her former marriage to be another credit in her favour. However, he decided it was time to change the subject.

"Is the workshop going well?"

"Very. Act IV of *Rigoletto* is in good shape, and the Beary girl and your son are enchanting in the Papagena/Papageno duet. *Merry Wives* needs more work. The final act of *Manon Lescaut* is as good as it's going to be considering the voices I've got to work with."

"What sort of talent are you working with?"

"The usual mix—a raft of reliable and unspectacular sopranos. Philippa Beary is delightful on stage and she sings well, but her voice is too light to take her into the big league. Still, she has the potential to carve out a decent musical career if she chooses her roles carefully. The tenor has a moderately good voice and a dynamic stage presence, but he's insufferable off stage. There's the usual quota of mezzos and baritones with adequate voices and sound techniques. I also have a couple of lightweights that are more interested in being the next Celine Dion than in training for the opera stage. However, on the up side, I have a couple of exceptional voices, your son being one, and the Trilling girl the other."

"Ah, Cordelia," sighed Robert. "Adam adores her."

"Yes," Katherine sympathized. "If only he could imbue her with his own dedication. Cordelia has world-class potential. That huge mezzo. If voices were all that counted, she'd go far, but of course she'll never make it. The temperament is all wrong. Did you know she's messing about with drugs? She was nervous and unreliable before, but lately she's been impossible."

"Yes," said Robert. "I tried to alert Adam to her shortcomings, but of course, being Adam, he quoted the bard at me: *Love's not love when it is mingled with regards that stand aloof from the entire point.* Cordelia's appeal for Adam is that she's a lost soul, like the assorted waifs and strays, both human and animal, he used to bring home as a child. Being the youngest of four children, he was always looking for someone or something smaller and more vulnerable than he was."

Katherine swung back into the fast lane and pulled ahead of a Chevrolet wagon.

"Adam does keep Cordelia under some semblance of control," she said. "My worst problem is my tenor because he creates friction among the other singers."

Robert had a reputation for not suffering fools gladly.

"Kick him out," he suggested bluntly.

Katherine took her eyes from the road and stared at him incredulously.

"You must be joking," she said. "David is a *tenor!*"

Robert placed a firm hand over hers on the steering wheel.

"Your Gilda may be prepared to die for him," he said, smiling, "but I'm not."

The car straightened out and resumed a steady course, but several seconds lapsed before Robert removed his hand.

Katherine blushed and put her eyes firmly back on the road.

*   *   *   *

Sergeant Martin looked appreciatively at the lady sitting opposite him. Rhonda Glenn was an exuberant redhead of the type the sergeant particularly appreciated.

"This is a very nice area, Mrs. Glenn," he commented, having mentally appraised the immaculate homes and manicured gardens of Acadia Circle on his drive to her house. "Have you lived here long?"

"Five years. Yes, it's a lovely spot."

"How long did the Grahams live next door to you?" Sergeant Martin asked.

"They moved here from Toronto a couple of years ago. They were quiet and kept to themselves, though as my husband and Hugh Graham were colleagues in the Geography Department, we saw them at faculty functions. I got to know Bobbie better than I knew her husband."

Sergeant Martin nodded and jotted a note in his book.

"What was Mrs. Graham like?" he asked when he looked up. "Describe her for me."

"Bobbie? She liked the open air. She was the clean-scrubbed, athletic type. A strong runner, and good at team sports. She coached girls' softball and grass hockey. She was something of a fitness fanatic—always ate health foods, and never went near a doctor."

"Did she go running regularly on the same route?"

"Every morning. She did four miles."

"Which way did she go?"

"Down Northwest Marine, past Cecil Green and the Chan Centre, then by the Museum of Anthropology—basically all through Pacific Spirit Park. She used to loop round the Japanese Gardens, cut through the student residences, and come back on the other side. There's a bike path and a dirt trail that runs all the way along the cliff. It's a popular spot for the students. That's where the beach access is."

"Wreck Beach. Yes, we're quite familiar with it," said Sergeant Martin, having had his phlegmatic personality tested to the hilt during eye-popping drug and alcohol checks at the nudist beach in his early days on the force.

"Bobbie never hung out there, though she often went to Tower Beach. On days when she had a lot of time, she used to go all the way down the steps and jog back up again. But either way, she always stopped to admire the view from the top of the cliff—then she'd do the rest of the run without a break. I saw her leave on the day she died. She looked in fine form." Rhonda stared meaningfully at Martin. "I'm amazed at her accident. She wasn't the type to faint or overbalance while admiring the scenery."

Martin paused and made another note in his book.

"What was your impression of Graham?" he asked when he had finished writing.

Rhonda Glenn shrugged.

"Good-looking, rather arrogant—not overly popular with his colleagues, according to my husband, but considered perfectly competent. I never took to him. He led his wife quite a dance. He chased other women."

Sergeant Martin nodded.

"One in particular, or women generally?"

"My husband often saw him with other women, and there was one knock-'em-dead brunette—a real fashion plate—who was seen with him on several occasions."

"You're a remarkably attractive woman yourself," Martin commented sincerely. "Did Graham ever make a pass at you?"

Rhonda Glenn laughed.

"You've hit my sore spot," she said. "No, he always treated me with the utmost respect. Actually, he seemed a bit of a cold fish, though once or twice when I saw him turn on the charm, I must admit he could be very engaging. But he kept his womanizing apart from his job. He was never linked with anyone on the campus."

"Are you sure the incidents noted by your husband weren't perfectly innocent?"

"Quite sure. After they'd been here about ten months, Bobbie broke down and confided in me. She burst into floods of tears and told me the whole story. She was a very unhappy woman."

"Were you able to help her at all?"

Rhonda smiled.

"Actually, I was," she said. "I gave her some advice, more because I thought it would boost her morale than improve her husband's behaviour, but everything worked out wonderfully. Or so I thought at the time. Now I realize we were deluded into thinking all was well."

Martin was intrigued.

"What was this wonderful advice?"

"To smarten herself up. At first she was reluctant, but once she got used to the idea, she took my advice with a vengeance. I took her to my hair salon and they gave her the full treatment—make-up and nails as well as hair. It was tremendous fun. She looked through pictures of the latest styles and picked out one that was diametrically opposite from her own. The stylist had a marvellous time making her over—how often do they get that kind of opportunity—to change nonde-script mouse-beige frizz to gleaming black with razor edges. Then we went to Mr. Clive's for clothes and accessories. We got the latest in dress suits and sportswear in flaming reds and wild magentas. Bobbie came back completely made over. Some of the other faculty wives were horrified initially. I think they thought her transformation was a pathetic attempt for attention. But they changed their tune in time because our strategy appeared to work!"

"Graham reacted positively?"

Rhonda nodded.

"Hugh seemed thrilled with his wife's new look. From that time on, none of us heard reports of him being with other women, and Bobbie never complained again. As far as we knew, they were getting along in perfect harmony. I still didn't particularly care for the man, and I thought he'd got off more lightly than he deserved, but then, it was their marriage, not mine. The main thing was that Bobbie seemed happy. But I suppose, what really happened was that he decided to be a lot more discreet. Poor Bobbie. We were all taken in by him."

Martin peered at her attentively.

"Just what are you suggesting, Mrs. Glenn?" he asked.

Rhonda stared back at him, wide eyed.

"I should have thought it would be obvious," she said. "I'm quite sure Hugh was responsible for Bobbie's death."

$$* \qquad * \qquad * \qquad *$$

"You should see the droves of book-toting Asians outside the Armory," said Sergeant Martin. "A far cry from the days when we used to bust poetry readings because the air was thicker than the *we-aim-to-shock* tripe being recited inside. This lot looks incredibly serious."

"They have to be serious. Look at the problems they're going to face in their lifetime."

"Speaking of problems," said Martin, "I got some interesting insights into the Grahams' marriage this morning. The next-door neighbour is convinced Graham murdered his wife."

Richard nodded.

"Having met the man," he said, "I can appreciate such an attitude. Graham has a perfect motive and he's doing little more than putting on a token performance of the sorrowing husband. Three months ago he took out a large insurance policy on his wife. Her death has made him a rich man. However, Graham also has a perfect alibi. On the morning his wife died, one of his colleagues, a John Pritchard, picked him up at six a.m. and drove him to the airport prior to taking the plane to Edmonton. The plane left at 8:15—two hours before Mrs. Graham fell to her death. Mrs. Graham was seen by the mailman at nine o'clock."

"And by Mrs. Glenn around nine-thirty," Martin interjected.

"Exactly. And at the moment Bobbie Graham fell to her death, her husband was several thousand feet up in the air with reliable witnesses to prove it. There's no way Graham could have done it."

"A hit man?" said Martin.

"That's the logical conclusion," agreed Richard, "but nothing I can pick up from any of our information network connects Graham with any known hired killer. I have a gut feeling that the man is guilty, but we may never be able to touch him."

"How should we proceed?"

"We'll turn every stone there is to be turned, but we may not get anywhere through orthodox means. I think I'll brief Philippa. She's on the spot. Her dainty little ears might pick up something useful."

*   *   *   *

Walter Denby liked being a techie. He left the lighting booth and found a cluster of singers draped over the orchestra seats. Walter lit a cigarette and mercilessly blew smoke at the singers. Oblivious to their discomfort, he peered earnestly over his round glasses and pontificated.

"You people are too young to identify with the characters you portray," he announced. Walter, who had failed enough courses to qualify as a professional student, was a superior twenty-five. "The longer you live," he continued, "the more sensitive you become."

"If you were sensitive, Walter," said Cordelia, "you'd realize that people who have spent three hours performing the hard physical labour of singing opera are not in the mood for philosophic debate."

Walter continued as if Cordelia had not spoken.

"I sometimes feel like an antenna," he said, "picking up waves of unhappiness from the rest of the population, yet I often wonder how genuine that unhappiness is; do we feel for others, or simply fear for ourselves through others."

Adam liked to bait Walter.

"I think we enjoy therapeutic benefits from the sufferings of others," he said.

Walter took Adam seriously.

"And by relating tales of others' griefs, See if 'twill teach us to forget our own?" he declaimed. Having taken English 365 three times, Walter had an unlimited supply of obscure Shakespearean quotations.

"Exactly. Wallowing in other people's misery is a wonderful way of alleviating one's own problems."

"Only if the misery is articulated in the form of tragedy," said Walter, "and then it's not the misery that diverts you, it's the expression of that misery. That's why the tragedy of *Lear* can still provide an uplifting evening. Ideas, well expressed, are like mirages. They can always provide a momentary alleviation of depression."

"Personally," said Adam, "I can get as much entertainment from a sordid murder in the press as I can from the antics of Goneril and Regan."

"Speaking of murder," said Cordelia, "have you heard anything more about Mrs. Graham, Philippa?"

"Very little," said Philippa, who had in fact heard a great deal, but was not in a position to repeat the theories that Richard had expounded to her.

"Good looking woman, that Mrs. G," said David Kean, strutting down the aisle in his Duke's costume. "Once she fixed herself up, of course. The older type, but I wouldn't have minded playing Octavian to her Marschallin." He completed the comment with a vulgar gesture.

"Lechery and crudity," said Adam. "A nasty pair of defects, David."

David smiled complacently.

"Don't be jealous, Adam, just because I have personality."

"Personalities are not like mathematical principles. Two negatives do not make a positive."

Not having understood the insult, David looked blank.

Katherine materialized from the wings.

"Come on stage," she called to him, "and you too, Cordelia. I want to go through the duet before we work on the Act as a whole."

Sensing another fifteen minutes of inaction, Adam pulled out the evening edition of the *Vancouver Sun*. Katherine came down into the auditorium and paced up and down the aisle, stopping David periodically to instruct him in his role.

Philippa leaned over Adam's shoulder and started to read a lengthy account of the Graham's university life. She stared at the large photograph of Bobbie Graham. It was taken before her transformation, and indicated a plain woman, quite different from the dazzling creature she had become in the last few months before her death.

"Strut! David," Katherine called out. "Exude arrogance. Every move has to let the audience see what a heel you are."

"You can do it, Davy boy," Adam grunted into his paper. "Be yourself."

David and Cordelia continued their duet, and Katherine, caught by Adam's *sotto voce* rumble, glanced down at him, and then peered more closely at the newspaper article.

"Is that Bobbie Graham?" she asked. "I never met her."

"Yes," said Philippa. "It's not that good a picture, though."

"No, it can't be," agreed Katherine. "From what I've been told, she was quite glamorous."

Katherine moved back down the aisle and frowning, this time at Cordelia, stopped the duet again.

"You're too bland, Cordelia," she criticized. "We need sex appeal."

Adam folded his paper and looked up. To Philippa's chagrin, when Cordelia was under fire, Adam watched like a hawk.

Cordelia tried to look sexy. She stuck her chest out and set one hip at a provocative angle, but she merely succeeded in looking uncomfortable.

"You don't have to use weird contortions," said Katherine, not unkindly. "I wish you'd been with me at the Seattle airport last week," she said suddenly, launching into a description of the girl she had seen by the baggage counter. "Modern as she was, that girl had the Maddalena quality. It has to come from within," she urged. "Sexy, and also ruthless. Stand up straight, use eye contact, and think yourself black, gleaming and glittering."

Cordelia frowned.

"She isn't that ruthless," she protested. "She wants to save the Duke—doesn't she?" she finished uncertainly, peering at Adam for confirmation.

Adam backed up Katherine.

"Of course she's ruthless, Cordelia darling. We know *you're* soft-hearted, but you must get it through your head that you're not Cordelia Trilling acting a part. You're an amoral low-life. Rather than spoil your immediate pleasure, you let some other person die. How ruthless can you get? *Any* body will do."

Philippa had been sitting in a trance since listening to Katherine's description of the Seattle Maddalena, but with Adam's words, she came to life. Leaping to her feet, she turned and stared at Adam.

"Adam, I think I've got it."

"Got what?" Adam looked bewildered.

"The connection. What you just said. *Any body will do.* Are you quite, quite sure that the Grahams were devoted to each other?"

"Yes. I already told you that. Hey, where are you going? You can't take off. We open next week."

In response, Philippa picked up her cape, blew him a kiss, and eased her way from the row of seats. Then she trotted up the aisle and disappeared through the lobby doors.

*   *   *   *

Opening night, the auditorium was packed. Cheers greeted the final curtain.

"Stay put," hissed Adam, gripping Cordelia firmly and pulling the line back into place. "We can probably go one more."

Sure enough, the auditorium curtains creaked apart and there was a renewed burst of applause from the partisan audience of fellow students and proud parents. The curtains inched their way shut once more, and this time the auditorium fell silent. The singers drifted apart and filtered toward the wings. Philippa pulled off her cap as she followed Adam toward the stairs.

"What's wrong with Katherine tonight?" she asked Adam. "She seems dreadfully subdued."

Under the layers of sweat and greasepaint, Adam looked guilty. Philippa stared closely at him.

"Adam, you've been up to something! Yes, of course, your father usually comes round to wish us good luck, but now I think of it, I haven't seen him backstage tonight."

"I must have made them self-conscious," said Adam analytically. "I hope I didn't overdo it."

"Overdo what?"

"I spoke to Katherine about Dad."

"What did you tell her?"

"That he'd told me how crazy he is about her and that it's only because of their age difference that he's reluctant to make a move."

"Your father actually told you that?"

"No. He's much too discreet to talk like that. I made it up for Katherine's benefit," said Adam.

Philippa was aghast.

"Adam, that's terrible," she said.

Adam looked defensive.

"No it isn't. The facts are true. I only invented the bit about Dad telling me how he feels."

"But why should talking to Katherine like that make your father stay away from her this evening?"

"Well, I suppose that's because of what I told him."

Philippa managed not to groan. With considerable effort, she contained herself and waited patiently.

"Go on," she said.

"I told him that the word via the grapevine was that Katherine only accepted the university workshop job because she was in love with him."

"Adam, that's not true."

"It's true that she's in love with him," argued Adam. "I admit I embroidered the rest a bit. Well I had to do something," he said indignantly, seeing Philippa's ferocious stare. "At the rate they're going, they'd never get together."

"Get together! You've taken a perfectly good friendship and driven them so far apart they'll never be comfortable working together again. I would never have thought you could be so stupid, Adam."

The conversation was interrupted by the arrival of Richard. Unaware of the quarrel in session, he hugged Philippa and shook Adam by the hand.

"Wonderful show, you two, both onstage and off."

He pulled them aside and found a quiet corner at the back of the stage.

"Do you want to hear the conclusion of your mystery, seeing as the two of you were responsible for bringing the truth to light?"

"Ah, our body," Adam purred, relieved to have the subject changed. "So did she fall, or was she pushed?"

"Neither, actually," said Richard. "She was hit in the face with a rock with sufficient force to knock her over the edge."

"So it was murder."

"Yes, and Hugh Graham was in on it. Philippa gave me the lead last week. We followed it up, and the details fell into place. Once we confronted Graham with what we knew, he broke down and gave us the whole story."

"I still can't believe Hugh Graham was a party to the murder of his wife," Adam said mulishly. "Those two were devoted to each other."

Philippa smiled.

"Listen to what Richard has to say," she said. "You were right."

"You're confusing me."

"Mrs. Graham wasn't a victim. She was a murderess."

Adam gaped.

"What are you talking about? I identified her."

Richard interjected.

"You identified a body of a woman with a heavily made-up face that had been disfigured by striking against a rock. The hairstyle was that of Mrs. Graham, and the body was wearing Mrs. Graham's jogging suit. The woman who died was a Louise Brummet. The motive for her death was money. The Grahams developed a complex scheme to defraud their insurance company, but to do it, they needed a body."

"*Any* body," Philippa cut in, "just like Sparafucile."

"I don't understand," said Adam. "How did the Grahams manage to get a body that looked like Mrs. Graham?"

"They began the scheme a long time ago," said Richard. "Ever since they arrived on campus, they've been acting the roles of the philandering husband and the distraught wife. But there was a sinister reason behind the husband's philandering. He was looking for a particular type of woman."

"One who looked like his wife."

"She didn't have to resemble Bobbie Graham very closely. The similarities had to be in height, build and age. Bobbie Graham had no outstanding features. There were probably many women who would have fit the criteria."

"No outstanding features?" said Adam. "The whole look of the woman was outstanding."

"No," said Richard. "The outstanding look didn't appear until a few months ago. You see Graham could be charming when he wanted to be, and he used that charm to go scouting for a victim. Once he met Louise Brummet, he settled down to a steady relationship with her. She fit the criteria exactly. She was single. Her relatives were in Australia, and she had few friends. She was athletic, similar in build and height to Mrs. Graham. The basic differences were stylistic ones. Louise Brummet wore flashy clothes and a lot of make-up. Her most distinctive feature was her stylish black hair. Rhonda Glenn still believes that the suggestion for a new look and a makeover was her own. She doesn't realize how cleverly Bobbie Graham manipulated her."

"Ah, *comprendo*," trilled Adam. "They didn't make a body look like Mrs. Graham. They made Mrs. Graham look like the body."

"Yes. That was the reason for the transformation. Then all that remained was for Graham to stop the public philandering and maintain discreet contact with Brummet on a regular basis until the time came to carry out the murder. He told Brummet that Bobbie had found out about them and was behaving irrationally, and he made it sound as if his wife's act of imitating his mistress was that of an unbalanced women. He told her Bobbie had even threatened suicide. Graham convinced Brummet that he intended to run away with her, but that they must be discreet because he was afraid of what his wife might do. They planned to go to South America, with Brummet leaving first, and Graham joining her there, going in various stages from Edmonton so that Bobbie Graham couldn't follow his tracks. Brummet bought her ticket, got her passport in order, and prepared for the trip. She resigned from her job and told her associates and friends that she was going back to Australia."

"How did they get her to come to the university and dress up in Mrs. Graham's jogging suit?" asked Adam. "Why did she go out for that run? Graham was already on a plane by then."

"I'm coming to that," said Richard. "The night before they were due to leave, Graham called Brummet. He told her that Bobbie Graham had committed suicide in the garage, and that things could look very bad for him. He asked for Brummet's help. Once Brummet agreed to Graham's scheme, Bobbie Graham left and spent the night in a hotel, disguising herself with a grey wig and drab clothes. Brummet drove to the university and parked her car a couple of blocks away to avoid suspicion. Then she spent the night with Graham. In the morning, she put on Bobbie's dressing gown and saw Graham and Pritchard off at six a.m. Waving from the doorway in poor light, it would have been impossible for Pritchard to detect the deception. Then two hours later Brummet, dressed in Bobbie Graham's jogging suit, left to duplicate Bobbie Graham's usual run. She made sure people saw her because the whole purpose, as she thought, was to give Graham an alibi in case he was accused of killing his wife. Her intention was to finish the run, then dress in her own clothes and leave unobtrusively, driving straight to the airport to catch her plane. Poor woman. Graham had even drilled into her that she must pause at Bobbie's usual spot on the cliff. When she did, Bobbie Graham, still in grey wig and hiking gear, was waiting in the bushes. You have to remember that Bobbie Graham was strong, and an expert pitcher. She walked out, called Brummet by name, and as Brummet turned, she smashed a large rock into her face, ensuring that not only would she overbalance and fall, but that her features would be sufficiently marred as to ensure no complications with the identification. Then Bobbie Graham calmly walked back to her own house, took

Brummet's suitcase and purse, complete with passport, plane tickets and car keys, and drove Brummet's car to the airport. In the airport washroom, she disposed of the grey wig, changed her clothes, and made up her face. Finally, using Brummet's passport, she got on the plane for South America. She was lucky she didn't run into Dean Craig. Katherine Marshall had never met her, but she did notice her, thinking her a perfect model for Maddalena. Katherine didn't realize how accurate her assessment was. It was a very wicked scheme."

Adam grinned broadly at Philippa.

"I was right," he crowed. "And if it hadn't been for my insistence that the Grahams had a close marriage, you would never have twigged."

"OK," said Philippa. "For once, you were right."

There was a choking noise behind them, and they looked round to see Walter Denby, flushed and pink, staring with embarrassment at Adam.

"What's the matter, Walter?" Adam asked.

"It…it's your father," Walter croaked, the words coming out with difficulty.

"What about my father?" Adam asked, suddenly alert.

"He's in the stairwell with Katherine," said Walter, turning even redder.

Adam's eyes gleamed.

"So?"

Walter finally managed to get the words out and they poured forth in a surging torrent.

"He's kissing her. Not just congratulations, and that sort of thing. I mean really kissing her. They're carrying on like a couple of teenagers!"

Adam whooped and tossed his wooden dagger into the air. Then he picked up Philippa and twirled her round the stage. Adam's joy was infectious, and in an instant, Philippa's amazement turned into delight.

"OK. So twice you were right," Philippa gasped. "Just don't gloat, Adam," she said.

Adam kissed Philippa exuberantly.

"Why not?" he boomed. "I told you, didn't I? My instincts are infallible. Sparafucile always hits the mark!"

Bow, Bow, Ye Upper Middle Classes

▼

"Hide your wallets," said Beary. "Here comes Gordon Rummel."

Edwina's expression became frosty. She had not yet recovered from the results of the civic election, and she was particularly offended that the former Provincial Finance Minister was now the local Mayor. Breakfast in the Beary household had become a ritual of gloom while Edwina pored over announcements of new council initiatives and delivered angry monologues about zealots with propaganda pamphlets for brains.

"How could the local electorate put him back in office?" hissed Edwina. "It's beyond belief."

Beary watched curiously as Rummel worked his way through the crowd in the hotel ballroom. "It's that toothy smile," he said. "Look. He's outshining the chandeliers."

"Nonsense," snapped Edwina. "Everyone loathed him when he controlled the money in the Legislature...yet the city election was practically a left-wing sweep."

"Not quite," said Beary smugly.

Gordon Rummel stopped at an adjacent table and began an animated conversation with its occupants. It was impossible to hear what was said for the ballroom was filled with the roar of voices struggling to be heard over the local symphony orchestra which was churning out selections from *Iolanthe*.

Beary hummed a few bars; then spoke reflectively.

"When W.S. Gilbert wrote that every babe was a little Liberal or a little Conservative, he obviously didn't anticipate the emergence of the labour forces in politics."

Beary continued to watch the next table. Rummel's attempt to socialize had been interrupted. A tall man with steel-grey hair had stopped by the table and accosted him.

"Isn't that Penelope Beech's husband?" said Edwina.

"Penelope Who?"

"Penelope Beech. The Arts Assembly President. Really, Bertram, you must keep track of these community people if you want to keep your council seat."

"I did keep my council seat. I was the only non-partisan candidate who managed to hang in there. Give me some credit. Anyway, why do I have to keep track of Penelope Beech's husband?"

"Because he's a wealthy doctor and he helps our slate at election time. My goodness," Edwina added, nodding approvingly toward the next table, "Edward Beech is really telling Rummel off."

"Rummel is impervious to verbal assaults," said Beary. "He's protected by the shield of his ideology. It doesn't matter how many broadsides I fire on Monday nights, they bounce off him like ping pong balls."

Demonstrating the truth of this observation, Rummel continued to smile until the doctor's tirade wound down, then he allotted a few carefully chosen remarks to the people at the table, and expertly manoeuvred himself toward Beary's group.

Taking liberties with Gilbert's lyrics, Beary carolled a few bars with the orchestra.

"Bow, Bow, ye upper middle classes! Rummel, will kick you in your…"

"Beary, you wicked old anarchist," crooned Rummel. "Good to see you. So glad you made it back on council. The term would have been terribly boring without you stirring up the civil servants. Practically an institution, aren't you? How many years is it now?"

"Twenty-two," said Beary. "Not all of us can graduate to the Province…and slither back again."

Rummel ignored the dig and smirked. "It was exciting to be part of the provincial government," he admitted, "but I missed the old days on council. I must say it's great to be back for the Mayor's Arts Ball. Two mayors and two cities joining forces to promote the local arts groups. Wonderful to see these community organizations again."

On the far side of the table, Joan Dorset looked grim. Joan was president of the local historical society.

"If you persist in your plan to slash arts funding and put all the taxpayers' money into subsidized housing and pay hikes for unions, most of these community organizations will have folded a year from now."

Rummel's smile did not waver.

"We have to priorize," he said. "There are tough decisions to make."

Joan Dorset stiffened and opened her mouth to retort, but Rummel, being a seasoned politician, had already segued to the next table.

"Nasty little snake," Joan said venomously. "He means someone has to pay for all the socialist rot they plan to introduce in the form of new programs."

"Heathens, the lot of them," grunted her husband, Timothy, his eyes squinting angrily and disappearing into the folds of his fleshy cheeks.

"Now, now," crooned Beary. "Let us separate Church and State. Rummel's cohorts are many things, but you can't call them heathens. One of his council colleagues is a lay minister. He's also a pompous ass, but he's extremely devout and absolutely sincere."

Timothy reddened, and the slits where his eyes were located glittered dangerously, but before he could respond, a hearty voice interrupted. Beary looked around to see the familiar face of the president of Komtrac Developments. Behind him stood his wife, Miriam, who chaired the local opera board. George Thurwell walloped Beary on his broad back and waved at the two vacant seats at the table.

"Are these taken?" he asked. "This looks like a congenial right-wing table."

"Help yourselves," said Beary, "but watch your labels. Joan and Timothy are most certainly several leagues to the right of Attila the Hun, but Elton and Tania Worthing are bureaucratic neutrals," he continued, waving his hand toward the young couple beside the Dorsets, "Elton being the assistant planner at the hall. As for Edwina, far from being right-wing, she is a bastion of the type of liberalism that sees the flaws in the extremes of all other parties and never offers any concrete measures as alternatives."

"Don't talk rot," snapped Edwina.

"It's not rot, my dear. How else do you think you could have moved up into the administrative heights of your chosen profession if not for your magnificent ability never to offend anyone in a position of authority?"

Edwina glowered furiously, but Beary ignored her.

"I myself," he continued, "belong to no political party other than the non-partisan association that sponsors my council candidacy, having realized at an early age that no party has a monopoly on intelligence or integrity, and all parties have their share of crooks, hypocrites and idiots." Beary heaved himself to a standing position. "So sit here at your peril," he added. "And on that eloquent note, it's time for a refill."

"The social hour is supposed to be for table-hopping," Edwina reproved him. "Everyone else is out there networking."

"Table-hopping is for socially ambitious toads," said Beary, "and networking is for fishers-of-men-with-money. I am merely a thirsty frog-who-would-a-woo-ing-go in the direction of the bar. Besides, if all the other guests are springing from cluster to cluster, we can greet them in the comfort of our chairs as they leap past our own table."

Edwina went pink. As Beary lumbered away to the bar, Elton Worthing tactfully changed the subject.

"Is your daughter singing tonight, Mrs. Beary? I see her over there looking spectacular in black and silver. How on earth does she keep that gigantic bow on her shoulder standing upright?"

Edwina smiled proudly.

"She's doing a couple of numbers after dinner, but she didn't give me any details. She's a soloist with the Bellemere Opera. What are they performing tonight, Miriam?"

"Highlights from *Merry Widow*."

"I'm so glad the opera company is doing well," said Tania Worthing. "It's wonderful to have a small company for local professionals. Genevieve Marchbanks deserves a medal."

Miriam Thurwell nodded.

"She certainly does. Genevieve is a wonderful singer and musician, and she's neglected her own career to create this company. She's an artist with real vision."

"She must be devastated by the announcement about the grants," said Joan Dorset. "It's bad enough for the historical society, but we're a small community group that will survive, albeit on a lesser scale. But I imagine the opera will die if it loses its major fundraising source."

"Yes," said Miriam. "Bellemere Opera isn't guaranteed federal government funding like the main company. But it's not just the grant. It's the new taxes and the changes to incentives for partnerships between business and the arts. The individuals and corporations that support us will tighten their belts and the donations and ticket sales may well fall off. I have to admit the future looks bleak."

Penelope Beech materialized at Miriam's elbow. She was a generously proportioned middle-aged woman whose unfashionably sculpted hairdo and beaded pink evening gown made her appear even larger than she was. She had heard the tail end of the conversation and she pursed her lips disapprovingly.

"It's an outrage," she spat. "It's not just the opera company that will be hit. There's a host of arts organizations that may go under. It's going to take every ounce of my self-control to sit at the head table and keep a smile on my face. If they put me next to Rummel, I'll be tempted to slip arsenic in his drink."

"Genevieve Marchbanks looks like she's plotting something of the sort," said Edwina. "Look at her."

They swivelled round and peered at the entertainers' table, which was set immediately below the head table. Philippa Beary was standing by the table, chatting with an incredibly handsome young man who was one of the junior members of the City Finance Department. The other singers were socializing with the cellist, a willowy brunette in wine-coloured velvet who was to play a solo prior to the opera excerpts. The ballet dancers had drifted away, and the only person actually seated at the table was Genevieve Marchbanks herself. She was dressed in a severe navy-blue suit and her face was white and grim. Her eyes, like two black stones, watched Rummel as he circulated about the room.

"She's an old school friend of the Rummels," said Penelope, "and she's always supported Gordon politically. She's taking his latest initiatives as a personal betrayal."

Beary rejoined the table, fortified by a large Glenlivet.

"Penelope Beech. How nice to see you again. Are you joining us?"

"Don't be silly, Bertram," said Edwina. "Penelope is at the head table."

"Of course you are. This is an Arts Assembly event, isn't it? Lovely occasion. Well done. How did you ever get Mrs. Thatcher, the Sequel, to cooperate with a joint Mayors' Arts Ball?"

Penelope blinked.

"Who?"

"Darling Gwendolyn."

"Oh. You mean Mayor Pye."

"Who else?" said Beary. "Dear Gwennie. Queen of the Royal City. She spends her whole life being alternately revered or reviled for her miserly thrift in allotting tax dollars to anything other than basic necessities, and for her fervent enthusiasm for any measure, however unpopular or environmentally unsound, that brings money into the community. I cannot conceive of a threat or bribe large enough to get Gwendolyn to help fund the Arts Ball."

"Oh, she only has to lend her name to the occasion," said Penelope. "That's all Rummel did too. Neither city government contributed. We raised the money through local corporations. I think it must be getting close to that time," she added, glancing at her watch.

She patted her coiffed head, straightened her pink chiffon skirt, and proceeded in stately fashion in the direction of the head table. As she passed the orchestra, she crossed paths with the stout figure of Gwendolyn Pye, who was working the room with the power and determination of a seventy-ton M1A1 tank. Mayor Pye hovered on the spot and exchanged a brief word with Penelope; then rolled forward to congratulate the orchestra leader.

"Gwendolyn's smile is a little forced, isn't it?" said Joan.

"What do you expect," said Beary. "In thirty minutes flat she's gone around every table in the ballroom, and look at her—what artistry—she's finishing up by shaking hands with each member of the band, and she's even got the instruments lined up so she'll wind up right by her spot at the head table. What a pro!"

"Gwendolyn enjoys mingling with the public," said Edwina. "It's a pity you don't try to emulate her," she added reprovingly. "The only reason she looks cross tonight is because she's having to share the spotlight with her ideological opposite."

"Gwennie's problem is more than political," said George Thurwell shrewdly. Thurwell knew Gwendolyn's husband, Desmond, for they were both partners in Komtrac. "Our company is going to lose a bundle under Rummel's new regulations."

"Actually," Beary commented, watching as the VIPs began to take their places at the head table, "Rummel is surrounded by people who would cheerfully string him up by his little left wings and dangle him over hot coals. Look at that row of cross little countenances. Penelope and Edmund Beech have turned their backs on him, Desmond Pye is mangling his napkin and Gwendolyn, bless her, looks as if she's sitting on a barbecue fork."

As they stared at the assembled dignitaries, a portly, balding man in an ill-fitting tuxedo crossed the speaker's platform and circled back around the head table, taking a place three seats from the end. He was nervously chewing his lip and he kept his eyes fixed firmly on the flower arrangement at the side of the microphone. His rather protuberant eyes were black and brooding.

"Who's that?" asked Thurwell. "Whoever he is, he gave Rummel a wide berth."

"Oh dear," said Beary. "Another thundercloud. That's Donald Merrick, the chairman of the Parks Commission. I suppose he's moderating tonight."

"What's Donald got against Rummel?" asked Joan Dorset coldly. "They're both slimy lawyers with labour ties. I'd have thought they'd be in complete harmony."

"The only thing they have in common is their party membership," said Beary. "Donald was Rummel's former partner in the law office, and he suffered a major financial loss when Rummel split up the firm. Besides, Rummel trounced Donald when he was trying to get the provincial nomination four years back."

"That's five out of eight at the head table that hate Rummel's guts," said Timothy Dorset with vindictive satisfaction.

"Who's the good-looking blonde?" asked Tania Worthing, eying a stiletto-thin fashion plate wearing a lime-green St. John knit that was the pecuniary equivalent of a plane ticket to Australia. "She doesn't look as if she hates Rummel. Rather the contrary."

"That's Ingrid Bjornson," said Thurwell, naming the local member of parliament, "and you're right. Rummel gets along fine with her. Too well they say. It's more than just a political attachment."

Joan Dorset looked shocked.

"But she's married to a local schoolteacher."

"They're separated. The marriage couldn't stand the strain of her commuting to Ottawa."

"Yes, well Rummel is married too. What's more, his wife paid his way through law school, and raised their children virtually single-handed while still holding down her own job. She works all hours and knocks herself out for him. She's an absolute sweetie and he's very lucky to have her."

"What does she do?" asked Edwina.

"She's a pharmacist. She copes with shift work and runs the home front without any help from him. She's the one that kept the family together while Rummel was gadding about promoting his political career."

"Many women hold down jobs and raise families these days," Edwina pointed out with acerbity. "I myself raised four children and have continued a successful career."

"That's different," said Joan. "Beary was well-established when you started out and he's been behind you all the way."

"You put it so aptly," said Beary. "I am always behind Edwina. Like Prince Philip, I am ever three paces to the rear and constantly at her disposal."

"Don't be facetious, Bertram," said Edwina. "All that is quite irrelevant. I wanted to work, and I organized my family life so I could do so."

"Exactly," said Joan Dorset. "You wanted to work. But Susan Rummel would much rather have been home with her children. She isn't a liberated woman; she's a liberated drudge. Rummel owes her loyalty."

"I wonder," said Beary, watching the head table as the rest of the VIPs took their seats. Ingrid Bjornson's blonde head gleamed at the far end of the table, and even on the other side of the ballroom, Beary could see the smile she flashed toward Rummel, and the tight line of Susan Rummel's mouth where she sat on her husband's right. A waiter darted along the table, filling the wine glasses of the special guests, but even a full wine glass could not animate the members of the head table. The VIPs sat stony faced as Donald Merrick introduced them and stood stiffly and self-consciously as Merrick invited the head of Bellemere's largest United Church to come forward to say the Grace.

Beary downed the rest of his Glenlivet and bowed his head piously, thankful for a moment's respite to close his eyes.

A moment later, the room came back to life as waiters and waitresses balancing large trays surged into view and began to deposit salads on tables. Beary continued to watch the head table. Merrick stepped to the microphone once more and called on Gordon Rummel to deliver the toast to the Queen.

Edwina snorted.

"How ridiculous. If that nasty little anti-monarchist had his way there wouldn't be a Queen."

"Calm down, old girl," said Beary. "Didn't I just hear Rummel tell us to charge our glasses? First sensible thing he's said in weeks."

Beary liberally splashed wine into his and Edwina's glasses and the assembly rose for the toast. Rummel raised his glass and flashed his gleaming smile.

"Ladies and gentlemen," he said, "I give you Her Highness, Queen Elizabeth."

Edwina turned purple.

"Her Highness! Ignorant lout. I hope he chokes to death on his wine."

Beary downed his own wine and glanced toward the head table where there seemed to be some agitated movement. Rummel had dropped his glass and was clutching his throat. The gleaming teeth were still visible, but the smile had become a grimace. Susan Rummel appeared to be hysterical, and was clutching her husband and screaming for help.

"My dear," Beary said to Edwina, "I think that's exactly what he's doing."

*   *   *   *

"This is outrageous," snapped Joan Dorset, "treating us all like criminals. When are they going to let us go home?"

"It looks as if they're planning to talk to all the witnesses," said Beary. "If that turns out to be the case," he added morosely, "it was certainly inconsiderate of them to close the bar."

"Your son is a DI," said Timothy. "Don't you have any influence?"

"Not here, old chap. This jurisdiction is city police. Richard won't be on the case."

"Ridiculous. Surely they can't be intending to question everyone. We'll be here all night."

Beary sighed and stared at the nightscape on the far side of the plate glass window that traversed the side of the room. The waters of Vancouver Harbour were an inky black mass, only identifiable by the yellow halogen lights on the docks and the illuminated windows of the SeaBus, which resembled a gleaming glowworm crawling across the inlet. The lights of North Vancouver twinkled on the far shore, and the beaded line of the Grouse Mountain chair lift was the only hint to delineate where land met sky. Beary turned away from the window and looked longingly in the direction of the bar, which was now a barren expanse of laminate with not a bottle, glass or stir-stick in sight. Two staff members were still in evidence however, a man wearing hotel regulation white shirt and black bow tie, and a woman who Beary recognized as the head waitress who had overseen the serving of the banquet. They appeared to be having an altercation.

"Isn't that the wine waiter who was serving the head table?" said Beary, nodding towards the man who was gesticulating hysterically at his supervisor.

"He seems rather put out," said Joan. "Very emotional."

"Greek," said Timothy. "What do you expect?"

"Well, he doesn't exactly have the stoicism of Hector in *Troy*, but he's probably a mine of interesting information if any of you would shut up long enough to listen," said Beary.

Timothy looked offended, but fell silent. Beary leaned forward and tried to hear.

The waiter was hissing at his supervisor, but his words were quite audible.

"I tell you, I never take my eyes off the glasses. You tell me to stay in case people need refills, and I stand there the entire time. I watch the head table until it is time for me to pour the wine for the toast."

The supervisor took a deep breath. "No one is accusing you…" she began.

Arms flailing, the waiter interrupted her. His voice rose several decibels and carried clearly across the room. "The pigs accuse me of lying, but I know what I see. There was nothing in the glasses. They are all empty. I swear. No one had any chance to poison that drink."

The double doors at the side of the ballroom swung open and Genevieve Marchbanks came through. In the light of the tinted lamps in the wall brackets, her pallor took on a greenish hue. There was an empty armchair beside Beary, and she collapsed into it and leaned her head back.

"Tough session, love?" asked Beary. "Rack and third degree, was it?"

"No. I haven't even been questioned yet. I've been with Susan."

"Susan?"

"Susan Rummel, of course," said Joan Dorset. She turned back to Genevieve. "How is she doing, poor dear?"

"She's quieted down, but the tears keep coming. She's been through a lot lately. She was pretty fragile even before this happened."

Joan nodded sagely and made a disapproving moue with her lips.

"The Bjornson woman. Yes, we heard all about it."

"Gordon got what he deserved," Genevieve said harshly. "I still can't believe that he was ready to abandon Susan and his family for that politically correct Barbie doll. She doesn't have a single opinion between her Tiffany pearl studs that hasn't been spelled out by the party manual."

"Rummel was going to leave his wife!" Joan was aghast.

"Yes. Susan was facing a divorce. After all she'd done for him. I used to have such faith in him. I worked with them on elections, and I thought he had such high principles. But the man was an utter louse."

"Still talking about the murder victim?" said Edwina, coming to join them from the far side of the room where she had been visiting with Philippa. "Are they any closer to finding out who dispatched him?"

"I doubt it," said Genevieve shortly. "Excuse me, I'd better go and speak with Penelope. If anyone knows what's going on, she will. After all, she was coordinator for this 'Two Mayors' Ball.'" She stood abruptly and moved to the far end of the hall where Penelope's large pink form could be seen firmly entrenched beside an apple-cheeked constable who looked extremely uncomfortable.

"One mayor now," said Beary. "Where is Thatcher, the Sequel, anyway? I can't imagine her sitting quietly waiting her turn to be interviewed. Even Police Commissioners quail when she enters the precinct. Pity the officer who ever had to arrest her."

"I wouldn't put it past Gwendolyn Pye to slip poison in a drink," said Edwina. "She's a very hard-nosed lady. And the Pyes are not only Rummel's political foes. They stand to lose a fortune if his new regulations go through."

"Nonsense," said Timothy. "The Pyes are the salt of the earth. There are much more likely suspects. Look at Donald Merrick. He's already lost a fortune through the law firm, and on top of that, Rummel publicly humiliated him at the labour convention."

"What about Penelope Beech?" suggested Joan. "She's worked for years to promote the arts in this community. Rummel has destroyed her efforts with one policy decision. And we all heard her talk about putting arsenic in Rummel's drink."

"There's her husband, too," said Edwina. "Look at the way he was going on earlier."

"You've got him on the list," sang Beary. "Good old Gilbert had a phrase for every occasion."

"We shouldn't leave out Genevieve Marchbanks," Edwina added. "I know she wasn't at the head table, but her group was adjacent to it and she was standing within three feet of Rummel during the toast. She's quite a neurotic woman, for all her artistic brilliance."

Beary stopped singing and looked sidelong at his wife.

"What about you, my dear?" he said wickedly. "You were clearly heard to say that you hoped Rummel choked to death seconds before he actually did so."

Edwina flushed.

"I suppose you'll never let me forget that, will you?"

"Never!" said Beary with relish. "I shall dine out on that story for the rest of my life."

*   *   *   *

In spite of the late hour, there were a surprising number of cars on the road as Beary and Edwina made their way home. Edwina was driving, even though many hours had passed since Beary's liberal intake of Glenlivet and Mission Hill Cabernet. Beary was still humming tunes from Gilbert and Sullivan, but had now switched to *The Pirates of Penzance.* He leaned back against the headrest. The headlights from the oncoming traffic hurt his eyes.

"So it was cyanide in the bubbly," he said, abruptly stopping his song. "A rapid end to a rapid rise. Today's media sensation, and by this time next year, none but the political crowd will even remember who Rummel was. Even the police seemed to be losing interest by the end of the evening. Not that that is surprising, after interviewing a ballroom full of over-inflated political egos."

"You weren't very long with the detective inspector," said Edwina.

"He was city police. The minute he found out that my son was an inspector with the RCMP, he made a point of indicating that he didn't need any help, thank you very much, and that he was quite capable of solving the crime unassisted." Beary chortled. "He appeared to be well and truly stuck," he added complacently.

"Is it such a difficult case?"

"Not at all. Crystal clear. Ah well, they'll figure it out eventually."

"It isn't that straightforward," said Edwina. "A man murdered at a public function while surrounded by enemies, any of whom might have done it. It's no easy task to find a killer in a crowd like that."

"Yes, well when you have a wealth of motives and a wealth of suspects, you have to turn your attention to means and opportunity…and it appears that there was a singular dearth of opportunities. There was only one person, to misquote W.S. Gilbert again, who had the 'first rate opportunity, to do murder with impunity'."

"Nonsense. Surely anyone had the opportunity to poison Rummel's drink. The glass was there on the table all through the social hour."

"True. But the wine wasn't poured until the VIPs were taking their seats. The waiter swears there was nothing in the glass. Moreover, he had instructions to stand to one side and keep an eye on the glasses in case anyone at the head table needed refills. Although there was some movement at the table prior to Merrick coming to the microphone, the waiter insists that no one went near Rummel's wine glass."

"He's obviously mistaken."

"I don't think so," said Beary. "I was watching the head table during the few minutes in question, and I didn't see anyone approach Rummel. Besides, think of the risk. Granted there was a lot of noise and confusion, but how could a murderer guarantee that not one single person would notice him slip something in the drink? No, nobody went near Rummel's place at the table. Therefore, there was only one moment when the drink could have been doctored and therefore, only one person who could have been responsible. I wonder if the police will ever be able to prove it. Could it be the perfect crime to dispatch a perfect rotter?"

"Don't be aggravating, Bertram. If neither the Pyes nor the Beeches, nor Donald Merrick or Genevieve Marchbanks went near Rummel's glass, then how could any of them possibly have murdered him?"

"They didn't," said Beary. "The murderer had to be within reach of the glass. Only one person meets that description. Rummel's glass was only inches away from the left hand of the person who was seated on Rummel's right-hand side."

"On his right? But that was Susan Rummel. His wife! She was hysterical when Rummel collapsed."

"Wouldn't you be hysterical if you'd been living on the edge for months and had finally been driven to such a degree of insanity that you planned to put poison in your husband's drink? Wouldn't you be hysterical if having tampered with the wine, you had to watch your husband die of cyanide poisoning?"

Edwina gave an icy smile. She remained silent as she steered the car into Lakeside Drive. Beary looked hurt.

"Susan Rummel has neither your nerves of steel nor your heart of stone," he said huffily. "She loved her husband and slaved for him until she became a nervous wreck. She would have continued holding down a job and running his house and managing the family until she dropped, but there was one thing she would not tolerate."

"I suppose he really was having an affair with that awful Bjornson woman. I knew it," said Edwina. "I always said that man was a cheat and a liar."

"It was more than an affair. Bjornson was divorcing her husband, and Rummel was planning to marry her. He was going to leave his wife."

"The louse," said Edwina. "Rummel would never have achieved success if it hadn't been for his wife. All those years she worked as a pharmacist putting him through law school...Oh, of course, she's a pharmacist!"

"Yes, I expect even the city plods will finally twig to the significance of Susan Rummel's profession."

"Well, I hope she gets away with it," Edwina said firmly.

"Edwina, you old radical. I believe you're finally learning something from living with me."

Edwina sniffed.

"Heaven forbid," she said. "You still haven't told me when Susan Rummel managed to doctor her husband's drink."

"Use your brain, old girl," said Beary. "We're only talking about a five minute period. Think. When was the brief few moments that Susan Rummel could be sure that no one, not even the wine waiter, would be looking in her direction. Recreate the scene in your mind. What did we do just before the toast to the Queen?"

Edwina pulled into the drive of the Beary residence and turned off the engine. She sat frowning for a moment, then with a gasp she turned toward Beary.

"We said Grace!"

"Exactly," said Beary. "As the pastor directed us, we all bowed our heads in prayer. And that was the one moment that Susan Rummel could safely reach out and poison her husband's drink."

"While we were praying!"

Edwina's expression changed from triumph to one of outrage. She snapped off the headlights and swept her purse from the back seat. Once out of the car, she slammed the driver's door and sniffed indignantly.

"Timothy was right," she said. "Socialists are heathens."

Edwina tossed her stole over her shoulder, thrust her granite jaw forward and marched down the driveway.

Beary sighed, and bent to pet Henrietta Plop who had prowled from behind a rose bush and was meowing at them in the driveway. Then, three paces behind, he followed Edwina into the house.

CONSTABULARY DUTY

▼

Richard Beary wished his sister had never met George Spragg. Ferociously, he banged a nail into the ruined chapel.

"There," he snarled. "That should do it. Solid as a rock."

George Spragg eyed the structure doubtfully. "A bit too solid," he said finally. "It does have to be moved, you know."

"That's the stage crew's problem," said Richard. "I'm a policeman, not a set designer. Besides, I'm off. Philippa asked me to donate a couple of hours and I've been here all day. The cast is arriving for the evening rehearsal and I haven't even had dinner yet. I'm supposed to be on holiday," he added morosely.

"We could send out for something," said George.

"Enough is enough," said Richard firmly. "I'm going to go home, have a beer, cook myself a steak and watch the hockey game."

He dropped his hammer and detached his jacket from a nearby brace. George was about to argue, but the doors at the back of the auditorium opened and abruptly, his attention shifted away from Richard.

"Here's your sister now," he said, his owlish face becoming distinctly ovine. "I find it amazing that someone so pretty and talented should also be so clever. Margery was ecstatic when Philippa appeared at the audition," he went on rhapsodically. "She considered her perfect for Mabel. It's too bad it's only an amateur group," George continued, "but it's still good exposure for her. Besides, it's such fun the way everyone pitches in to help."

Richard scowled, but his expression softened when he noticed the striking brunette who had joined Philippa in the auditorium.

"Who's that?" he asked George.

"Janet Green. She does the lights. Nice-looking if you go for the older type."

"She's gorgeous, you callow youth," said Richard, briskly dusting the sawdust off his jeans. "Besides, I *am* the older type," he added as Philippa and her companion approached the stage.

"George," Philippa called sweetly, "The light in the green room has blown. Do you think you could find us another bulb?"

As George dropped his glue gun and hurried away, Richard smiled wickedly and carolled with an ease borne of years of familiarity with Gilbert and Sullivan operettas:

'Here's a first rate opportunity,
To get married with impunity.'

"Don't be silly," Philippa retorted. "George and I are friends, that's all."

"Ah, but does *he* know that?" asked Richard.

Before Philippa could reply, Janet introduced herself to Richard. Her voice was pleasantly mellow.

"I'm in a spot," she said. "I need someone to help me in the booth during the show and Philippa said you might be available. It would involve several evenings, but if you could I'd be awfully grateful. And if you do decide to help, I'd appreciate it if you could stay this evening so I can show you the ropes."

"You'll never get him to stay tonight," said Philippa. "He's been here all day and he hasn't eaten yet. Besides, there's a hockey game on."

Richard glanced at Janet Green's slender ringless hands.

"That's all right," he said. "I can always send out for something."

*   *   *   *

The lighting booth was tucked at the back of the auditorium. The stage was visible through the glass front of the booth, but Richard was more interested in the vast array of switches and levers that ran the length of the counter.

"This is a first class set up for an ancient theatre," he said, as Janet slid open a door in the end wall and revealed an elaborate tape deck. "You've got top-notch equipment."

"Too top-notch," said Janet. "The circuits are all overloaded. That's why I need someone to help me during the performances. I need an able body to run below stage and switch plugs so we don't blow all the fuses."

"Below stage? How do I get there?"

"Through that door, down the steps and along the hallway. The box is at the end. I'll take you down and show you later."

"And where does that go?" asked Richard, pointing to a ladder that disappeared through the roof of the booth.

"There's a passage that takes you above the auditorium and into the fly gallery—not that we need it for this show. The sets are fairly simple. It's how we light them that counts."

"Do I have to switch plugs tonight?" Richard asked.

"Heavens, no. I can't set lights until the scenery is there. But I'll show you how the board works and I'll explain the cues. Other than that, just watch the run through and familiarize yourself with the show. When you're not checking the hockey score, of course," she added, sliding open a door beneath the counter and revealing a small television set.

"Now I'm really impressed," said Richard.

"With me, or the accommodations?"

"Both. This equipment must have cost a fortune."

"The Modern Major General donated it. He owns Mayberry Electric and CM Sound."

"Does he?" said Richard with interest. "I wonder if I could talk him into a discount on a new stereo."

Janet's eyes twinkled.

"You'd do better to work on me," she said. "I manage the downtown store. You see, Cliff Mayberry is my uncle."

"So that's where you get your technical expertise. It runs in the family. And now I think of it, didn't you introduce me to another Mayberry before we came up here?"

Janet nodded.

"Steve Mayberry," she said. "Uncle Cliff's brother. He manages the West Vancouver store."

"Then he's your uncle too? Isn't he rather young?"

"He's thirty-five. Steve was the afterthought in a large family. My mother was the oldest, and next came Uncle Cliff. Then there was another sister, Bella, who ran away from home after my parents and grandparents were killed in a car crash.

Steve and I were very young at the time, but Uncle Cliff was already a young man, so he's been like a father to both of us."

Richard nodded.

"One tends to feel a sense of responsibility toward brothers and sisters who are a great deal younger," he said. "I'm fourteen years older than Philippa, so I know exactly what it's like."

"It was hard for Uncle Cliff because he was just starting his business. I'm sure he never married because he was run off his feet trying to cope with two children while he was busy establishing his chain of stores. He had to rely on a series of housekeepers, and some were pretty hopeless, though of course, the quality improved as he became more successful."

"It must have been difficult for you and Steve too," said Richard.

"I think Steve really felt it," said Janet. "There are some emotional scars. I'm afraid he's a bit of a family embarrassment. He and Uncle Cliff have had their ups and downs."

"What does Steve do on the show?"

"He's the stage manager."

"Is that the one who gives you the lighting cues?"

"That's right. There are headsets on stage right, stage left, and in the booth, so the stage manager, the ASM, and the lighting technician are in constant communication during the performance."

"The ASM?"

"Assistant stage manager. Young George Spragg. Sssshh," Janet hissed suddenly. "They're starting."

A tall blonde girl had moved into the pit and was conducting with a sweeping circular motion, but as the sole beneficiary of her elusive beat was a toothy creature at the piano, the introduction to the pirate chorus was far from stirring. As Richard watched the rehearsal, he found himself more fascinated by the interruptions than by the performance itself, though he was pleased to see that his sister performed well. However, to his surprise, the musical director was rather short with her.

"Philippa's charming on stage, isn't she?" said Janet.

"The conductor doesn't seem to think so," said Richard. "What's she doing wrong?"

Janet sighed.

"Not a thing," she said. "Charlene's going through a personal crisis and she's taking it out on everyone else. She won't even speak to me at the moment."

"Why ever not?"

"Because I'm related to Steve. Silly, of course, because I'm as disgusted with his shenanigans as she is, but she's too upset to be logical. You see, she's been his live-in girlfriend on and off for the past ten years. Steve's a terrible womanizer. I could point out three of his former lady friends on stage right now, including one who's married to the tenor."

"That's what you meant by a family embarrassment?"

"Yes. Steve can't leave the girls alone. He even had a go at Isobel Drummond," she said, nodding toward the statuesque woman who was playing Ruth, "and she's a good five years older than he is. Not that he got anywhere with her, but he tried. Charlene has always forgiven him and taken him back because she was convinced he'd ultimately reform and marry her, but now he's dealt her the lowest blow of all."

"No reform?"

"Oh, he's reformed all right, but he's become engaged to Nancy Street." Janet pointed at a chorus girl standing by the proscenium. "She's young, nubile, and a perfect dear, but she's also extremely determined. She won't tolerate the kind of nonsense that Charlene put up with. She's also informed me that she wants six children. Steve is about to settle down with a vengeance, which is good from the family's point of view, but Charlene is understandably bitter. So is her brother, Stewart, who's playing the pirate king."

"Good God. The atmosphere on stage must be poisonous. I'm glad I'm going to be in the booth with you."

"Yes," she agreed. "It's a hotbed of blazing feuds down there. It's much more peaceful where we are."

Richard enjoyed his evening, pleasantly alternating between the hockey game, the operetta, and Janet's technical lectures. However, during the second act, while he was watching an exciting play between the Toronto Maple Leafs and the Vancouver Canucks, he became aware that the action on stage had ground to a halt. He watched the television until the Toronto team scored, then looked up to see what was happening. The director was haranguing a line of woebegone men, all of whom carried truncheons.

"What's bothering your director?" Richard asked Janet.

"The sergeant," said Janet. "Allan Sturdy would try anyone's patience." She turned down the sound on the television so they could hear Margery Bevan's penetrating voice.

"You're supposed to be British Bobbies, not the Canadian Army Reserves. And Allan, you're the worst of the lot. It's beyond belief. Haven't you ever seen an English movie?"

Richard thought of his associate, Sergeant Martin.

"I know someone who'd be perfect for that part," he said.

"Of course," said Janet. "You're an RCMP Inspector, aren't you? Is your friend British?"

Richard nodded.

"His accent is as thick as a London fog."

"Too bad we can't borrow him. Look, Margery's given up. They're going on. Now," she added briskly, her tone becoming business-like, "this is the spot where you'll be switching plugs below stage."

Richard watched as the pirates made their entrance.

"It's a split second change," said Janet, "but the cue is very easy. After the pirates sing, 'With cat-like tread', they thump down like a herd of elephants, the orchestra plays a loud chord, and the cymbals crash—and that's when you change the plugs."

"Easy," said Richard. "I must say you picked a great spot for me to be under the stage," he added ruefully.

*   *   *   *

"Steve Mayberry has a gun tucked under the counter on stage right," said Philippa.

Richard set down his wine glass abruptly. Making the most of fleeting leisure, he and Philippa had descended upon their parents for Sunday dinner. A week of makeshift meals had made their mother's cooking appear particularly tempting.

"What sort of gun?" Beary asked curiously.

"I don't know," said Philippa. "I only caught a glimpse of it as I was retrieving my purse. Besides, I'm not very good at recognizing weapons."

"What did it look like?" coaxed Richard.

"It was very small. The sort of thing ladies carry in their handbags in private-eye movies."

"Probably a stage prop," said Edwina, handing Beary a large platter of vegetables and pointing to a spot at the centre of the table.

"It might be," said Philippa, "but somehow I don't think so."

Richard frowned.

"I know Steve Mayberry isn't popular," he said, "but I didn't think matters were that serious. Does he strike you as a man in fear of his life?"

Philippa thought for a moment. Finally she said: "He might be. On the surface he's snide and full of bravado, but he must be aware that he's made a lot of enemies."

Richard helped himself to a generous serving of roast beef.

"A lot of enemies?" he repeated.

"Well, Stewart and Charlene Grey, anyway. They're definitely out to get him."

"Hell hath no fury, and all that?"

"No, there's more to it than that. There's money involved. I had a long gossip with Nancy Street one night. Personally, I don't know how she can stomach Steve, but she's certainly got no delusions about him. She knows what she's getting and she's quite sure she can keep him in check. Anyway, she filled me in. Evidently, Charlene paid most of the expenses while she and Steve were living together."

"Foolish girl," said Edwina with feeling.

"Yes," said Philippa. "But that's not the worst part. Steve borrowed money from both Charlene and Stewart—all their savings, in fact—and lost the lot on bad investments. Now they claim they're owed ten thousand dollars, and they're prepared to go to court if Cliff Mayberry doesn't make good their losses. It's all very unpleasant."

"Why did Steve have to borrow money from Charlene and her brother?" Richard asked curiously. "Surely he's far better-heeled financially than they are?"

"He is, but he lives beyond his means. Both he and Janet get good salaries, and they also get a percentage of the profits from the stores they manage. Janet's doing really well—I gather she has her uncle's flair for business—but Steve is lazy and inefficient, and he lets money slip through his fingertips. I suppose the stock market seemed enticing to him because it offered quick returns, but he had to have some capital to get himself started. When he failed to get an advance on his inheritance from his brother, he persuaded Stewart and Charlene to let him invest their savings."

"Will Clifton Mayberry pay them off?" asked Beary.

"Yes, but he's so furious with Steve that he's cut him out of his will. Janet's portion—she gets forty percent—remains intact, but Steve's share will be held in trust for thirty years, then divided equally among his children, assuming he has any, of course."

"He will if he marries Nancy," said Richard. "Six, I believe, is the projected number. Oh well, sixty percent will divide very nicely."

"Forty percent," Philippa corrected him. "There was a delinquent sister who ran away from home at the age of sixteen. Clifton still has a soft spot for her, so twenty percent goes to her—or to her children if she predeceases her brother."

"Is that a new provision?"

"No, it's always been there. It's only Steve's inheritance that's affected by the new will."

"Ugly," said Beary. "And provocative. The Mayberry family relations must be strained to their limits."

He tossed a large chunk of gristle at MacPuff, who caught it and swallowed it in one gulp.

"Yes," Philippa agreed, "but I feel very sorry for Clifton. He's terribly upset about the whole business. Especially as Charlene is deliberately trying to stir up trouble. Her latest piece of vindictiveness has caused no end of bother. She's told the tenor about Steve's affair with his wife."

"That was exceedingly spiteful of her."

"Yes, especially as the affair ended two years ago."

Edwina looked appalled.

"No wonder the atmosphere is unpleasant," she said. "How do you concentrate on your part?"

"With difficulty," said Philippa. "It's bad enough being cast opposite a reedy-voiced tenor with a face like a weasel, but when he's angry and indifferent as well, the love scenes become impossible. In fact, everywhere I turn there's someone in a state of turmoil. George Spragg stands on stage left and makes sheep's eyes at me. Then there's Charlene glowering in the pit and Steve Mayberry scowling on stage right—only during Act One, of course. I get a break in the second act because the stage manager's corner is hidden by the ruined chapel."

"I noticed that," said Richard. "Steve's quite isolated during Act Two, isn't he?"

"Completely. Now that the legs are drawn back to make room for the set, his corner isn't even visible when we're standing backstage. Every so often, Nancy disappears in there and we all stand in the wings, pretending we don't hear the giggles, but nobody else dares go near the place."

"What about entrances?"

"They're all made from the upstage side of the leg."

Beary carved himself another slice of beef.

"I think," he said thoughtfully, "that Richard should take a look at that gun."

*   *   *   *

"Gun?" said Steve Mayberry. "You mean the old .38 Special? It's been tucked under the counter since the club did *The Maltese Falcon*."

One point for Philippa, thought Richard.

"So it's just a stage prop," he said.

Steve gave Richard the sheepish smile that made sweet young girls long to mother him.

"Not exactly," he said. "I mean, they used it for a prop, but it's a real gun. I hope you're not going to pull me in for possession of a restricted weapon."

"I could," said Richard shortly. "Is it licensed?"

"I think so," said Steve. "At least it was. Maybe not now though."

"Who owns it?"

"Larry Reed. The club drunk. He had a gun collection, and he offered to lend us the .38 for the show."

"Why wasn't the gun returned to this man?" asked Richard.

"Because he died."

"Died? How?"

"He shot himself," said Steve, and emitted a raucous hoot of laughter. "No," he modified quickly, seeing Richard's expression, "actually it was a heart attack. Anyway, no one wanted to intrude on the grieving widow. Not at first, that is, and afterward we just kept procrastinating. So the gun's still there. It's been lying around for more than a year now."

"I assume there's no ammunition for it," said Richard glacially.

"You assume wrong," said Steve. "Larry Reed was a no-brain. When he brought the gun in and gave it to the stage manager, it was loaded. His idea of a joke. Luckily for the actors the SM was an observant type."

Richard flinched.

"Good God," he said finally. "What happened to the bullets?"

"I don't know. You'd have to ask the SM who did *Falcon*."

Janet's pretty face bobbed round the wall of the ruined chapel.

"I know where those bullets are," she said. "We put them in a box and brought it up to the booth because that's the one area we can lock up. We tucked the box in the cupboard above the tape recorder. I hardly ever use that cupboard, and I don't think I've looked in there since. We can get the box when we go up to the booth."

"We'll go now," Richard said firmly, "just as soon as I've retrieved the gun."

He bent down and peered under the counter, then reached in and felt through the debris on the shelf. After a moment, he stood up and stared, tight-lipped, at Steve.

"It's not there," he said.

"What!" Steve dived toward the counter and rummaged underneath. "But I saw it a couple of days ago."

"I hope you realize how serious this is?" said Richard.

Janet frowned.

"I did the lights on that show," she said, "but I wasn't around on strike day. I just assumed the gun had been returned to its owner."

"Let's go and get those bullets," said Richard.

He and Janet moved toward the front of the stage. As they went down the steps, George Spragg ambled down the aisle. He was carrying a cassette recorder.

"I've recorded the noises off from the tape in the booth," he told Janet. "This should do the trick if I turn the sound way up. For tonight anyway."

"What's the problem?" asked Richard.

Janet explained as they moved up the aisle.

"Margery wants noises off during the second-act dialogue—the forest at night, owls hooting, and so on. Normally we run sound effects from the booth, but the speakers on stage are out of commission. George was in this afternoon and he says the sound didn't come through on either one, so tonight we'll have to settle for his cassette player. Steve's going to run it on stage right. It won't be as good, but at least Margery will know we're trying."

"How many speakers do you have on the stage?"

"Two. One right and one left. I'll check them before I go home tonight."

Richard and Janet passed through the swing doors into the lobby, and from there they climbed into the lighting booth. Reading Richard's mind, Janet pointed to a small door above the cupboard that enclosed the tape deck.

"The box is up there," she said. She stood on a stool and opened the cupboard door. She peered inside; then she stiffened and rapidly shifted the contents of the cupboard. After a moment, she turned back toward Richard. Her face was pale.

"It's gone," she said.

*   *   *   *

Later that evening when Richard returned to the booth, having synchronized his third plug change with the pirates' distinctly unfeline leap, Janet looked at him sympathetically.

"You're worried, aren't you?" she said.

"Yes. A missing gun isn't something to be treated lightly, especially when there are so many frayed tempers and ill feelings smouldering on that stage. I feel extremely uneasy."

"I wish I could do something to cheer you up."

"You can," said Richard with a sudden smile. "Let me take you out for a drink after the rehearsal."

Flashing a radiant smile, Janet pulled off her headset and placed it on the counter. "What a lovely idea," she said.

"Won't you miss your cue?" said Richard.

Janet shook her head.

"There's nothing for a few minutes," she said. "Besides, no one's on the other end at the moment."

"Where have the others gone?"

"Steve has sneaked off for a cigarette, and George is playing Errol Flynn above the proscenium."

"Why?"

"One of the Fresnels is depositing light on the top of the tree. I don't know how it got out of alignment, but Charlene grumbled about the glare all through the break so I asked George to fix it. When Charlene's in a mood, it's best not to inflame her unnecessarily."

"I know. I got a display of her temper before the rehearsal. She overheard me phoning headquarters."

"So I gather. She had no business being so rude to you. Everyone's heard about that phone call now."

"That's all right," said Richard. "It won't hurt the cast to know that the police are aware of the gun's disappearance, or that they're checking its registration. Whoever's taken it might have second thoughts about using it now."

"Do you really believe someone might get shot? Surely the whole business is just a silly prank. I can't imagine any of the people in the club contemplating murder. They're hardly criminal types."

Richard laughed.

"Criminals aren't any particular type," he said, "and they don't spend twenty-four hours a day engaged in homicidal pursuits. You should listen to the lyrics of that wretchedly bad policeman's solo."

Richard burst into tuneless song:

When the Coster's finished jumping on his mother,

He loves to lie a basking in the sun...'

Janet put her headset back on and sang in stentorian tones:

'Taking one consideration with another,
A policeman's lot is not a happy one.'

"You don't have to be rude, George," she added. "I didn't know you were back. OK, Steve, I heard you."

Janet adjusted a switch on the panel, and instantly, a shimmering green light hovered around the entrance of the chapel. The Major General, candle in hand, came into view.

As Janet leaned back in her chair, there was a sudden explosive sound in the headset.

Flinching with pain, Janet ripped off the headset and clutched her ears. Richard was off his chair in an instant, but as he started to comfort the white, shaking girl, he noticed that chaos had broken out on stage. The show had stopped, and a series of high-pitched screams was coming from the stage-right corner.

Janet was still dazed, but she had seen what was happening on stage.

"Go on," she muttered. "I'm all right. No," she added, as Richard headed for the door of the booth, "go that way." She nodded toward the ladder. "The overhead walkway. It's faster."

As Richard left, Janet was still rubbing her ears.

Quickly Richard climbed the ladder and raced along the passage. At the far end, he emerged onto a metal walkway, high above the proscenium, that extended around the grid. To the left, Richard saw a ladder, and as he moved toward it he looked down. Many feet below, he saw a cluster of pirates, policemen, and Victorian maidens, interspersed with the odd figure wearing blue jeans. At the centre of this oddly assorted group lay the motionless form of Steve Mayberry.

*   *   *   *

With a director's instinct for taking command, Margery Bevan cleared the stage area. Then, having carefully noted Richard's instructions, she hurried away to phone the police.

Richard remained with the body, and being careful not to touch or disturb anything, he looked around the stage manager's corner. The .38, which must have been pressed against Steve's right temple, now lay like a paperweight at the centre of an open score on the counter. Curiously, Richard glanced at the score. He could not read music, but he recognized the lyrics of the Major General's song. The only other item on the counter was a battered gardening glove. It's mate lay on the floor beside the body, as if Steve had collapsed against the counter and dragged the glove away with him when he slid to the ground. As he had fallen, the headset had been pulled off, and it now hung against the defunct speaker. The speaker reminded Richard of something, but though he checked the area thoroughly, the item he was looking for was nowhere to be seen. Thoughtfully, Richard turned his attention elsewhere.

He looked at the side wall of the theatre. Beside the ladder that descended from the fly gallery hung a black curtain, and above this curtain was an exit sign. Before Richard could investigate further, Margery returned.

"I phoned your headquarters," she said, "and yes, they do want you to take charge. I'm sorry," she added penitently. "We've managed to ruin your holiday, haven't we? Is there anything I can do while we're waiting for your cohorts to arrive?"

"Yes," said Richard. "You can answer some questions. First of all, what are those gloves for?"

"They're for handling the lights," said Margery. "Janet keeps a box of old gloves in the booth, but Steve always has a pair on stage right and George usually has two or three pairs on stage left because he tends to leave his lying around and then he can't find them when he needs them."

Richard nodded; then abruptly changed the subject.

"Where does that exit go?" he asked, indicating the black curtain.

"To the fire escape. The stage is only one flight above the ground, but the fire escape goes up the side of the building to the fly gallery too."

"I wish I'd known that before I climbed down the ladder," said Richard. "What a descent that was."

"The ladders aren't bad when you're used to them," said Margery. "The crew zoom up and down them in less time than it takes me to walk up the aisle."

"Is this the only ladder that goes to the flies?" asked Richard.

"No. There are two others. One upstage centre and one on stage left."

"And any of them can be reached from the walkway round the grid?"

"Yes, but you're stretching credibility if you're supposing the killer used a circuitous route like that. Even if he'd got to stage right without being seen, he could never have made a speedy getaway. The people on stage must have reached Steve's corner within seconds of the gunshot."

"Is there an exit door near the bottom of the fire escape?" Richard asked thoughtfully.

"Yes. There's one right beside it."

"How do you reach that exit from inside the theatre?"

Margery pointed upstage.

"You go down the stairs, but instead of going straight at the bottom, you turn right and go down the hall past the green room. The fire exit is at the end."

"Does any other route lead there?"

"Yes. The emergency exit at the foot of the auditorium takes you through into the backstage hall."

Before Richard could ask any more questions, the chapel door was wrenched open and the bulky form of Sergeant Martin appeared.

"Oh, there you are, sir," he boomed, awkwardly circumnavigating the exit. "I could hear your voice but I had a bit of bother finding my way in."

Richard introduced his colleague to Margery.

"I want to look around the theatre," he added, turning to Sergeant Martin. "Stay here until the rest of the crew arrives. Then I want you to start getting statements from the members of the company."

"Being an operetta," said Martin dourly, "I suppose it's a large cast."

"Very." Richard turned to Margery who was staring with undisguised fascination at the newcomer.

"Will you see that Sergeant Martin gets everything he needs?" he asked her.

Margery blinked.

"Yes, of course," she said eagerly. "I'll get one of the cast members to show him around. No, really," she insisted, as Martin demurred, "it won't be any trouble at all."

✳   ✳   ✳   ✳

From the stairs Richard could hear the excited voices of the performers, and when he reached the hall, he quickened his step to escape the potent atmosphere of sweat and turbulence that emanated from the green room. At the end of the hall was a door bearing the sign, 'LOO—Please Do Not Flush During Performance', which Richard correctly judged to be a reflection upon the theatre's ancient pipes. Beside the washroom he noticed the heavy swing door that led to the auditorium and a smaller door that opened into the orchestra pit. Opposite these was the fire exit. Richard opened the door and peered outside. It was dark, but he could see a mass of cigarette butts at the base of the fire escape. Wedging the door open with a block of wood, which was probably kept nearby for that very purpose, Richard went outside and climbed the first section of the fire escape.

On the first landing he found himself outside the door that led to the stage manager's corner. The door could not be opened from the outside, but the landing was well used for there was another pile of cigarette butts at the foot of the door.

Thoughtfully, Richard returned the way he had come.

*   *   *   *

The following evening, Richard tracked Janet down in the green room. She had dark circles under her eyes and her normal glow had faded to an unhealthy pallor, but when Richard appeared, she looked up from her clipboard and smiled.

"I seem to recall that I invited you out for a drink last night," Richard said apologetically, "before the reason for our sudden parting erased everything else from my mind."

"That's all right," Janet said gently. "I fully intend to take you up on your offer, but let's get this wretched investigation out of the way first. You look exhausted," she added sympathetically.

"Four hours' sleep. Rather less than my usual quota. You look a little weary yourself."

"We had a late production meeting last night. The club president is determined to open as planned, so while you and that delicious sergeant were interrogating witnesses, we were going over the technical cues."

"Who's going to stage manage?"

"Margery. She knows the show better than anyone." Janet paused. "And her assistant will help me in the booth," she said finally.

"Probably more competently than I could."

"Perhaps," said Janet. "But I shall miss you."

Richard felt a sudden surge of anger against the killer of Steve Mayberry.

"How I wish this horrible business had never happened," he said vehemently.

Sergeant Martin appeared in the doorway and coughed loudly. Startled, Richard swung round. To his surprise, he saw that his normally phlegmatic colleague was showing signs of strain. Martin was glancing nervously over his shoulder.

"What on earth is the matter?" Richard asked him.

Martin cautiously entered the room.

"I'm dodging the bloke who showed me around yesterday," he replied.

"Why? What's wrong with him? Didn't Mrs. Bevan find you a willing slave?"

"Yes, sir. Rather too much so. There's something funny about the man."

"In what way?"

"He watched me every instant, sir—constantly asked questions, and offered to get me cups of tea every five minutes. He dogged my steps all evening." Sergeant Martin went a shade redder than his normal florid hue. "He even followed me down to the loo—the one downstairs with the British Rail-type sign on the door. The whole evening was most unnerving, sir."

"Who did Margery assign to you?" Janet asked curiously.

"His name's Sturdy," said Martin. "Quite demented. He kept asking if I could say *Tarantara*."

Janet sputtered and disappeared behind her clipboard. Not sure whether he felt irritation or admiration for Margery Bevan, Richard reassured his colleague.

"We'll be working together this evening," he said, "so I'll be able to keep Mr. Sturdy at bay. Now, let's go somewhere we can talk undisturbed. We have alibis to break."

*　　*　　*　　*

Philippa spread her belongings across the counter and in leisurely fashion, began to apply her make-up. Then, as she smeared pancake across her freckled nose, she was startled to hear Clifton Mayberry's voice as clearly as if he had been in the room with her.

"I'm sorry to see you in this predicament, Stewart," he said. "I feel responsible for the whole mess."

Philippa suddenly realized that although the entrance to the dressing-room was around the corner from the green room door, the two rooms were adjacent. The backstage walls were merely thin partitions. On the other side of the dressing-room, the girls constantly chatted with the men in the next room, but it had never occurred to her that the conversations in the green room would be audible if the dressing-room were silent.

Stewart's voice sounded harsh and strained, but it carried as distinctly as Clifton Mayberry's.

"You?" he said. "Why should you feel responsible?"

"Because Steve's behaviour was a result of my own neglect. He was so young when our parents died. He needed love and care and attention, but I never had any time for him. What was worse, I couldn't always get suitable people to care for the children. They must have been desperately unhappy."

"Some people have failure born into them. Janet survived the same conditions, and look how well she turned out."

"Janet has a good brain and she's always been resilient, but Steve was the slow, insecure one. He needed care and direction. So did Bella. If I'd been more understanding with her, she'd never have run off the way she did. I failed them both, and I blame myself for what's happened now."

"Charlene didn't kill Steve," Stewart said abruptly. "She was angry, and she may have threatened him—but she didn't kill him."

Clifton's voice sounded thoughtful.

"No, I don't believe she did," he said, "though from my point of view it would have been better if she had."

There was a pause, and when Stewart spoke again, the sound was muted. Realizing that he had deliberately dropped his voice, Philippa set down her sponge and strained forward toward the mirror. She could hear the urgency in Stewart's voice, but she only caught his last few words. "You ought to tell the police," he concluded.

"I don't know anything—that's the trouble," said Clifton. "It's just a resemblance I've noticed. A hunch. It's probably nothing and I certainly can't prove anything. You see, I've already had two operations for cancer, and though the doctors speak with great optimism, I know I haven't got a great deal of time. Oh, I may be good for three or four years—more if I'm lucky—but I'm not going to live to a ripe old age."

"Cliff, you're rambling. I don't know what you're talking about. What does your life expectancy have to do with Steve's murder?"

"A great deal, if he was killed for my money. I made a very serious mistake when I changed my will. By doing so I put Steve and Janet in terrible danger."

"Janet? How is she in danger?"

"Isn't it obvious? Surely you can see the implications of what has happened? If my theory about the killer is correct, Janet will be the next victim."

With tantalizing abruptness, the conversation stopped, and after a moment, a third voice could be heard in the green room. However, to Philippa's intense disappointment, the subject had been changed to an innocuous discussion of the weather.

*   *   *   *

"This appears to be an impossible crime," Richard grumbled to Sergeant Martin. They were seated in a small office adjacent to the theatre lobby, which had served as an interview room and had become their unofficial headquarters during the investigation. "There are no fingerprints on the murder weapon, and such an abundance of them everywhere else that they're no help to us at all. We have scores of motives, but we're also inundated with cast-iron alibis. Margery Bevan is out, because she was sitting with her assistant in the auditorium. The policemen and pirates were on stage, albeit hidden behind trees and pillars, and Clifton Mayberry was performing his solo in the centre spotlight. The tenor was in the upstage left corner with Nancy Street, my sister, and the rest of the ladies chorus. Stewart Grey is our most likely suspect because he was in the wings on stage right, but one of the chorus girls was late coming up the stairs and she insists that she saw him just before the shot was fired. Of course, his sister, Charlene, probably hated Steve Mayberry more than anyone, but she was conducting the orchestra in the pit when the shot was fired, so we have to eliminate her. Young George Spragg is accounted for because Janet heard him over the headset at the crucial time. And who else…ah yes, Isobel Drummond. She'd just made her exit, but she'd immediately headed downstairs and gone out the bottom door for a cigarette."

"In mid-winter?"

"They have strict no-smoking rules backstage. The Drummond woman was the last person to see Steve Mayberry alive. The two of them were the company's nicotine addicts. They were both out for a smoke on their respective landings during the policeman's number a few minutes earlier. Unorthodox behaviour for a stage manager, but these amateur groups seem to make their own rules. They're either so loaded full of jargon and protocol that you can't move an inch, or lax to the point that the only serious deadline is to finish the show before the pubs close. Anyway, Drummond came back upstairs for the pirates' chorus. She says Steve remained outside, but we know he came in before the end of the pirates' number because both Janet and George heard him give the next cue over the headset. Clifton Mayberry also heard him give the cue. He couldn't see him, of course, because he was on the other side of the leg, but he heard Steve's voice. But that brings us to another point. Clifton Mayberry insists that no one entered the stage manager's corner via the stage-right wing while he stood there, which was practically the entire second act. So if no one passed Clifton Mayberry, how did the killer reach Steve's corner? And how did he get away afterward?"

"Over the top?"

"If the killer had come down the ladder from the flies, Steve would have seen him and been suspicious, yet there was no sign of a struggle. And the murderer couldn't have escaped that way because he'd have been seen by the people who got to the wings within seconds of Steve's death. Even Superman couldn't have shot up the ladder that fast."

"What about the fire escape?"

"Isobel Drummond was outside. She'd have seen anyone who came out onto the landing above her, but she says there wasn't another soul in sight. She was out there for some time too, because she was the one member of the company who didn't realize what had happened."

"Could she have done it? Come up the stairs, like, and in through the fire door?"

"How would she have opened the fire door from outside?"

"Perhaps she knocked."

Richard grinned at Martin.

"That's so simple it's logical. She'd have had a valid excuse for coming through. But why? The woman has no motive. Anyway, I'm still convinced that Steve didn't know what was going on. However the killer got there, he managed to stay unnoticed, then crept up behind his victim..."

"With cat-like tread?"

"That wouldn't have been necessary. Steve would have been watching his score—he was also wearing a headset. He would have been an easy target. The gun would have been pressed to his temple before he knew what had happened. Exit the stage manager."

"And then there were two."

Richard swung round and saw his sister standing in the doorway. She was neatly dressed in a demure white gown and her gloved hands clasped an extravagantly frothy parasol, but the pretty effect was marred by the anxious frown on her face.

"Two what?" asked Richard. "I presume from your enigmatic entrance line that you have something to tell me."

"Two little Mayberries," said Philippa.

"You mean Janet and Clifton?"

"No. For one thing, Janet isn't a Mayberry. She's a Green. I meant Clifton and Bella. Richard, I really think you ought to trace Bella Mayberry."

"Did I hear someone mention Bella Mayberry?" a voice asked brightly. George Spragg's round head bobbed around the door. Without waiting for an answer to his own question, he threw Philippa a yearning look and addressed himself to her. "Philippa, I simply have to talk to you," he said. "Every time I track you down, you're busy. I know you have a lot on your mind, but this can't wait any longer."

Philippa looked imploringly at Richard, who ignored her expression and abruptly addressed George.

"Before you go…" he said.

George reluctantly pulled his eyes away from Philippa and turned to listen to Richard. "Where's your cassette player?" Richard continued smoothly. "I couldn't see it on stage right."

George blinked. "I took it home," he said. "We didn't use it after all. Steve and I tried it out before the rehearsal started, but the sound was inadequate."

"And what happened to the cassette?"

"I erased it," said George.

Richard nodded.

"All right," he said. "Off you go. He's all yours, Philippa."

Like Marie Antoinette being led to the guillotine, Philippa raised her head and walked out the door.

∗   ∗   ∗   ∗

The following day, Philippa drove to Granville Island and met a friend who had just returned from Toronto. Having negotiated a difficult scene with George the previous evening, she was glad to be with someone who was not associated with the show.

It was a glorious day, only one fluffy cumulus cloud, so white and symmetrical that it looked like it belonged in a child's picture book, broke the smooth surface of the sky. Philippa and her friend strolled around the boardwalk, watching the small craft darting about the water and enjoying the view of snow-capped mountains, which formed a distant backdrop behind the apartments of English Bay. Then, having bought a plush frog at Puppets and Kites for one of Juliet's daughters who had an imminent birthday, they strolled through the market and settled at a table in a restaurant overlooking False Creek. Having devoured a spinach salad, followed by a shrimp and lobster crepe the size of a football, Philippa sat back contentedly and watched the Aquabus chugging back and forth between the Island and the far shore. Her friend, who had just completed an engagement with COC, produced an envelope of photographs, and over coffee, Philippa browsed through the pile, admiring the ornate period costumes and lavish sets.

"Those are spectacular," she said enviously, as she returned the thick wad of pictures to the girl opposite. "How did you manage to get them?"

"I was dating the stage manager. He let me stand in the wings and click away all through the dress rehearsal."

"Didn't the singers complain?"

"No. I was very discreet. I held off during the quiet bits. But most of the orchestration in *Rondine* is sufficiently heavy that no one heard a thing. One section of the second-act waltz is so explosive that you could fire a cannon and no one would notice a...Philippa? Is something the matter?...Now what did I say that was so earth-shattering?"

Philippa sat staring into space.

"So that's how it was done," she said. "Just like that old Hitchcock movie."

"How what was done? What movie? Really, Philippa, you're behaving most oddly."

"I'm thinking. Just a minute." Philippa frowned. "But no," she said, "we heard the shot, and...Oh my God." She stopped, looking stricken.

Her friend looked at her anxiously.

"Philippa, are you all right?" she said. "You look quite ill."

"I *feel* ill," said Philippa. "You've just given me the solution to a problem—not that there's any way of proving it—but now that I know the answer, I'd give anything to know nothing at all about the whole affair."

Philippa glanced out the window and sighed. Appropriately, the sun had retreated behind the solitary cloud, which now cast a pall on the scene below. She signalled to the waiter and asked for the bill. She was not looking forward to her next meeting with her brother.

*   *   *   *

"How very Dame Aggie-ish," said a willowy policeman, pulling off his bobby's helmet and filling it with potato chips from the dish on the green room counter. "Of course, it's hardly one's typical opening-night reception, but it's too, too terribly exciting. I wonder what that dishy inspector is going to say to us."

He peered around the green room, which was bulging at its seams, and his eyes lit on Philippa who was sitting unobtrusively in the corner.

"You're very quiet, Pip," the policeman said insinuatingly. "Do fill us in. Is your brother going to dazzle us with his deductive skills, present us with overwhelming proof of some intricate solution, and drag the killer handcuffed and snivelling from the room? *So* dramatic."

Philippa, who was feeling wretched, felt like screaming at her interrogator. If Richard had proof, she thought, he'd make his arrest quietly. He wouldn't be forced to go through this miserable farce and confront you all in the hope of getting a confession. And furthermore, you nasty pile of bile, he doesn't take any pleasure in showing off his deductive skills, as you so acidly put it.

However, being a well-brought-up young lady, she merely said: "Richard will explain when he gets here."

The policeman pouted in a manner highly unbecoming to his uniform.

"I see you've lost your shadow," he added spitefully.

He smirked with satisfaction and pointed at George Spragg who was sitting at the far end of the room. George, who had studiously avoided Philippa all evening, appeared to be engaged in an earnest conversation with Clifton Mayberry.

Philippa was saved from the effort of a reply, for at that moment, the door opened. The actors fell silent as Richard and Sergeant Martin entered the green room.

*   *   *   *

"Steve Mayberry had many characteristics that caused people to dislike him," said Richard, once he had everyone's attention, "but his murder seemed to be tied in with a particular sequence of events: his engagement to Nancy Street, the breaking-off of his relationship with Charlene Grey, the financial fracas that ensued, and the quarrel with his brother that resulted in Clifton Mayberry making a new will. There has been a great deal of talk about this new will, and this led me to consider two questions: Who would benefit financially by Steve Mayberry's death? And who would be affected by the change in Clifton Mayberry's will? The answer to the first question was obvious. The remaining legatees—Janet Green and Bella Mayberry. But the second question posed a problem. Janet, of course, had known about the contents of both wills, whereas Bella, who hadn't seen her family for more than twenty years, knew nothing about her future inheritance—but the fact remained that neither Janet nor Bella's portions had been altered in any way. The change didn't seem to affect either of them. Yet I was still convinced that the new will had precipitated Steve Mayberry's death. Then the significance of the change struck me. Steve Mayberry was not a discreet young man. In fact, he was the kind of person who aired his frustrations to anyone who would listen. He was angry and bitter about the new will, and before long the entire company knew of the family quarrel. The contents of Clifton Mayberry's will became public knowledge."

"I fail to see the significance of what you're saying, Inspector," said Clifton Mayberry.

"Think," said Richard. "Even though your changing the will didn't affect your sister's inheritance, it was possible that the change and all the ensuing controversy resulted in her *hearing* about the inheritance. Who knows how she might have reacted if she had suddenly learned that she was still included in your will?"

Clifton Mayberry paled.

"Bella?" he said. "You're talking nonsense, Inspector. Bella loved Steve. You'll never convince me that she killed him."

"No," said Richard. "She didn't. I'm afraid I have bad news for you, Mr. Mayberry. Your sister, Bella, is dead. Do you remember the bus crash in Peru last year that claimed the lives of more than a dozen Canadian tourists. We learned yesterday that your sister and her husband were two of the victims. Of course, even if you had read about the casualties, you wouldn't have recognized the names. The newspapers listed them as Mr. and Mrs. Bernard Spragg. But you know their son, however. He's sitting beside you at this very moment."

As all eyes turned toward him, George Spragg shifted uncomfortably; then looked nervously toward Clifton Mayberry.

"Yes," said Clifton. "I think I knew all along. You look so very much like your mother. But why?" he added with sudden intensity. "Why didn't you tell me who you were?"

"I...that is, my mother...I didn't know..." George faltered and stopped.

"You didn't know whether you'd like us or not?"

"I suppose so," said George. "But I was going to tell you. I fully intended to..."

"Until you heard about the inheritance," said Richard. "And then you decided to remain silent."

George looked up sharply. Suddenly his voice lost its nervous tremor.

"You can't pin this murder on me," he said. "I was on stage left. Janet can back me up. She heard me over the headset just before the shot was fired. Didn't you?" he added, turning toward Janet, who was staring at him with undisguised amazement on her face. Richard realized that Clifton Mayberry had never revealed his suspicions to his niece.

"Yes, that's true," said Janet. "You were with me at the time, Richard," she added. "You must have heard me answer him. It was only seconds before the shot was fired."

"No," Richard corrected. "It was some time after the shot was fired. You see, we all assumed that Steve was killed during the Major General's solo, but in reality, the murder occurred several minutes earlier."

"But that's impossible," said Clifton Mayberry. "We'd have heard the shot."

"Not if it were timed correctly," said Richard. "Think of what happened during the previous number. The orchestra played a loud chord, the cymbals crashed, and the pirates thumped down together like a herd of elephants. And at that precise moment, Steve Mayberry died."

"Now wait a minute," said George. "I heard Steve speak after that. So did Janet and Cliff."

"He's right," said Janet. "Steve gave me a cue, right at the end of *Cat-Like Tread*."

Clifton Mayberry nodded.

"Yes. I heard his voice just before I went on stage."

"You see," said George. "And what about the shot we heard. If Steve was killed earlier, how do you explain that?"

"Pure theatre," said Richard unrelentingly. "Both the voice and the shot were merely sound effects. Something you're an expert at."

Janet went white. Trembling, she turned toward George.

"The cassette player," she said slowly. "You must have recorded Steve's voice at one of the previous rehearsals. Then later, you put a gunshot after it. That's how you did it. You put it right into the sound-effects tape. And to think I was the one who sent you up into the flies. You must have climbed down the ladder while Steve went out for a cigarette, then hidden behind the door as he came back inside. You killed him—then you climbed back over the top to stage left, knowing that the sound-effects tape would proceed on cue and make us all think Steve was murdered later."

George glowered angrily.

"Come off it," he said witheringly, sounding completely himself again. "That cassette player couldn't record a gunshot clearly, let alone replay it convincingly. You'd need some first class speakers, like the ones on stage, if you were going to pull a trick like that. And as I already told you, the stage speakers were out of commission."

"Only the one on your side of the stage," said Richard. "The stage-right speaker was in perfect working order."

"You're still talking rot," said George. "How would I have turned on the tape…by remote control? It would have…"

Brutally, Richard interrupted him.

"But you slipped up in one very significant way," he said. "The stage manager used a score to follow the show, and that score was as good as a clock. Steve Mayberry stopped turning pages during the pirates' number—and that's when the murder occurred."

"But that's impossible," cried Janet, her voice suddenly shrill. "I turned…" Paling, she fell silent, her eyes riveted on Richard.

Richard's voice became steely as he turned toward Janet and forced himself to go on.

"Yes, Janet," he said. "Impossible, because after you killed Steve, you turned the pages of the score ahead to the Major General's solo."

Richard stopped, and a bleak expression clouded his blue eyes. Finally, George Spragg broke the silence.

"That's what I was about to say," he muttered. "About the tape, I mean. A trick like that would have to be controlled from the booth."

*   *   *   *

Three days later, Margery Bevan found Philippa sitting alone in the green room long after the night's performance had ended.

"What are you sitting around for?" Margery asked briskly.

"I'm waiting for Richard. He said he'd give me a ride home tonight."

"Your poor brother," sighed Margery. "Still, I suppose his case is wrapped up. Janet really gave herself away at the end, didn't she? He took her off-guard when he went after George Spragg. It's incredible," she added. "Janet always seemed such a charming, steady girl. I suppose underneath she was as emotionally deprived and morally deficient as Steve."

"Yes. She just covered it better. She was really the most logical suspect," said Philippa. "She had her own set of keys both to the theatre and to the booth, so she above all people had the opportunity to make the tapes, disconnect and reconnect the speakers, and adjust the Fresnel. She was an expert at setting the technical side of a show. This time, she created her own show, carefully plotted and meticulously timed, to run concurrently with the operetta."

"I'm still confused," said Margery. "How did she actually do it?"

"She knew Steve went outside for a cigarette during the policemen's number, so once he was off the headset, she told George to fix the Fresnel, which she herself had moved earlier. She had to get him out of the way in case he called her over the headset and discovered she wasn't on the other end. Also, no matter how loud the orchestra was, George would have felt the impact of the shot if he'd been wearing his earphones. Richard had already been taken care of because he had a plug change at the very moment the shot was to be fired. Janet sent him down well ahead of time. Once he'd gone, she climbed the ladder to the upper passage, went across the top, wedged open the fire door that opened off the flies—then descended the ladder on stage right. She waited behind the exit door so Steve wouldn't see her as he came inside. I imagine she remained behind the black curtain until the pirates' number began and only crept out as the chord approached. Once she'd killed Steve, she had to hurry. She flipped the score ahead and hung the headset against the speaker. Then she went out the fire exit, ran up the fire escape, and came in through the upper door. She raced along the passage, returned to the booth, and probably just had time to switch on the tape and put on her headset before Richard returned."

"Then he became her alibi."

"Exactly," said Philippa. "She was so sure of herself. After the fake shot, she sent him along the same route she'd taken so he could get to the stage quickly. Then once he'd left, she erased the tape and the evidence was gone."

"But she seemed genuinely fond of Steve. Why did she do it?"

"She wanted to control her uncle's business. Clifton's first will would have enabled her to do that because Steve would have willingly sold his share in the company; but once the new will was in effect, Steve's portion was tied up for thirty years. Steve couldn't sell it and Janet couldn't touch it. She would have been stuck with her forty percent and Steve as a partner, unless she could have bought out Bella, but there was no guarantee of that. So she decided to kill Steve before he could marry and have children."

"Very logical," said Margery. "*I* wouldn't want Steve forced on me as a business partner, and someone as bright as Janet would have been devastated by such an arrangement. I can almost feel sorry for her."

Margery did not notice Richard enter the room, but Philippa glanced up and caught his expression as he overheard the director's words. Margery did see Philippa's reaction, however, and sensing another presence, she swung round and stared at Richard. He gazed at her blankly, frozen by the recollection of green eyes turning black with fury. Then his vision cleared, and Margery's animated face came into focus.

"Don't delude yourself," Richard said stiffly. "It was a cold-blooded, wicked crime."

"Um," said Margery, looking embarrassed. "Well anyway," she added briskly, "George is going to be a rich man one day. Cliff says he's going to leave him the lot. George is a smart boy too. He'll do very well taking over the Mayberry enterprises. A good catch," she said firmly, looking pointedly at Philippa.

Philippa sighed.

"Too late," she said. "I rejected an impassioned proposal three days ago."

"That's not irrevocable," said Margery. "I had the impression that he adored you."

"Adored, past tense. I used my extreme youth as an excuse, but even so, he was very offended when I said I only wanted to be friends. He withdrew his offer to take me out for a drink tonight."

"Oh dear. What bad luck."

"Ah well," said Philippa. "I never fancied marrying for money. Well, not *just* for money, anyway."

Richard tousled his sister's hair.

"Come on," he said. "I'll buy you that drink. My pubbing plans went awry too."

As Richard and Philippa left the green room, Allan Sturdy bobbed out of the men's dressing-room. Whistling exuberantly, he lumbered down the hall. He overtook them at the corner, nodded cheerily, and disappeared up the stairs.

Philippa looked after him thoughtfully.

"You know," she said, "for someone who was abysmally bad at the start of rehearsals, he made a remarkable improvement. Just in time for opening night too. I wonder how Margery did it."

To his amazement, Richard found himself laughing.

"If you haven't figured that out," he said, "you'd better throw in your sleuth's cap forever."

As they ascended the stairs, they heard Allan's heavy footsteps plodding across the stage. Suddenly the thudding steps stopped; then began again with a rapid and uneven rhythm, as if the owner of the feet had whimsically broken into a hobnailed-boot shuffle. Allan's wobbly bass reverberated above the noise:

"When constabulary duty's to be done...to be done,
A policeman's lot is not a happy one...haa-peeeey one."

Richard Beary wished his sister had never met George Spragg.

Mortality Play

▼

"How does one conclude a play in a church?" asked Victoria. "Does the congregation applaud, or is it considered infra-dig to take bows? Do we just fade discreetly into the stained-glass windows?"

"They'll applaud," said Philippa. "People are informal here."

"They seem so. Very different from what I remember of Sunday school when I was a child. Of course, that was thirty years ago. This group has been most gracious, welcoming a heathen like myself back into the fold. The things you find yourself doing when you marry and have children. I was afraid the vicar would refuse to baptize Fiona when he realized neither Larry nor myself had been near a church in three decades."

"Reverend Dunne knows a useful prospective parishioner when he sees one," said Philippa. "A professional actress is too good to pass up. Look how he's commandeered you into producing this Morality Play for Lent. I bet you never envisioned yourself organizing your schedule between *Blithe Spirit* at the Playhouse and *The Seven Deadly Sins* at St. Margaret's Anglican Church."

"'Thus conscience doth make cowards of us all'," said Victoria. "Though I must say," she continued, "I'm enjoying St. Margaret's. You have to admire the theatrical slickness of a church service. Amazing talent too. Leaving aside yourself—after all, you're their hired soloist, so you don't count—the others are very good performers. John Hewitt is magnificent—such a resonant voice—and Glynis Thorpe is a real trouper. Can't you imagine her as the nurse in *Romeo and*

Juliet? Ah, my props," she added, swinging round and looking toward the door-way.

Philippa turned to see Laura Hewitt coming toward them up the aisle. A long, black cloak was draped over one arm, barely concealing the coil of picture wire clasped in her hand.

Her other hand held a macabre-looking leather whip and a sack covered with glittering stars and moons.

Victoria slid from her pew and relieved Laura of her bizarre oddments. "I didn't ask for this," she said, frowning at the picture wire.

"That's for Howard and Len," said Laura. "Reverend Dunne asked them to put up some pictures in the office."

Laura was a fresh-faced girl in her early twenties. Like her father who was one of the lay clergymen, she was devoted to parish duties.

"Dad said to tell you he'll be here in ten minutes," she added. "He's winding up a meeting with the Bazaar Committee. Glynis will be here any minute too. She's training a new Sunday school teacher."

"The joys of church theatricals," sighed Victoria. "*The play's the thing,* but everything else comes first. I suppose you wouldn't have any messages why Stuart Hindley is delayed?" she added.

Laura flushed.

"No," she said shortly, and disappeared.

"What did I say?" asked Victoria.

Philippa enlightened her. "Laura was Stuart's fiancé before Sue James came along."

"Oh, heavens," said Victoria, rolling her eyes upward. "I need an assistant to fill me in on the Parish gossip so I don't put my foot in it. I asked Reverend Dunne for background information, but he was hopeless. Even his list of pro-spective actors was useless. I finally rounded up a cast through Glynis Thorpe."

"Naturally," said Philippa. "Sunday school superintendents are much more practical than vicars."

Victoria shifted her statuesque figure to a more comfortable position. She ran her fingers through her tawny blonde hair and frowned.

"Why did Stuart Hindley break off with Laura Hewitt and take up with Sue James?" she asked. "Laura is perfect for him, and the other girl—well, I can't think of a less suitable companion. She looks like a refugee from an MTV rock video—all boobs and make-up, but without the frenetic vitality."

"I don't know Stuart that well," said Philippa, "but I suspect his choice was an act of rebellion. When you consider how Mabel has kept him under her thumb all these years, it's hardly surprising that he should bust loose at least once."

"Mabel's a dragon," admitted Victoria, "but she does wonderful things with her choir."

"She's a good organist," Philippa acknowledged, "but I feel sorry for Stuart. Mabel had him late in life, and she lost her husband shortly afterward. Stuart has been reared with a combination of intense maternal devotion and fanatic religious fervour. Mabel guides his every step. He sings in her choir, works diligently at his office job—acquired through Mabel's brother—and he became obediently engaged to Laura. Actually, Laura is probably the perfect girl for him, if they could have got together without help from Mommy Dearest."

Victoria stared at Philippa.

"Philippa, you're normally sweet and charitable. What has Mabel done to get to you?"

Philippa scowled.

"She plays my solos at the wrong tempos and destroys my breathing," she said. "That's her way of getting even for having a professional soloist thrust on her. She's annoyed about this play too. She's only doing the music because Reverend Dunne insisted, but you watch, she'll do something to muck it up at the service tomorrow."

"I thought churches were supposed to be benevolent places," sighed Victoria. "No wonder Stuart went off the rails. Tarty as she is, Sue probably does wonders to reduce his tension. How on earth did a girl like that come to be a member of this congregation?"

"This is a big downtown church," said Philippa. "There's an incredible mix in the congregation…Shaughnessey millionaires like the Loewens and their son, Howard, well-to-do professional types such as the Hewitts…even politicians. You've met George and Angela Tivett, Len's parents. Then we get the oddest assortment of types wandering in off the street, some of whom have serious problems."

"What sort of problems? Drugs? Crime?"

"Those are the top two," said Philippa. "Sue floated in last year—and, believe me, I mean floated. She was quite the pothead when she first arrived, though she does seem to have improved. She's been pretty thick with all the members of the youth group, particularly the men. She hangs out quite a bit with Howard and Len, but Howard's such a weasel, for all his money and privilege, so she'd never get the upper hand with him. And Len's had a track record with drugs, much to his parent's mortification, so she can't teach him anything."

"Good Lord," said Victoria. "I thought they were such nice, helpful young men. They're great techies."

"Oh, Len's straightened out. His parents got him involved at St. Margaret's and he's stayed out of trouble ever since. Howard, I think, just puts on a show of piety and usefulness because Mummy and Daddy are hard-nosed types that wouldn't think twice about disinheriting him if he didn't meet their standards and expectations. But Stuart is another story. He's led a sheltered life. Sue James had him dancing attendance within two months and he's been her slave ever since, except for occasional timeouts when they've had a fight. Their relationship is rather volatile."

A bang from the door cut the conversation short. A pink, frilly infant raced into the church and flung herself into Victoria's arms. She was followed by an amiable giant in a tweed jacket.

"Hello, dear," said Victoria. "Philippa, have you met my husband?"

Philippa nodded.

"I thought you were rehearsing," said Larry, eyeing the empty nave.

"We are," said Victoria. "I'm waiting for three-quarters of my cast. Don't jump on the pews, Fiona," she added.

"Here's one more quarter," said Larry.

A stout lady appeared in the doorway. She had fiery hair striped with grey streaks. She was towing a rickety cart with two large, wobbly wheels.

Victoria jumped up and examined the cart.

"Perfect," she pronounced.

"Isn't it?" said a velvety voice from the doorway. "A means of travel for the travelling players."

"Another quarter," said Larry. "Here's your devil, Vicky."

John Hewitt strode majestically into the church. His appearance was Machiavellian, partly because of his dark beard, and partly because of the cynical arch of his eyebrows and his sardonic smile. His resonant voice and dramatic appearance had served him well during a long career as a lawyer. Only those that knew him realized what a gentle, devout man lay under the formidable exterior.

"Where are the others?" said Victoria looking at her watch.

"Here's Stuart and Sue," said Glynis.

Stuart entered quietly and mumbled an apology. Sue James said nothing, but slid into a pew beside Stuart, stretched purple legs and smiled a feline smile.

"Is your mother coming?" Victoria asked Stuart.

"She's talking to Reverend Dunne," he replied.

"Not any more," boomed the vicar, bursting into the church. He was followed by a hatchet-faced woman in brown tweeds who marched to the organ and slapped a pile of music on the bench.

"Carry on, Victoria," ordered Reverend Dunne. "You're doing a magnificent job." He eyed the whip and the star-spangled bag and his round face split into a grin. "That'll shake up a few of the parishioners. The people's warden will be apoplectic. Good show. Keep it up."

He beamed at the ensemble and sailed out the door.

A smile flickered on Victoria's majestic countenance.

"You heard the Rev," she said briskly. "Clear the pews. Places, please."

*   *   *   *

By nine-thirty Sunday morning, the church daycare was a hive of activity. Outside, the day was wet and dreary, and the cast of the play was sharing the room with boots, umbrellas, anxious churchwardens and hyperactive children. Victoria surveyed the scene and sighed. She had been buffeted and blown by so many distractions that she felt completely disoriented. She found it impossible to reconcile the secular world of theatre with this ecclesiastical domain of committee meetings, food banks, hospital visits and Bible study groups. Even Philippa, she noticed, who was normally professional in her attitude, was laughing gaily with an elegant young man who had arrived with the Beary family that morning. Beside them stood a dazzling brunette who appeared to belong to Philippa's brother, Richard.

Victoria glanced around the nursery. In a far corner, Sue James reclined languidly on a table while Howard Loewen and Len Tivett explained the intricacies of the church's lighting system. Her expression did not inspire Victoria with confidence. Stuart Hindley glowered from a far corner of the room. He and Sue had been fighting again. In the centre of the room, Laura Hewitt checked props and costumes. She was cool and efficient, at any rate.

Victoria shifted her glance to her husband, who had removed his raincoat and, with the help of Richard Beary, was using picture wire borrowed from the Rector's office to tighten the wobbly wheels on the cart. Behind the cart, Fiona hopped back and forth, resisting John Hewitt's efforts to make conversation and keep her out of her father's hair.

Once the wheels were steady, Larry packed his tools and helped Fiona clamber onto the cart. Richard Beary straightened up and joined the dazzling brunette who was now talking earnestly with his mother, while his father stood on the sidelines glowering at Philippa's young man. Sensing eyes on them, Philippa glanced up. She moved to her father, took him by the arm, and firmly led him across the room. She planted him in front of Victoria, introduced them, and immediately drifted back to her young Adonis.

"How can an intelligent girl be taken in by a face like that?" growled Beary. "They have absolutely nothing in common."

"He is rather manicured," murmured Victoria. "Not really Philippa's type. Still, looks like that pre-empt any necessity for compatible character traits. Who is he, anyway?"

"His name's Mark Brennan. She met him at the Hall when she dropped in to meet me for lunch one day."

"The Hall? Oh, you mean City Hall. You're a councillor, aren't you? Is Mark Brennan on the council too?"

"Good God, no. He's an underling in the Parks Department. He dreams up initiatives to waste taxpayers' money. He took Philippa out for dinner last week, and she invited him to hear her sing today."

"I'm not surprised. This play is quite a showcase for Philippa. All those soaring psalms. He'll be struck dumb with admiration."

"He couldn't be struck any dumber than he already is."

"Who's the spectacular brunette with your son?" Victoria asked, tactfully changing the subject.

"I'm not sure where Richard found her," said Beary. "Barbara something or other. She's pretty enough, but a bit serious. She hasn't laughed at any of my jokes and she's getting along much too well with Edwina. That's definitely a danger sign."

"Ah well," said Victoria, "You may disapprove of your children's choices, but you have to let them live their own lives."

"I don't see why," said Beary. "Not that there's much I can do to interfere. The four of them are going out to lunch after the service."

"Didn't they invite you and your wife too?" Victoria asked, amused.

"They did, but being a long weekend, Edwina and I had already planned to visit Juliet—that's our daughter who lives in Sechelt. We have to rush to catch a ferry as soon as the service ends."

The double doors swung open and Glynis Thorpe bustled into the room. She was followed by three children: a boy in a navy and white sailor suit and two girls in matching sailor dresses. Glynis marched the children over to Victoria.

"This is Mrs. Marsh, children," she announced. "She's in charge, and I want you to do exactly what she tells you."

Victoria looked bewildered.

"What am I supposed to do with them?" she asked.

"They look so nice in their sailor outfits," said Glynis. "I thought we'd put them in the play."

"We're not doing *The Sound of Music*," said Victoria.

"Now, use your imagination, Victoria," said Glynis. "They can run alongside during the procession and wave to us all the way up the aisle. It'll look more like travelling players if you have spectators milling around."

Victoria had to acknowledge the validity of the point.

"What are their names?" she asked.

"Christopher, Clarissa and Christabel."

"How alliterative," said Beary.

Victoria eyed the smallest girl sceptically.

"Isn't this one a bit young? How old is she?"

The child stared upward through straight blonde bangs and fixed almond-shaped blue eyes on Victoria.

"Christabel is three," said Glynis.

"She has presence," Victoria acknowledged, wilting under the child's disconcerting gaze.

"She'll be fine," said Glynis. "She'll hold her sister's hand and go wherever she goes. Do use them, Victoria," she hissed as an aside. "They're Marvin and Ida Loewen's grandchildren. They belong to Howard's older brother. He and his wife are going through a marriage breakdown, so Marvin and Ida look after the children every weekend. Taking part in the play will be good for them."

Victoria weakened.

"All right," she said, resigned. "Let's round up the heavenly throng."

Glynis boomed a summons, and the inhabitants of the nursery drew near.

"Gather round, everyone," said Victoria. "Let's review the procedure."

Glynis pulled the children into a circle on the mat, and the adults gathered round them.

"Now, remember," Victoria began, "there's no sermon today…"

"We *are* the sermon," John Hewitt interjected helpfully. "The message is in our play."

"Yes, exactly," said Victoria. "As I said, there's no sermon—by Reverend Dunne," she added quickly as John appeared ready to interrupt again. "And the order of the service is changed. Our play comes after the offertory hymn, so during the hymn, you must slip out. You don't have to worry about costumes as everything's loaded on the cart. The only thing that won't go on the cart is the wooden tree, and Stuart will carry that. You get into costume when you reach the sanctuary. It's all part of the play. Sue, you have to black out the house—I mean church—lights…"

"The nave, actually," corrected John Hewitt.

Victoria took a deep breath.

"The lights in the *nave*," she paused and gave John the stare that she used on actors who liked to hold up rehearsals with endless discussions on motivation, then continued, "*before* the procession comes in. You do that from the dimmers behind the rear pew, right by the door where you'll be lining up for the procession. You don't have to worry about bringing up the lights above the altar because Len will be downstairs counting the collection money and he's going to slip across to the control room and bring up the chancel lights from there."

Sue looked anxious, as if a problem had suddenly occurred to her.

"What about at the end?" she said. "I'll be in the control room. I'll be able to turn off the sanctuary lights, but who will turn on the lights in the church?"

Victoria sighed, having already explained the procedure on several previous occasions.

"By that time," she said patiently, "Len and Howard will have rejoined the service, so Len will bring up the main lights. Not to worry, Sue. You come in with the procession and do John's devil make-up in front of the altar, but keep his back to the congregation so they don't see the result until he turns round. When the dialogue begins, you slip out the side door and go below to do the lightning flashes from the control room. Now, the rest of you, remember—if anything goes wrong—ad lib. Stay in character no matter what. Lots of energy, lots of volume. It'll be just great," Victoria concluded with a robust enthusiasm that she did not feel.

"Before we leave," boomed John Hewitt, getting to his feet and gesturing for the others to rise, "let us all join hands and pray."

Victoria found herself drawn into the circle as John delivered a short yet moving prayer. Then the group dispersed and Victoria was left standing with Beary.

Beary chortled at the expression on Victoria's face.

"It's incredible," said Victoria. "They don't attend rehearsals, they wait till the last possible moment to learn their lines, they throw in improvisations when there's no time to see if they work, and then they say their prayers and go out of here with utter confidence that the thing will be a success. The craziest part of it is that I felt better after John's prayer than I did after my own pep talk—in fact, I felt as if my pep talk was utterly redundant."

"Remember," said Beary wisely, "we *are* in church. God has to have the last word."

*   *   *   *

"Good sermon today, Reverend," Beary said tactlessly. Edwina flinched, but Reverend Dunne merely chuckled.

"They did wonderfully well, didn't they," he agreed. "Not a hitch, apart from Mabel jamming the organ before the opening procession. But so clever of John to stride in and sing the march until Mabel could start the music. He's always so on top of things."

"That procession was delightful," trilled Mrs. Dunne, peeking out from behind her husband. "With John booming Mozart, and the children running up and down, and that little tree with legs coming up the aisle. We loved it," she added to Victoria, who was following Beary through the receiving line.

"The navy was a nice touch," said Beary.

Victoria blinked.

"Oh, you mean the children?" she said, catching on.

"Weren't they sweet?" cooed Edwina. "Particularly that little one who wasn't sure what to do when she came adrift from her sister. She managed very well."

"A regular Gertrude Lawrence," Victoria agreed, remembering the determination with which Christabel had lunged free and executed a pirouette before sitting down, pulling a marble from her pocket and playing with it through the entire performance. "No one will have to teach that child the meaning of the word, *upstaging.*"

"She displayed real genius when she dropped her marble down the peep-hole into the control room," said George Tivett, moving into the space vacated by the Bearys who were now drifting toward the coffee aroma emanating from the hall. George had a politician's appreciation for good timing. "Most appropriate too…just as John delivered his line about *ever doing ill being his sole delight.* Her wail of rage topped his line beautifully."

"Not to mention the display of frilly knickers as she tried to rescue her marble," gurgled Angela Tivett.

"Seriously, though, Victoria, it was well done," added George Tivett, assuming the earnest expression that had won him three consecutive elections.

"Your family did its bit," Victoria acknowledged. "Your son and Howard Loewen did a great job on the lights, not to mention training Sue James. The final blackout was too sudden, but otherwise the lighting was very effective."

"Wasn't it, though," said Mabel, pushing her way through the line. "Excuse me shoving through," she apologized. "I must go downstairs and change my gown. So sorry about the trouble with the organ, Victoria," she added with a smirk. "I've never had that problem before. I can't think how it happened."

Victoria grunted.

"No matter," said Reverend Dunne. "The little flubs merely served to highlight the chaotic, worldly aspect of the play. That's why the travelling players with the cart worked so well. A really motley crew. And then when the sun came out just in time to let light from the clerestory fall on Philippa as she sang the psalms—magnificent! The timing was perfect and the contrast was really meaningful. The beauty of the words and the music transcended everything. It worked, Victoria, it worked. The message came through."

Suddenly remembering how moved she had been toward the end of the play, Victoria realized that the Reverend was right. She flashed him a grateful smile, and relaxing, she went into the hall and poured herself a cup of coffee. Laura Hewitt passed the cream and sugar across the counter to her.

"Have you seen Stuart?" Laura asked her.

"No," said Victoria. "He disappeared after the service and I haven't seen him since. Maybe he's downstairs. Why don't you run down and check?"

"It's not that important," said Laura, flushing. "I just wanted to collect his props, that's all."

"He's probably sulking in a back room somewhere because he and Sue had a lover's tiff," said Ida Loewen with complete lack of tact. "Check the sacristy. He might be there." She poured a cup of coffee and sniffed expressively. "I thought I told you children to play in the nursery," she added sharply to Clarissa who was gathering large portions of cake to share with her siblings.

"The lights were out," said Clarissa.

"Well, they're on now," snapped her grandmother. "Off you go."

"Come to think of it," said Victoria, still concentrating on Ida's first remark, "I haven't seen Sue for ages either. In fact, I haven't seen her since she went down to the control room. Odd. Still, they must be around somewhere."

She peered about the hall but neither Sue nor Stuart was anywhere in sight. As she glanced across to the far corner, Victoria saw with amusement that Bertram Beary had cornered Mark Brennan, and was obstinately monopolizing him while his daughter looked on in fury.

"Was someone looking for Stuart?" said Angela Tivett, materializing at Victoria's elbow. "He's been helping Dorothy Thomas sort Sunday school books ever since the service ended. They just this minute went downstairs to store the boxes."

She moved to the counter to help herself to cream and sugar for her coffee. Then she paused. Abruptly she set down her coffee cup and put her head on one side.

"What's that noise?"

Victoria listened. Gradually, over the hubbub created by the people in the hall, she became aware of a high-pitched note coming from somewhere distant.

As one by one, people became aware of the sound, the chatter diminished and the hall became quiet. When the talking stopped, the sound became recognizable. Someone was screaming in the basement of the church.

$$* \qquad * \qquad * \qquad *$$

"This is a fine kettle of fish," grumbled Richard Beary. "In an attempt to make a good impression on the most gorgeous girl I've ever met, I bring her to church to hear my sister sing and end up being forced to abandon her while I investigate a murder."

"You didn't have to volunteer," pointed out Sergeant Martin. "It is your day off."

"I didn't volunteer," said Richard. "My father volunteered me—with alacrity, I might add, just before he skipped off to catch his ferry."

"Well, of course, you do have a bit of a feel for the situation."

"Don't I just. An ex-junkie who was passionately adored by one member of the congregation, hated equally passionately by three other members, and sufficiently disliked by the rest of the congregation that no one seems willing to help apprehend her killer."

"She was probably killed by the one that passionately adored her," said Sergeant Martin philosophically. "That's usually the way it is."

"It would simplify my job if you were right," said Richard, "but the method doesn't fit. She was garrotted with a noose made from picture wire. That doesn't tie in with a crime of passion. Besides, the boy didn't have the opportunity to kill her."

"How many people were in the church basement while the girl was there?"

"The sidesmen, Howard and Len, were counting the collection money in the rector's office as she went down. The control room is opposite the office. They saw her go in and Len spoke to her before coming back up. That was approximately 10:35. No one went down during the course of the play, which took the next half hour. The lightning flashes occurred on cue around 10:55. The play ended at 11:05. At that time, John Hewitt slipped downstairs to the room where the choir members gown themselves so that he could wash off his devil's make-up, change and return to the service, which he did approximately 10 minutes later. His daughter also went down after the play ended and returned the props to the basement storage room. She came back upstairs and rejoined the service during Communion. After the service ended, the members of the choir went below, but they all vouch for each other. None of them went anywhere other than the change room, which is right at the foot of the stairs. None went down the far end of the hall where the control room is located. However, Mabel Hindley went down to change a little later by which time the others had come back upstairs, so she was alone in the basement. Stuart himself returned to the church immediately after the play ended and remained there for the duration of the service. He didn't go looking for the girl because they'd had a fight. After the service, he helped Mrs. Thomas sort books. He discovered Sue James' body when he went down to return a case of books to the control room, which is also used to store Sunday school supplies. Mrs. Thomas, following almost immediately afterward, found him on his knees, holding the girl and sobbing his heart out. No wonder she started screaming her head off. As for Hindley, we've hardly got a word out of him since."

"Shock?"

"Ostensibly, but I don't know for sure. There is a curious anxiety about his silence. I think he realizes that his mother, and Laura and John Hewitt are all suspects. Though which one did it, and how to prove it is not going to be easy."

"Because they'll stick together like glue and protect each other right down the line."

"You have it in a nutshell," said Richard.

"Are they the only people that went to the basement?"

"Yes. There is no lower entrance to the basement. The control room is a small booth with an assortment of dimmer switches and a largish spy-hole that looks up through the base of a choir pew toward the altar, but it has no windows. The only basement window is in the rector's office, but it's sealed shut. The only way down is via the stairway, and the ladies selling church calendars set their table up at the top of the stairs shortly before the service ended. They assure me that they would have seen anyone going downstairs."

"But what about the time between the end of the play and the end of the service?"

"Nothing doing. One of the elderly ladies was feeling faint and came out during the play. She couldn't go home as she gets a ride with the church van, so she sat quietly in the armchair by the top of the stairwell. She didn't move until the service ended, and she insists that the only people that went below were the ones I mentioned."

"Then there are only three possibilities for the murderer. Mabel Hindley, or Laura or John Hewitt."

"It would appear so," said Richard, "unless…"

Sergeant Martin peered quizzically at him.

"Unless," Richard continued slowly, "there is trickery afoot."

*   *   *   *

At the main entrance, trouble was brewing. The weather had turned foul again, and Barbara's expression matched the storm clouds overhead.

"Philippa," snapped Barbara, "have you any idea how long Richard will be? I thought we had a lunch date."

"I'll go and check," said Philippa. "I don't want to keep Mark hanging about either," she said. "Though there are a couple of people I need to speak to. I'll only be a moment."

Barbara looked exasperated.

"Why do you have to speak to anyone? This whole nasty situation has nothing to do with any of us."

"It's something my father asked me to do," said Philippa. "He has an instinct for these things."

"It's all very well for your father. He's headed for the Sunshine Coast. We're stuck here in filthy weather, and after sitting through that service, I'm starving. We should be tucked up in a restaurant lounge with a large fireplace, not standing around in an ancient stone pile with no central heating. You'd better tell Richard I'm not going to wait around here forever."

"Why don't you wait there?" suggested Philippa. She gestured to a dark alcove beside the main entrance where cushioned benches lined the walls beneath the lancet windows. Then, without waiting to see if Barbara was following her suggestion, she turned and went in search of her brother.

As she crossed the vestibule, she saw Howard and Len giving their enthralled parents an animated replay of the morning's events.

"Howard," she interrupted, "did you and Len actually see Sue go into the control room?"

"Yes," said Howard, "we not only saw her, we talked to her."

"That's right," said Len. "There was a good twenty minutes until she had to do her bit with the dimmers, so I reviewed her cues and the use of the board."

"Was this after you'd counted the collection?"

"We'd almost finished. I took a couple of minutes out to help Sue. Then Howard and I completed the count and came back upstairs. But before we came up, I stuck my head into the control room again to make sure Sue was confident of what she was doing. She seemed fine, so we came upstairs."

"Were her cues really that complicated?"

"No," said Len. "They were easy. It was just a matter of her peeking through the spy-hole, listening for her cue and flicking the altar lights several times. But Sue wasn't a particularly bright girl, so Victoria wanted us to double-check everything."

"How long after she came down did you go upstairs?"

"Five minutes at the most," said Howard.

Len nodded assent. "That's right. You were just starting your first psalm, but the sound system was acting up, so I had to spend the rest of the play monitoring it from the alcove beside the font. I didn't have a very good view of the play, which was disappointing as I'd been looking forward to it."

"So Sue was alone for about fifteen minutes before she had to create the lightning effects," said Philippa.

"At least that long," agreed Howard.

"I wonder what she got up to during that time," mused Philippa.

"Other than being hit in the eye by a marble," chortled George Tivett.

"Oh dear, poor girl. We shouldn't laugh," said Ida Loewen remorsefully.

Angela Tivett giggled, barely disguising a note of hysteria, and began a blow-by-blow description of the antics of Christabel. Philippa left them to it. Thoughtfully, she turned right, and proceeded through the swing doors that led into the nave. She walked up the aisle until she reached the choir pews. Glancing down, she saw light shining from the spy-hole at the base of the first pew.

Curiously, Philippa knelt down and peered through the spy-hole. She got a clear view of the lighting board and rows upon rows of dimmer switches. Otherwise, the room was empty. The forensic crew had departed.

She straightened up to see Victoria staring at her from the end of the aisle.

"Victoria, you were standing at the back of the church all through the play," said Philippa. "You must have seen anyone moving in and out. Are you sure no one left?"

"Absolutely," said Victoria.

"When did Len and Howard come in? They weren't here for the start of the play because they spoke with Sue after she'd gone down to the control room."

"That's right," Victoria nodded. "They came through the back doors while you were singing your first solo. It would have been four or five minutes after the play began."

"Did they come in separately?"

"No. They arrived together."

"So they were definitely here when Sue did the lightning effects from the control room."

"Goodness, yes. I'd say they were here a good fifteen minutes before. I sent Len into the alcove to monitor the sound controls because we were getting a lot of static, but I could see him the whole time. And I stood Howard by the house controls so he could bring up the lights at the end of the play."

There was a rustle from the back of the nave. Philippa swung round and saw Mark Brennan standing in the shadows.

"Philippa," he interjected testily, "do you intend to stay here all day? We did have a lunch date. It's only your brother who's on duty, you know, and I gather he's given everyone permission to leave now."

"I'm sorry, Mark. I'm coming. You've been wonderfully patient."

"So has Barbara," said Mark. "I think she's rather miffed that Richard has been put in charge of this case when he's supposed to be off duty. You could do a little fence-mending if we all went out together."

"Yes, of course. I'll come right away," said Philippa. "If only we'd known what was going on down below," she added as she followed Mark toward the door. "You'd have thought we'd have heard something. After all, down in the booth you can hear everything that is happening at the front of the church. Just think, if we'd got our nose to the floor and peered down the spy-hole, we might have seen the murder."

Philippa stopped suddenly and clapped her hand to her forehead.

"Oh, my God," she said reverently.

"What is it now?" snapped Mark.

"Perhaps somebody did."

Ignoring Mark's expression of fury, Philippa shot off toward the church nursery.

*   *   *   *

The nursery was empty, except for Glynis Thorpe who was tidying the toys.

"Where are the Loewen children?" Philippa asked her.

"Clarissa and Christopher have been in and out all afternoon," said Glynis. "Christabel was here with me, but she left a couple of minutes ago."

"By herself?"

"No. Len Tivett came to take her to her parents."

"Len Tivett! But that's impossible."

"Oh, no it isn't."

Philippa swung round to see her brother standing in the doorway. His face was grim.

"Come on," he snapped.

He turned and raced off down the hall. Philippa hurtled after him. They ran up the stairs and shot past the Dunnes who were conversing with another couple in the vestibule. Richard sped through the church doors with Philippa close behind.

The traffic din from the road was so loud that the impact of the noise hit like a physical blow. The rain was coming down in torrents, and it was hard to see anything beyond the grey downpour and the blur of vehicles. Then, on the far side of the road, Philippa saw a sight that made her blood run cold. Len Tivett was pushing a wriggling Christabel into a black sports car. Richard surged forward and tried to make his way through the traffic, but he had barely crossed the first lane when help came from an unexpected quarter.

Suddenly, without warning, two small figures shot into view on the far pavement. Moving simultaneously, young Christopher executed a violent head butt into Len Tivett's back while Clarissa grabbed Christabel's arm and pulled her clear of the car.

As Len Tivett recoiled, Christopher hurled his Sunday School Bible at his opponent's head. His aim was sound, and Len Tivett overbalanced and tottered onto the sodden pavement, just as Richard reached him and read him his rights. Christopher leapt away and joined his siblings at the edge of the sidewalk.

Watching from the church steps, Reverend Dunne took the spectacle in his stride.

"It is fortunate," he intoned, "that the Good Book is weighty in mass as well as in content."

*   *   *   *

"Why did Len Tivett want Christabel?" John Hewitt asked Philippa the following Sunday after the service had ended. "Don't tell me the child actually saw the murder through the spy-hole?"

"No," said Philippa, "but what she saw would have identified him as the killer."

"What did she see?"

"Absolutely nothing."

John Hewitt stepped back to allow Philippa to go first through the main portal. They emerged into the sunlight and continued their conversation on the front steps. Unlike the previous Sunday, the traffic was light, the air was clear, and the waters of the inlet formed bright patches of blue between the skyscrapers. The sun beating on the brown masonry of the church created a patch of warmth that turned April into August.

"Don't be enigmatic, Philippa," said John. "Explain yourself."

"The lights were off in the control room. She couldn't see anything."

"But how could Sue have operated the dimmers if the room was in darkness?"

"She couldn't, and in fact, she didn't." Philippa stepped aside to make way for the steady stream of parishioners who were filing past and paying their respects to Reverend Dunne. John followed her, his expression perplexed.

"But the lightning flashes were magnificent. And she did the final blackout too, if somewhat abruptly," he insisted.

"Sue didn't do them," said Philippa. "Len did. Sue was already dead. She wasn't killed after the play ended. She was killed near the beginning of the play, while Len and Howard were in the basement counting the collection money. Len left Howard counting the envelopes and slipped across the hall, ostensibly to review the cues with Sue. That's when he killed her. Then he put out the lights and returned to the Rector's office."

John still looked confused.

"But according to Howard, they talked with her a couple of minutes later, after they'd finished the collection."

"That was another of Len's tricks." Philippa noticed that Reverend Dunne's head was inclined in their direction, though he continued to shake hands and mutter appropriate responses to the members of his flock.

"Trick?" said John.

"Yes. When they emerged from the office, Len allowed Howard to go ahead of him down the hall. Then he opened the door of the control room, stuck his head in and said a few encouraging words. Howard could hear and see him, but was too far along the hall to realize that the room was in darkness. The illusion was that Len and Sue had engaged in a brief conversation. Then Howard and Len returned to the service together and Len stayed in view until the body was found."

"How monstrously devious," said John. "Are the horrendous rumours true, that he was involved in a drug ring, actually operating it here at St. Margaret's and bringing his minions into the congregation knowing they'd blend in among the assorted waifs and strays we attract in this parish?"

"Yes. Sue was one of his pushers. He brought her here, but he didn't bargain for the fact that Stuart Hindley would not only attach himself to her, but also do a first class job of rehabilitating her. When the poor girl died, she was no longer an addict and she was ready to blow the whistle on Len. Knowing she would be alone in the control room during the play, he grabbed his opportunity."

Having dispensed his last benediction, Reverend Dunne joined them. He had clearly been following every word of their conversation.

"Why didn't Sue take Stuart into her confidence?" he asked. "He was so anxious to help her."

"I suppose she wouldn't tell him anything for fear of involving him. I think she must have been a more decent sort than we all gave her credit for."

"Foolish child," said the Reverend.

"She was indeed," said Mabel Hindley, appearing in the doorway and butting into the conversation. "Still, every cloud has its silver lining. Amid all this grief, Laura and Stuart seem to have come back together."

"It would have happened in time anyway," said the Reverend. "It's unfortunate that their coming together evolved through tragedy."

Mabel turned toward Philippa.

"Speaking of romance," she smirked, "am I right in thinking that the young man you brought to the service last week is now seeing the brunette that was here with your brother? I hear they went to lunch together and have been constant companions ever since."

"Yes," growled Philippa.

"What a charming couple they'll make," cooed Mabel.

Philippa felt a pang as she visualized Mark Brennan's perfect face, but then, superimposed on his chiselled features floated a vision of Christabel's almond-shaped blue eyes, and she suddenly realized that she did not regret her actions one bit.

"Actually," said Philippa with spirit, "I ended up having lunch with a creature of far greater beauty than Mark Brennan."

Mabel flinched.

"Well, really," she said. "Some people are rather inconstant, aren't they?"

She looked meaningfully at the Reverend and sailed off, battle flag flying, in the direction of the parking lot.

John Hewitt raised his Machiavellian eyebrows.

The Reverend chortled.

"I think Philippa is referring to the fact that she took Christabel and her siblings to the White Spot after the service," he explained.

"Very sensible," said John.

"They deserved it," said Philippa. "The three of them had worked out the solution long before the rest of us," she said. "They're very bright children."

"Christabel's only three," John demurred. "Surely she didn't understand the significance of what she'd seen?"

"She didn't, but her older brother and sister did. Christopher is an electrical whiz and he realized how Len had created the illusion that Sue was at the controls until the end of the play. But they were troubled about the implications of what they knew because Len Tivett is a family friend. They were going to tell Marvin and Ida after they'd got home. Then, when they saw their suspect making off with their little sister, it became a case of open warfare."

"It did indeed," said Reverend Dunne. "*Fight the good fight*. Of course, one abhors violence on principle, but in the circumstances, Christopher's actions were entirely justified."

"Why did it take Len so long to realize Christabel might have some damaging evidence?" asked John.

"It was only when Ida Loewen started talking about Christabel's antics during the play that he realized she'd been peering through the spy-hole. He'd maladjusted the sound controls before the play started to give himself an excuse to be in the alcove for the remainder of the performance, so even after he came upstairs, he was tucked beside the font and he couldn't see Christabel. There you have it," she concluded.

"Wait a minute," said John, "You still haven't explained how Len managed to do the lightning flashes and the final blackout. How could he be in two places at once?"

"He wasn't in two places at once," said Philippa. "After Richard and I retrieved Christabel from Len's clutches, Christopher took us to the alcove at the back of the church. He'd become suspicious after the service because the nursery lights were off and the switch wasn't working, yet shortly afterwards the lights came on again. Christopher realized they would be on a circuit that controlled more than one area of the church."

"I begin to see the light," said Reverend Dunne. "Or rather, the lack of it. How devilishly clever."

"Exactly," said Philippa.

She paused, her performer's soul relishing the transfixed gaze of her attentive audience.

"You see," she concluded, "the alcove contains several items besides the sound controls, and one of them happens to be the church fuse box."

FATAL INTERVAL

▼

Richard Beary's head swivelled as the woman walked by. She could have been anywhere between thirty and fifty, an ageless beauty with translucent skin, platinum hair, and an ivory gown. Her face was illuminated by startling blue eyes and a radiant smile.

"*Age cannot wither her, nor custom stale her infinite variety,*" declaimed Bertram Beary, whose eyes had followed his son's glance. Richard was not the only man present who appeared captivated by the blonde siren. Heads were turning with such symmetry that the males in the theatre lobby began to resemble the chorus of waiters from *Hello Dolly.* Ticket-takers smiled and nodded as she passed. A tuxedoed, middle-aged Adonis at the fundraising table, who was encouraging two bejewelled matrons to participate in a raffle for the silver Mercedes that stood gleaming and resplendent at the foyer entrance, froze in mid-spiel, and abandoning his customers, moved forward to offer the blonde temptress one of his brochures. Even the bartender's eyes seemed riveted on the woman who had created such a stir.

Edwina Beary paused in her monologue on modern education. She stared at her husband.

"What did you say, Bertram?"

"You, my own," said Beary. "A veritable Cleopatra. *Other women cloy the appetites they feed, but she makes hungry where most she satisfies.*"

"Don't be ridiculous," snapped Edwina. "And don't have another Glenlivet before the opera starts. There are three intermissions, and I'd like you to be able to walk to the car at the end of the evening. Besides, the theatre bar charges ridiculous prices for drinks."

"Fortification," said Beary. "*Trovatore* is a five-Scotch work."

"Well you already had three of them with dinner," Edwina retorted. Richard had treated his parents to a sumptuous pre-opera dinner at the William Tell Restaurant.

"Ah, but those drinks have already been absorbed by Portobello mushrooms and a rack of lamb—which I must say was delicious—but as Richard's ticket is a comp and we're here courtesy of the City, we can afford some additional refreshment."

Richard came to his father's defence.

"Think of it this way," he said. "Dad's got you the most expensive seats in the house. The council gets two comps in exchange for a $1,500 grant. That's $750 per ticket, and you get them gratis."

Edwina sniffed.

"To the taxpayer," said Beary, raising his glass and emptying it. "My, my," he added. "The things you see when you haven't got your Uzi."

A young giant loomed beside them. He had a wild mane of light brown hair, and his massive bulk was encased in an ice-blue tuxedo, ruffled shirt and silver bow tie. He lumbered by and disappeared in the direction of the bar.

Edwina ignored Beary and waved to a distinguished grey-haired gentleman standing by the coat check.

"Who's that?" asked Richard.

"Robert Craig. Charming man. A widower. Not for long though. He's engaged to Katherine Marshall, that delightful lady who runs the Opera Workshop. His son is a fine bass baritone."

"Ah, Adam Craig. The one Philippa hangs about with."

"You must be feeling very proud this evening," said Edwina as Robert joined them. "Isn't tonight Adam's professional debut?"

"Yes, if one doesn't count chorus work. Of course, the messenger only has a couple of lines, but it's a start. At least he's getting paid for singing, instead of waiting on tables or serving cocktails."

"Well, thank goodness for the service industry," said Beary heartily. "Where would the theatre be without it? Performers have to pay the rent, even when they're 'resting'. Too bad we don't have Adam on the bar tonight. The chappie they've got is totally incompetent. I had to repeat my order three times before he managed to retain the information, and then he still got it wrong. However," he added, eyeing the bar, "things are looking up. There appears to be a sudden dearth of patrons." A second bartender was now in place behind the counter and the line was appreciably shorter.

"I don't think you have time, Dad," said Richard, reading his father's mind. He turned back to Robert. "Philippa says Adam sings his two lines very nicely," he added. "Though of course, she's prejudiced."

Robert chuckled.

"Young Philippa's very fond of my son, isn't she? I expect one of these days Adam will wise up and notice her. He did tell me she makes a spectacular gypsy in the second act. How is Philippa these days, anyway?"

"Doing quite nicely," Edwina said proudly. "She's on a regular contract with the opera, and she's doing some work with CBC, plus quite a few roles have come her way—and of course, she has her church job. She's feeling sufficiently secure that she's taken the plunge and rented a condo at New Westminster Quay—with a girlfriend from the chorus naturally. She couldn't afford it on her own, but I think she'll do all right."

"The plunge indeed. She'll have to work hard if she's going to support herself from singing, but it's doable if she's really committed. Does she have any back-up for when work is scarce?"

"She's finished her degree, so she could teach if the musical career doesn't work out. And she's very good with computers. She's taken several courses, so she could do marketing or administrative work in between singing jobs."

"Good for her. She's a clever girl, your youngest. Are the other family members here to cheer her on?"

"No," said Edwina. "Sylvia is working on a case, and Juliet is in town, but she couldn't get a babysitter. They're coming closing night. Where's Katherine this evening?"

"In Banff, unfortunately. Conducting a master class. She'll be back next week, so she'll be here closing night too."

"We were so happy to hear of your engagement," said Edwina. "You must bring her to dinner one evening. Excuse me," she added, seeing Beary slithering toward the bar.

Richard and Robert watched in amusement, waiting for the inevitable confrontation. However, the warning chimes began as Beary reached the front of the line, so Edwina returned triumphant, with her husband at her side.

"What a waste of time that was," Beary grumbled.

"Don't gripe, Dad," said Richard. "I told you there wouldn't be time for another."

"There would have been plenty of time if the bartender's assistant hadn't ducked out to work the coffee bar. It was Cleo…" He paused seeing Edwina's suspicious stare. "That blond vamp you were admiring earlier. The minute she got in the line for a latte, the backup bartender couldn't shift roles fast enough. But even then I'd have made it if I hadn't been stuck behind the blue brocade Godzilla."

"He had an order to match his size, did he?"

"No. He knew the bartender. By the time they'd finished exchanging maudlin remarks about their love lives, the chimes were ringing. It's bad enough that we're going to have to listen to an anal-retentive baritone harping on the same subject all through the opera. We don't need a preview in the lobby."

"Come along, Bertram!"

Edwina took Beary's arm and propelled him into the crush that was heading through the doors of the auditorium.

Their party had aisle seats, so Richard moved ahead and took the seat furthest into the row. The seat beside him was empty, but the adjacent ones were occupied by a pair of sullen, jean-clad women who were studying a dog-eared libretto. The plainer of the two, by virtue of granny glasses and a dirtier sweater, stared contemptuously at Richard's tuxedo. A modern-day harpy, Richard decided, and proceeded to read his program.

As the lights dimmed, there was a shimmering movement in the aisle, and a lady was ushered into the row. As she squeezed by, Richard was aware of a light but tantalizing fragrance, and with a start, he realized he was sitting next to the vision of elegance that had caught his eye in the lobby.

As the vision sat down, Richard heard the harpy mutter a comment about people who came to the opera to show off their wardrobes, but if his elegant neighbour heard, she gave no indication. As the conductor entered the pit and the audience broke into applause, the lady's program slipped off her lap. Richard scooped it up, returning it with a smile. He was rewarded with a warm smile and a 'thank you' that revealed a gloriously mellow voice. Suddenly pleased with the world, Richard settled back to enjoy the first act.

*   *   *   *

When the curtain fell, Richard turned toward his attractive neighbour.

"It's a good production, isn't it?" he said.

She smiled and nodded. The applause continued, and while they clapped, she and Richard managed snippets of conversation.

"Are you coming out, dear?" asked Edwina. Beary was already standing in the aisle.

"The boy's busy," said Beary. "Come on, Cleopatra. To the bar. The hiccups in the soprano's cabaletta made me thirsty."

"Don't rush me," snapped Edwina. "There's lots of time."

"No, there isn't. I told you, the bartender is on another planet. I think he's been sampling the merchandise. If we get stuck at the end of a long line, we'll be out of luck."

The singers appeared for another bow, but Beary clasped his wife's arm, winked at Richard, and frog-marched Edwina up the aisle.

"Don't let me keep you from your party," the vision said graciously.

"I'm quite happy to sit," said Richard, genuinely. "There are two more intermissions. Perhaps I could buy you a drink in the next one."

"That would be lovely," said his companion. She paused, then added, "Didn't I see you at the William Tell earlier?"

Richard looked surprised.

"Yes, I took my parents there for dinner," he said, "but I'm amazed that I didn't notice you. Where were you sitting?"

"You wouldn't have seen me. I was with some of the directors from the opera board. We reserve the Crossbow Room on opening nights. It makes a nice evening out, not to mention being able to use the hotel valet parking instead of battling one's way into the theatre lot. It's such a short walk to the theatre, and we generally go back to have dessert afterwards." Her eyes sparkled. "Their meringues are out of this world," she added.

She smiled again, and Richard was dazzled by the warmth and charm the woman exuded. She must have been a few years his senior, and she was not beautiful in a conventional sense, but she was without doubt one of the most alluring creatures Richard had ever met. She introduced herself as Lorna Mainwaring. She was knowledgeable about music, having sung professionally before she married, and was now on the board of the opera. Richard had never enjoyed a discussion about music so much in his life.

When his parents returned, Edwina looking cross, and Beary smiling seraphically and smelling of Glenlivet, Richard and Lorna were still engrossed in conversation. The lights dimming for the second act seemed an unpardonable intrusion. If Richard had not had the interest of picking out his sister in the gypsy chorus and seeing her friend, Adam, play the messenger, he would have passed the second act in a blur, only conscious of the competing scents of Chanel No. 5 and expensive Scotch.

When the lights came up, Richard turned to his elegant neighbour but to his surprise, she was facing the harpy who was addressing her with quiet vehemence. Richard could not hear what was said, but Lorna appeared startled. After a moment, her expression became impassive and she turned purposefully toward Richard.

"I would love to have that drink," she said. She stood and faced the aisle. It was a queen's command. Like a sheepish Mark Anthony, Richard followed her out of the auditorium.

Once in the lobby, Richard introduced Lorna to his parents. Beary was already clutching a glass.

"You'd better hurry up," he advised. "The bartender is in even worse shape than before. I take back what I said about him sampling the goods. More likely a dose of the flu. I saw his assistant slip him a couple of aspirin. Good job alcohol acts as a disinfectant."

Lorna smiled, and Richard went to buy the drinks, having carefully memorized Lorna's intricate directions for her gin and tonic. In spite of his father's warning, he had no difficulty obtaining the drinks. With both bartenders in position, the line moved quickly. As Richard neared the front of the line, he did a rapid count of the patrons in front of him and calculated that he would be served by the assistant bartender, who appeared to be several years older and infinitely more competent than his colleague. However, as he reached the counter, the assistant turned to pour more glasses of wine, and Richard found himself waiting until the original bartender finished serving the customer beside him. Still, when his turn came, his order was filled with speed and efficiency and his server was focused and attentive. Whatever the assistant had given the younger man had obviously been effective.

As he returned across the lobby, he noticed the two women who had the seats next to Lorna's. They were standing by the Guild membership table on the far side of the foyer, but they were staring at Lorna with disdain. He rejoined Lorna and handed her the gin and tonic. Curiosity got the better of him.

"Tell me," he said, "what did the harpy say to you back there?"

"Who?" said Edwina.

"We are sitting next to two rather horrid creatures," explained Richard. "They glowered at Lorna as if she were the Whore of Babylon and one of them was hissing something in her ear at the Act II curtain."

"Hissing describes it perfectly," said Lorna. "She was rather reptilian."

"But what did she say?" asked Edwina.

Lorna hesitated. Then she smiled.

"It was all quite silly," she said. "I have this awful tickle left over from my cold, and I came armed with cough sweets and my decongestant capsules in case the air conditioning irritated my throat. Half-way through the *Anvil Chorus* my eyes started to water, so I got out a cough sweet and popped it in my mouth."

"Did you?" asked Richard. "I didn't hear so much as a paper rustle."

"I'm not surprised," said Beary, nursing his Glenlivet. "Cymbals crashing and gypsies screaming their lungs out. A denuded Hacks couldn't compete."

"Well," continued Lorna, "I must have disturbed the draggletailed creature next to me because she took great pains to inform me that my rustling candy wrapper had destroyed her concentration and ruined the act for her. I was struck dumb. Then, to top it off, she informed me that it was obvious I'd never been to an opera before because I clearly didn't know how to behave." Lorna smiled mischievously. "I didn't have the heart to tell her about the great artists I worked with in my early days. How could one puncture such zealous self-importance? She would have been crushed."

"Would you like to trade seats with me for the next act?" asked Beary. "They can have the pleasure of hearing me snore in time to the *A l'armi* chorus."

"You'll do no such thing, Bertram," Edwina commanded. She changed the subject. "I thought your son sang his bit very well," she said to Robert.

"I can't say the same for the men's chorus," said Beary. "Did you notice how the tenors sang into their armpits? I bet they're reading the lyrics off the back of their shields. Still, you can't expect a tenor to coordinate his voice with his brain. After all, one is in his throat, and the other is in his bottom."

Over the rim of his glass, Beary noticed the harpies by the Guild membership table. They stared contemptuously, then turned their backs and became engaged in earnest conversation with the tuxedoed volunteer, who glanced nervously in the direction of the Beary party.

"Methinks I have offended the pseudo-intelligentsia," said Beary. He leered malevolently and raised his glass towards the Guild table.

"Nonsense," said Edwina. "Your stentorian tones, even amplified with alcohol, aren't loud enough to reach the far side of the lobby—not in this crush. They couldn't possibly have heard you."

"Actually, I think they were glowering at me, not you," said Lorna.

"What an insufferable pair," said Richard. "Are you sure you don't mind sitting by them in the next act?"

"No, really. Anyway, Timothy will put them straight."

"Timothy?"

"The gentleman selling raffle tickets. He knows me well. You watch, they'll be models of courtesy during the next act." Lorna's eyes glanced over Richard's shoulder. "Would you excuse me a moment," she said.

Lorna slipped away in the direction of the stairs leading to the restrooms. As she reached the stairwell, a tall, bronzed man wearing a dinner jacket loomed into her path. He stepped aside courteously, but the smile he gave her suggested familiarity. Lorna paused to speak to him briefly, then swept by and disappeared down the stairs. Richard's eyes followed Lorna's progress, and he continued to watch as the man followed her down the stairs. When he looked back, he saw that Robert Craig was watching him. His expression was enigmatic.

"She's a charmer, isn't she?" he said. "You'd better watch out, Richard."

"Watch out for what? Lorna appears to be a cultured and interesting woman."

"She is," said Robert. "She's a wonderful benefactor to the opera, but she does have a weakness for handsome young men."

Richard raised his eyebrows and stared quizzically at the older man.

"I'm complimented," he said finally. "I suppose you're trying to tell me that she's very much married."

"Very much married indeed. She and her fourth husband have recently separated, and I imagine she's out scouting for a fifth. That was husband number three."

"Who?"

"The tanned gentleman by the stairs. He was Lorna's third. The racing driver…the one before the actor."

"Why so many?" asked Richard, genuinely interested.

"She comes from a very wealthy family, so she's rich in her own right," said Robert. "Her first husband was a widower with two children. He was also a multi-millionaire. He died and left Lorna fabulously rich. She manages her money astutely, along with the trust funds her husband left for his daughters. From what I've heard, they've grown up into a couple of loutish rebels who delight in annoying her in every way they can, so she gets her fun in life by indulging herself in every romantic whim that strikes her. Actors, racecar drivers, musicians, ski instructors. Some she marries, and some she doesn't. But either way, when her men cease to be amusing, out they go. She'd make mincemeat of a mere detective inspector like yourself."

Richard grinned.

"Forewarned is forearmed," he said.

Robert moved away to talk with an elderly couple, who in spite of their frail appearance, were resplendent in formal attire, the white-haired gentleman in a tuxedo that appeared to date from the early twentieth century and his wife, tiny, vivacious and charming in a confection of violet chiffon. Richard smiled, and drifted over to the plate glass window that overlooked the courtyard. A panhandler sat on the wall by the fountain, his worn overcoat a grim contrast to the opulent dress of the theatre patrons inside. An enterprising fellow, thought Richard. He would have a long wait until the final curtain, but the domain of the beggar was as competitive as the business world, and he would be first in line when the theatre doors opened to release the audience.

As the chimes began for the third act, Richard turned his back on the window and scrutinized the inhabitants of the lobby; some were obediently depositing glasses and hurrying towards the auditorium doors, while others nonchalantly lingered over drinks and finished conversations.

After a moment, Lorna reappeared, and Richard watched with pleasure, once more taken with her graceful carriage and the elegant flow of her gown. She emerged from the stairwell and glided across until she was alongside the bar. Suddenly, the huge young man in blue brocade stepped backward into her path. The collision was unavoidable, and the man's drink bounced from his glass and spattered freely. Lorna sprang backward and in the scurry that followed, Richard lost sight of her. Both bartenders leapt round the counter, towels in hand, and the tuxedoed Timothy hurried forward and oozed solicitude. Suddenly Lorna's third husband appeared amid the throng, and Richard could see him talking to the brocaded giant who gesticulated wildly, while a circle of theatregoers stood fascinated by the scene. Suddenly, Richard heard Lorna's voice ring out over the general hum.

"I don't find this amusing."

Her tone was icy. Richard suddenly realized there was another side to his beautiful lady, and he had a vision of what it would be like to be designated to the *out* pile. But when Lorna reappeared, she gave Richard the most seductive smile he had ever seen, and as they returned to their seats, she leaned toward him and made small talk with an air that suggested a promising hidden message. Mentally, Richard completed his father's quotation. *For vilest things become themselves in her, that the holy priests bless her when she is riggish.* After all, he thought, I might as well enjoy being on the *in* pile.

During the third interval, the group reconvened in the lobby. Robert Craig took orders for refreshments and Richard accompanied him to the bar. Edwina appeared to have given up trying to control Beary, who was rumbling snatches of opera and ogling every pretty girl that passed by.

Richard and Robert found themselves in line behind the blue-brocaded giant. Richard estimated that the man must have been close to seven feet tall. In spite of his titanic stature, he had the face of an exuberant puppy. He fidgeted in the line, and Richard kept his distance for fear of being trampled. He noticed that Robert had stiffened, and at first he attributed his companion's rigidity to the antics of the ungainly young man, but then he became aware of discontented muttering and turned to see the harpies directly behind them.

The line was moving quickly again as the assistant bartender had abandoned cappuccinos and was pouring glasses of red and white wine, leaving his colleague free to dispense drinks from a well-stocked supply of hard liquor. Once the blue giant had been served, he set his glass on the counter while he put his change in his wallet. Giving him a wide berth, Richard and Robert ordered their own round of drinks. The harpies moved forward to the older bartender and asked for two glasses of wine. Efficiently, he passed them their drinks and turned to help complete Richard's order. While he waited, Richard became aware that he could see a vast expanse of the lobby. The night sky had turned the plate glass windows into a huge mirror, and sparkling lights and swirling bodies danced a continuously evolving picture before his eyes. He and Robert were reflected in the foreground, and beside them was the blue giant, still fiddling with his change. Richard noticed two other familiar faces by the bar. Tuxedo Timothy had abandoned his Mercedes and was engrossed in conversation with 'husband number three', the tanned racing driver. Richard could see some kind of exchange going on, though the men's hands were hidden below the counter. Tuxedo Timothy might have left his post, but he had not stopped peddling his wares.

A nudge from Robert brought Richard's attention back to the bar and he saw that the bartenders had lined the drinks along the counter. As Richard gathered the glasses, the brocaded giant turned and caught his arm. Richard's hand hit one glass, and it tipped slightly and righted itself again, but in his determination to hold onto his own drink, the huge young man let his wallet slip to the ground.

Cards spewed everywhere. Richard abandoned the drinks and, with the other members of the queue, helped the young man retrieve his paraphernalia from the carpet. The giant stuffed the cards back in his wallet, apologized profusely, clutched his drink and lumbered away. Richard and Robert waited until he had cleared the counter before they attempted to reclaim their drinks.

"Pity the director who tries to steer him through a scene," said Richard, as they walked away from the bar.

"I don't follow you," said Robert.

"He had a Canadian Actors' Equity card in his wallet. I picked it off the carpet. He must have a pretty limited repertoire."

"Oh, I don't know," said Robert. "David and Goliath. Frankenstein. The Jolly Green Giant."

"Wrong colour," said Richard. He chuckled at his own wit, but then, in an instant, his light-hearted mood evaporated. Lorna had moved away from the Bearys and was talking with her third husband. They were laughing, heads close together. With a feeling that Richard was honest enough to acknowledge as an excruciating pang of jealousy, he saw Lorna lean forward and drink from her former husband's glass. The intimacy of the exchange made Richard go hot, and then cold. He steeled himself into indifference as he watched the racing driver tap Lorna gently on the nose, then move away to greet a noisy group of people near the staircase, before loping with athletic stride up to the mezzanine.

But then, as he approached, Lorna turned and looked at him, and the world regained its roseate hue. The soft smile she gave him caused him to lurch inwardly and he found himself clutching the drinks tightly as if the internal tremors she was causing were manifesting in his hands.

They returned to the others and handed round the drinks. Beary took a deep swallow and sighed contentedly. Edwina, turning her back on him, addressed herself to Robert and reopened her diatribe on the education system. Lorna took her drink, her eyes on Richard, and touched her glass against his own.

"To a wonderful evening and a charming companion," she said.

The blue eyes continued to hold Richard's own as she raised her glass to her lips. Richard felt weak at the knees. The next five minutes passed with little conversation, though Richard had a sense of communication that would have shaken Edwina rigid if it had been verbalized.

When the chimes indicated the imminent start of the fourth act, Richard placed a hand firmly on the small of Lorna's back and guided her toward the auditorium doors. While they stood in the crush and inched toward the doorway, Lorna's blue eyes looked steadily into his own. They were beautiful eyes, wide, and bright and sparkling—the sort of eyes that would inspire poets to rhapsodize about sunlight twinkling on azure pools. Richard felt himself sinking, and did nothing to resist the glorious sensation.

Then suddenly, abruptly, the beautiful eyes glazed. The pressure on Richard's hand intensified for one brief second; then completely disappeared. Lorna fell against him and slid into his arms.

By the time the crowd had made a pathway and Richard had carried Lorna to a couch in the foyer, she was unconscious.

She died before the ambulance arrived.

*   *   *   *

A week later, Richard joined his family for Sunday dinner. After the meal, he related the end of the story.

"She died of a massive overdose of an antidepressant drug," he said sadly.

"In the drink that you bought her, I presume," said Beary. "Tragic. What a waste of a beautiful woman."

"It sounds as if she was no better than she should be," snapped Edwina. "I had no idea what sort of creature was ensnaring my son."

Philippa smiled sympathetically at her brother.

"What a good job you are who you are," she said. "If you'd been another of Mrs. Mainwaring's pretty boys instead of a detective inspector, you'd have been the first to come under suspicion."

"There was no danger of that," said Richard. "When the people in the bar line were questioned, it became obvious that something could have been slipped into Lorna's drink while the queue was preoccupied retrieving the contents of that blue giant's wallet."

"But how could anyone know that the drink was intended for Lorna Mainwaring?" asked Edwina.

"She was fussy about the way her drink was made. Anyone who knew Lorna and had seen us together would have known the drink was for her when he heard me ordering it. Though of course that became irrelevant once witnesses came forward to say that Lorna had recognized a member of the crowd during the altercation when she collided with the giant in blue brocade."

"Don't keep us in suspense," said Edwina. "Who killed her?"

"Ah," rumbled Beary. "Anyone with minimal powers of observation could have figured that out."

"I fail to see how your powers of observation could have been working considering the drunken fog you were in that night," Edwina said tartly. "And don't let that dog put its drooling mouth on the furniture."

Beary looked hurt, but he moved MacPuff's head from the arm of the chair onto his knee.

"It would be logical to suspect those who inherited her fortune," Edwina suggested.

"Her stepchildren!" said Philippa. "Let me guess. Those nasty young women were really Lorna's stepdaughters."

"Imaginative, but wrong," said her father. "They were unforgivably pompous musical snobs, but not murderesses."

Richard smiled.

"Well done, Dad," he said. "No, it wasn't her stepchildren. It was her husband. The one who had received his marching orders a few months earlier—and I don't think he even cared that much about the money. He was still insanely in love with Lorna, and he didn't want anyone else to have her. He was a young actor—not too successful, and rather unstable. The antidepressants were his own pills. He contrived to be at the opera, knowing Lorna would be there. I suppose he was still trying to get her back. He managed to speak with her briefly, and was given the deep freeze. That, along with the fact that she was getting along so well with me, was the last straw. He decided that if he couldn't have her, no one else could."

Edwina sniffed.

"How very lurid."

"It's operatic," boomed her husband. "We were wrong. She wasn't Cleopatra. She was Carmen."

Edwina slew him with a piercing glance.

"I knew you weren't talking about me," she hissed.

"It was a comparison, my own," Beary lied. "And naturally, you came off the better."

Edwina looked suspicious, but mollified.

Philippa chimed in.

"The husband must have been the blue giant. You said he was an actor. All that clumsy-ox behaviour was simply a cover."

"Not at all," said Beary. "Godzilla wasn't the murderer. Lorna's husband was the bartender."

Edwina, Philippa and Richard stared open-mouthed at Beary.

"Now how could you possibly know that, Dad?" Richard finally asked.

"I'm right, aren't I?" Beary said smugly.

"Yes, you're right. Now tell us how you guessed."

Beary patted MacPuff.

"During my first trip to the bar," he said, "I noticed the bartender appeared to be jittery. He couldn't concentrate. Don't you remember me complaining about him? And during my second frustrating and abortive attempt to get a drink, I noticed that Cle...I mean, Lorna, was standing nearby. I also saw that the nervous bartender kept staring at her. And I heard him complaining about his love life to the blue Godzilla who was obviously an acquaintance of his. We've since found out they were both actors. That's how they knew each other. I told you about their conversation."

"I recall you saying something rude about the baritone," conceded Edwina. "You said they had the same complaint."

"Not the same *complaint*," said Beary. "The same *plaint! Gelosia!* During my third trip to the bar, after my sprint at the Act I curtain when I made it to the counter ahead of everyone else, the bartender was sweating and pale. I thought he was sick…well, he was sick really. He was eaten up with jealousy. Yet according to Richard, *he* got served efficiently and the bartender was completely focused on his finicky instructions about Lorna's G and T."

"Because he'd made the drink many times before."

"Yes, and because Richard was the new man that was catching Lorna's attention. Of course the bartender was highly concentrated. I bet you had his total attention."

"Yes, I did," admitted Richard.

Beary continued.

"And during my fourth trip to the bar…"

"You didn't make a fourth trip to the bar," snapped Edwina. "Richard got the drinks during the second and third intervals."

"That third and fatal interval," mused Beary. "But you're wrong, my dear. I did make another trip to the bar. You were all busy fussing about Lorna. I knew nothing could be done for her, so I slipped back for a quick one before the ambulance and police arrived."

"Really, Bertram. You are impossible," Edwina began.

Beary halted her with a stern look.

"As I got my drink," he continued, "I told the bartenders that Mrs. Mainwaring was dying." Beary reflectively stroked MacPuff's ears. "The young one turned away," he said.

Beary paused and glared at Edwina. "But even in my drunken fog," he said reproachfully, "I could tell that he was crying."

OH, WHAT A BEAUTIFUL
MOURNING

▼

The woman in black drifted slowly through the rose garden. She passed the beds of pink floribundas, and turned onto the flagstone path that bisected a vast expanse of lawn where indolent Canada geese and lively squirrels cohabited peacefully. She followed the path as it snaked between pale Peace roses and vibrant Crimson Glories; then walked down the steps to the latticed arbour at the center of the flowerbeds. The arbour was a picturesque structure, with an open peaked roof supported by timber uprights in granite bases, and when the woman reached the entrance, she paused to examine a luminous white bloom; then disappeared behind the mass of climbing roses that lined the bower.

"There she goes again," said Philippa.

Adam stuffed another ham sandwich into his mouth.

"Who?" he mumbled.

"The Unmerry Widow. Don't tell me you haven't noticed her? Look, she's coming out the other end."

Adam looked up as the woman reappeared at the far end of the trellis. She moved like a sleepwalker, following the curve of the path, yet seemingly detached from her surroundings. Then she paused in the shade of a cluster of luxuriant hydrangea bushes, finally coming to rest on a weathered teak bench at the edge of the lawn.

"Oh, the woman in black. Now you mention it, I suppose I have seen her on and off during the run."

"She never misses. Six o'clock on the dot. Every evening without fail."

"She's putting on quite a show, isn't she?" Adam stared thoughtfully at the woman. "Very elegant mourning, and all that. I mean nobody dresses like that these days, except to go to a funeral, and not even then, more often than not."

"I wonder who she's grieving for," said Philippa.

"The rose garden has been here since 1920," said Adam. "Maybe she had a beloved father who was a founder of the Kiwanis Club."

"No. Lover or husband, I should say. Perhaps they used to sit together amid the flowerbeds. It's obvious that the garden means something to her."

The woman remained seated on the bench. From where Philippa and Adam lay on the grass, she appeared motionless. Suddenly a loud voice interrupted their reverie.

"Excuse me, aren't you Philippa Beary and Adam Craig?"

Startled, Philippa swung round to see a stout woman dressed in navy hiking shorts and a white shirt. A sandy-haired man stood some yards behind her. He hung back, looking embarrassed.

Philippa and Adam nodded cautiously.

"I thought I recognized you," said the lady. "We came to see *Oklahoma* last night. I just wanted to tell you how much we enjoyed the show. You were both delightful."

Adam looked mildly offended.

"I'm playing Jud Fry," he said. "I wasn't trying to be delightful."

The woman laughed.

"In your case, delightfully villainous," she amended. "You have a magnificent voice."

Adam preened. The woman's husband, looking more relaxed, stepped forward and spoke to Philippa. "You make a lovely Laurie," he said. "Utterly charming. You and the fellow playing Curly…"

"Andrew Bishop," prompted Adam.

"Yes, that's the one. The two of you were perfect. Every bit as convincing as Shirley Jones and Gordon MacRae."

"Thank you," Philippa said graciously. "It's enjoyable for us too. I love doing Theatre Under The Stars. There's something magical about musicals at Malkin Bowl."

The woman nodded.

"Singing love duets in real starlight must be so romantic," she said.

"Oh, yes. Very romantic," Philippa agreed. "Stanley Park is full of romance," she added, glancing toward the arbour. "We were just watching the woman in black. She comes to sit in the rose garden every evening. She's a terribly mysterious figure."

"Don't you know who that is?" asked the woman, surprised.

"No, should we?" asked Philippa.

"That's Althea Cray. George Cray's widow. We often see her when we walk around the sea wall."

"George Cray. The multi-millionaire!" exclaimed Adam. "What on earth is his wife doing in a public rose garden? You'd think they'd have all the roses they want on their private estates."

"The floribunda bed was donated to the city by George Cray," their fan informed them. "Rumour has it he proposed to his wife there."

"I told you the rose garden had a romantic connotation for her," Philippa said to Adam. "George Cray only died…what?…four months ago? Coming here must be her way of feeling close to him."

"She owns a penthouse in the West End," offered the woman, "in addition to an island off the Sunshine Coast and goodness knows how much real estate all over the world. I read a feature on the Crays in *Equity*. Mrs. Cray must be staying at the penthouse right now."

"Imagine having a heart attack at the age of forty-eight," Adam said gloomily. "Scary. Cray hardly had time to enjoy the money he made."

"You don't have to worry, Adam," said Philippa. "The stress of maintaining his millions probably finished George Cray off. You'll never work hard enough to be rich or to have a heart attack."

Adam looked hurt. Their fans took this as their cue to leave.

"We'd better be on our way. I expect you're in a hurry to get to the theatre."

"Not really," said Philippa. "It's our night off. *Pajama Game* is on tonight. We're here as audience."

The couple wished them good weather for the remainder of the run and strode off in the direction of Lost Lagoon. Adam's dark eyes twinkled as he watched them go.

"Romantic, eh?" he taunted Philippa. "What was the comment you made the other night? Something about singing love duets with a flaming fairy in the freezing night air, with mosquitoes biting elephant-sized chunks out of you, sea lions barking accompaniment from the zoo, and the nine o'clock gun going off in the middle of your high note? I believe you said it was the closest thing to living hell you could imagine?"

"They were nice people, Adam. I didn't want to disillusion them. And I never, ever called Andrew a flaming fairy. I like Andrew. It just irks me that he sings our duets to the conductor instead of to me."

"Well, they've lived together for ten years. What do you expect?"

"I expect him to act more," snapped Philippa.

"Why don't we rewrite the show for closing night," suggested Adam. "We'll burn Curly on the bonfire and race off to Jud Fry's shed and live happily ever after."

Philippa's eyes narrowed.

"When you want be romantic with me," she said sharply, "you can do it in your own character, or not at all."

Adam chortled.

"Come on," he said, unfolding his huge frame and leaping to his feet. "If we hustle, we'll just have time before the show starts."

"Time for what?"

"To go for a ride on the miniature train and visit the petting zoo."

"The petting zoo is for children," protested Philippa. "So is the train, come to that."

"Don't be a spoil-sport," said Adam. "Everyone likes baby goats, bunnies and trains."

He gathered up their garbage and lumbered down to the nearest bin to dispose of it. Philippa sighed. Adam was very attractive in his overgrown, bear-like way. She wished he would stop behaving like her big brother.

In the early evening light, the roses flamed and the lawns gleamed. The roof of the Mounted Police Stables glinted behind massed rhododendrons and a blue spruce that glowed violet in the setting sun. As Philippa waited for Adam to return, she noticed that the widow had left her bench and was now standing, staring at a huge gnarled stump in the center of the lawn. It was a nurse stump, covered with ivy and circled by benches, with five cedar trees sprouting from the top, and the black widow—*now why did I call her that*, thought Philippa—seemed fascinated by it. She seemed to pause there for an eternity; then suddenly she turned and started back along the path. She moved slowly, but her carriage was straight and her walk was youthful. She wore a slim-fitting black suit that revealed a full, but attractive figure, but her face was completely hidden by the heavy veil that hung from her pillbox hat.

Philippa remained seated on the grass, watching as the dramatic figure passed within a few feet of her. Suddenly, the widow lifted her head, and the angle of the sunlight against her veil momentarily rendered it transparent.

Philippa shivered. For fleeting seconds, she had been given a chilling glimpse of a beautiful face that appeared to be smiling.

*   *   *   *

The next day, Philippa decided to telephone her father. His position as city councillor made him a mine of useful information and he had contacts all over the Lower Mainland. If anyone knew the history of the Cray family, he would.

Philippa took her morning coffee and the telephone onto the balcony of her condominium. It was a glorious day, the clouds screening the sun, but not inhibiting the warmth, and the quay was a hive of activity. She stretched her legs and watched the boats on the river as she dialled and waited for her father to answer. Two enterprising tugs, like motorized sheep dogs, were herding the log booms, and she was fascinated by the acrobatic manoeuvres of the two boatmen with pike poles who were leaping from log to log as they connected the chains.

The phone at the other end kept ringing, and she was about to give up when her father answered. He had just returned from his walk with MacPuff and seemed perfectly happy to chat with his daughter while he made himself a cup of tea. Philippa came straight to the point.

"The Crays?" harrumphed Beary. "Why do you want to know about them? Not your type of people at all. He was a shark, and his wife is all jewels, furs and neuroses."

Philippa felt a surge of triumph.

"Then you do know them! I thought you might."

"I don't know them at all. I've run across them from time to time at the odd civic function. I could tell you a lot about George Cray's development projects, but other than that, I only have a general impression of the couple, and I already gave you that."

"Your impressions are pretty accurate, Dad," Philippa cajoled him. "Give it a try. Did they appear to be happy together?"

"I would think so. She was always with him at social functions. Good-looking woman. Cray seemed to consider her a vehicle for showing off his wealth."

"Was she a new wife? Younger than him?" The sun emerged, glaring, from behind its cloud, so Philippa swivelled round in the other direction and watched the SkyTrain arcing its way across the river.

"I'd put her in her late thirties," Beary estimated. "Don't think she was a second wife, but who knows. She seemed attached to him, but what can you tell from political functions? People can put on lovey-dovey facades in public and only communicate through the cook in their own home. I tell you what," suggested Beary, "if you're desperate for personal information, that old pirate, Horace Treadwell, was pretty close to the family. He operates at the same level of elevated sleaze as the Crays. I could call him and pick his brains."

"Would you? Thank you, Dad. You're a pet."

"I know I am," said Beary. "Talk to you later."

"I'll be leaving for the park at five," said Philippa. "Adam and I are having a picnic dinner before the show. If you don't hear anything by then, you can call me tomorrow. Not before noon, though. I'm sleeping in these days."

"I'll do better than that. I'll see you at the Bowl tonight."

"You're coming to see the show again?"

"Not exactly. I was called by some officious bully who told me you needed volunteers to run what she called *front of house*, so I agreed to tear up tickets for one night. Your nieces will be there too," he added. "Juliet is short a babysitter, so I said I'd bring them with me to give out programs."

"Aren't you a good sport!"

"Not at all," said Beary. "Your mother says participating in volunteer activity helps me stay elected."

*   *   *   *

Adam and Philippa took full advantage of the warm August weather. They walked around Beaver Lake, then strolled part way along the sea wall, before stopping at Lumberman's Arch to buy fish and chips.

"Let's sit here and look at the water," suggested Adam.

"No," Philippa replied. "I'd rather go back to our usual spot. I want to have another look at the Black Widow."

"You've changed her title since yesterday," noted Adam. "That smile really got to you, didn't it?"

They continued along the sea wall, dodging around the assortment of humanity that was travelling the route on foot, bicycle or roller blade; then cut inland by the salmon-spawning stream near the outdoor art display. They strolled past the rose beds and stopped at the small amphitheatre, north of the gardens that overlooked three large chessboards painted on concrete.

"Let's eat here," suggested Adam, pointing to the center chessboard. It lay under the cover of a triangular shake roof, which was supported by rustic logs, and the entire structure was ringed with rhododendrons and huckleberry bushes.

The forest floor around the area was covered with salal, and from here, Philippa and Adam had a clear view of the walkway.

Philippa nodded agreement.

"Cozy," she said. They unwrapped their dinners and tucked in enthusiastically.

Half an hour later, the food was all gone, but Althea Cray had not appeared. Philippa looked at her watch.

"It's 6:30. How very odd."

"Maybe she came early."

"We've always seen her at 6:00. Every day we've come here. You could set your watch by her. I wonder why she hasn't shown up."

"Who cares?" said Adam. "Let's go visit the otters before we go back to the Bowl."

In the zoo, they spied Andrew Bishop and Guido Cimaretti eating sandwiches and peering at the penguins. They went over to join them.

"That one looks just like you in your tux," Adam told Guido. "Look," he added, as the penguin flapped its wing at a fellow inmate. "It even conducts like you."

Guido laughed amiably, but before he could respond, the air was rent by shrill shrieks and two young girls raced down the ramp. They hurled themselves at Philippa, who lifted the smaller one up so she could get a better look at the antics of the penguins. Philippa was quite fond of her sister's children.

"Where's Grampus?" she asked them. Guido raised his eyebrows.

"A fat, huffing fish?" he asked in his lilting Italian accent.

"When you see their grandfather, you'll understand," said Adam.

Guido suddenly beamed and pointed, and Adam turned to see Bertram Beary puffing up the ramp. Behind him loped Macpuff, unleashed, and taking full advantage of his freedom to forage for popcorn and abandoned hot dog buns. A woman wearing a purple jogging suit stood beside Philippa at the railings. She sniffed disapprovingly.

"I thought dogs weren't allowed in the zoo," she said pointedly.

Philippa pretended she had not heard. Her father joined them and booted MacPuff into a sitting position.

"Have you listened to the news yet today?" he asked Philippa.

"No. Not at all. Did you manage to get hold of Horace Treadwell?"

MacPuff caught sight of the penguins and started to bark hysterically. The woman beside Philippa glowered at Beary for a moment. Then a startled look of recognition came over her face.

"Yes, I did," said Beary, ignoring the woman hovering at his elbow. "I found out quite a lot, but I'd really like to know what prompted your inquiry."

"Why are you suddenly interested?" Philippa asked. "What's happened?"

MacPuff's barks turned into agonized howls.

"Excuse me," interrupted the woman in purple. "Aren't you Bertram Beary, the city councillor?"

"No," said Beary.

He turned back to Philippa. "Althea Cray committed suicide last night," he said. "She jumped from the balcony of her West End penthouse."

∗   ∗   ∗   ∗

A half-hour later, with Beary ensconced at his post and dutifully tearing tickets as early-comers filtered into the enclosure, Philippa explained why she was troubled.

"It wasn't the smile of a woman about to kill herself," she said. "It was triumphant. That's the only way I can describe it. There's a story behind that smile."

Beary glanced toward MacPuff, who had been consigned to the care of Jennifer and Laura. The girls were taking turns issuing programs and marching the dog back and forth on his leash, which was a token gesture toward control, given that MacPuff was a Siberian husky and much stronger than either one of them. MacPuff appeared to be behaving, so Beary turned back to Philippa.

"I believe you," he said, "but the interpretation of the smile could be many things."

"Are you sure Althea Cray was happy with her husband? Could her elaborate mourning have been a sham?"

"Not according to Treadwell. He says she was devastated when her husband died."

"Was George Cray a good husband?"

"Passable. He upset her at times with his cutthroat business practices, but he was fundamentally loyal to her. There was no danger of him dumping her for a newer model or any nonsense like that."

"My dears, are you talking about the Crays?" Andrew Bishop hopped over the rope partition and joined Philippa and Beary.

"Yes," said Philippa. "Why? Did you know them?"

"Darling, Guido and I live in the same building. Several floors down, of course. My God, she could have sailed right past our window."

Philippa felt a surge of excitement.

"So you did know the Crays."

"Not personally…no. But Mrs. Cray always presented the Alice B. Warden scholarship at the TUTS awards night. Warden was her mother-in-law's maiden name. Big dollars in that family. You must have seen Cray there…all jewels and hairspray and the most divine gowns."

"No, actually I haven't. I've never been to the awards night. This is my first time in a TUTS show."

"Oh, you must come," insisted Andrew. "It's such fun. Besides, you might win something this year. Of course, you won't get to see Anthea Cray all tarted up. Isn't it awful what happened? They say she was absolutely glued to the pavement…blood all over what must have been the most exquisite blue lace nightie. And you know what else they say?"

"No," said Beary. "We obviously don't have our ears to the right bit of *terra firma*. What do they say?"

Andrew leaned toward them with a conspiratorial smile.

"They say her ghost is already haunting the West End!"

*   *   *   *

"Bilge and rot," said Beary, after Andrew had gone through the stage door. "He hasn't picked up that much gossip about the Crays, even if he does inhabit the same apartment block. Treadwell was much more informative."

"Go on then. What else did you learn about the Crays?"

"The biggest bone of contention between them," continued Beary, "was that Cray didn't want children. He liked to be number one and he wanted Mrs. Cray to be free to go everywhere with him. Treadwell says she kept hoping he'd change his mind, but then she developed some internal problem…or so his wife says…and after that, she couldn't have children, so the issue became irrelevant."

"She must have resented him for that," said Philippa.

Beary frowned.

"Perhaps, but you can't escape from the basic facts. Treadwell insists that Mrs. Cray loved her husband. Actually, the child issue resolved itself in an interesting way. Mrs. Cray's twin sister had a baby late in life, and she and the child moved from Toronto and came to live with the Crays about six months ago. That's the *ghost* your leading man was twittering on about."

"A twin sister! That's an interesting twist. Why did she come to live with them?"

"She'd just been through a traumatic divorce. The baby is a little over a year old, and there's an ongoing and difficult custody suit. Mrs. Cray was very happy to have her sister and the baby there. The sister doesn't have much money, and the Crays were willing to help her out as long as she needed assistance, forever by the sound of it. According to Treadwell, the sister—her name is Martha Trimble—was prepared to stay on indefinitely. Then three months after she joined the family, George Cray had his heart attack. There's no question of foul play. He'd been hustling real estate projects back east for a couple of years, and his health had been worn down by overwork and anxiety. Mrs. Cray and her sister were both deeply shocked and grieved. Now, if you can tell me how you can fit a 'wicked smile of triumph' and a murder into that scenario, you're a better man than I am, Gunga Din. Sorry, ma'am," Beary added to two ladies entering the enclosure. "You can't come through until you buy your tickets."

"That's Ado Annie and Aunt Eller," said Philippa, looking up and recognizing the pair.

Beary winked at the fluffy blonde who giggled back at him as she wriggled by; then he grandly kissed the hand of the stately lady who followed her through.

"Of course they are," he said grandly. "How could I fail to recognize such charming ladies? Lovely performances, both of you."

He ushered them through and escorted them to the stage door. Then he hurried back to retrieve MacPuff who had broken away from Laura and was growling at a large black horse with a policeman on its back.

"Come to borrow a cowboy hat, officer?" asked Beary.

The young policeman smiled.

"No, Councillor," he said, "just visiting with your attractive daughter."

"Officer Leach knows Richard," Philippa explained. Philippa's brother, Richard, was a detective inspector.

"Aha," said Beary, "you had a nasty shindig on your beat last night, I hear. Over at Beach Towers."

"The Cray suicide. Yes. A bad business. I wasn't on duty, but I heard about it when I came in today."

"It was definitely suicide?" Philippa asked curiously.

"Yes. Cray left a suicide note. Besides, the nanny witnessed the sister trying to calm her down before she jumped."

"Did she hear what they were saying? Are you sure Mrs. Cray wrote the note?" asked Philippa.

Officer Leach smiled at Beary.

"This girl does love a mystery, doesn't she?" he said. He turned back to Philippa. "We won't know anything for sure until after the inquest," he added. "You know that. Anyway, if you really want to know all about it, you should talk to your brother."

"Good idea," said Philippa. "I think I will."

"I wonder," mused Beary, "who inherits Mrs. Cray's fortune." He turned away and stared balefully at the line of people accumulating outside the enclosure.

"*Oh, the cattle are standing like statues,*" he carolled, ripping apart a lady's ticket and ushering her through. "Better go and slap on some make-up, girlie," he said to his daughter.

Philippa looked at her watch and gasped. She grabbed her bag and hastened toward the stage door.

*   *   *   *

The next day, armed with a Starbuck's triple latte and an oversized cheese bun, two of Richard's favourite indulgences, Philippa accosted her brother in his office.

"I thought you might like a coffee on your break," she said, plopping her offerings on his desk.

"You mean you want information," said Richard. However, he picked up his latte and took a long, appreciative swig.

Philippa leaned over the desk and fixed him with the look she usually reserved for erratic conductors.

"Something isn't right. Richard, you must check it out carefully."

"We are checking, but the evidence supports the sister's claim. After George Cray's death, Althea Cray wrote a new will and spent a great deal of time with lawyers to ensure it was airtight. It seems that death was on her mind."

"So who inherits?" asked Philippa.

"Her sister, Martha Trimble. Don't look like that. It's logical that she'd want her assets and business interests to go to her sister. Remember, her sister's child had become a substitute for the baby she could never have. And she and her sister were very close. She'd supported Trimble through an acrimonious divorce, and the two of them had mourned together after George Cray died."

"I know all that, but Trimble has the perfect motive. You know, something occurs to me. I keep seeing that horrible smile. Could it have been Althea Cray's sister that I saw in the park?"

"Not according to the nanny. Althea Cray took her usual walk that day and Trimble was at a doctor's appointment with the baby."

"Is the nanny reliable?"

"I think so. She's a young Philippino, but there's nothing dubious about her immigration papers. She's here legally and she has nursing qualifications. Cray hired her when Trimble came to live with them. Her English is excellent and her statement can't be ignored."

"What did she see that night?"

Richard sighed and abandoned the pile of papers on his desk. He took another sip of coffee; then gave Philippa the information she was seeking.

"She was with the child in the back bedroom. Cray and Trimble were in the living room. The nanny had just got the child settled when she became aware of sobbing in the other room. The crying became louder and more hysterical; then she heard Althea Cray shouting that she was going to kill herself. She rushed out and saw her employer going berserk. Cray kept crying that she couldn't go on...she didn't want to live any more. Martha Trimble was trying to calm her down. Then Althea Cray saw the nanny watching them and she turned and screamed at her."

"What did she say?"

"She told her to go back...to look after the baby. Martha Trimble repeated the order...a lot more calmly of course. She said she could manage, and for the nanny to make sure the child didn't become upset."

"Then what?"

"Althea Cray pulled away from her sister and ran out to the roof garden. Trimble followed. The nanny waited. She was unsure what to do. She said the voices outside became quieter. She could still hear Cray, but she was whimpering. She kept repeating that she was cold. Trimble was comforting her. The nanny decided the situation was under control and she started to go back to the child's room, but then the sobbing became louder again and the voice started to get shrill. Suddenly Cray shouted, 'No! I can't go on. I can't bear it any more.' She heard Trimble saying, 'No, don't do it. Althea, don't jump. Please...Oh my God.' Then there was a bloodcurdling scream. She rushed outside and saw Martha Trimble standing shocked and distraught by the balcony rail."

"It sounds cut and dried," Philippa acknowledged.

"It is cut and dried," Richard said firmly. "The suicide letter was on Cray's bedside table. The nanny knew her employer's handwriting. Althea Cray was determined to die."

＊   ＊   ＊   ＊

On the closing night of the show, Philippa went to the park early with the intention of walking the sea wall. Adam was at an audition, so she was alone, but she was glad of the solitude as she was trying to clear her thoughts. Philippa loved the sea wall, with its breathtaking view of the ocean and the North Shore Mountains, but today she found herself seeing little details. The picture seemed to be broken up, like a jigsaw, and the broader panorama eluded her. She stood to watch a cruise ship emerge from behind the gleaming white sails of the Trade and Convention Centre; then found her attention diverted as a red sea plane with white pontoons glinting in the sun soared overhead. Her eyes were drawn to the fuelling floats in Coal Harbour, the gantry cranes for loading and unloading shipping containers, and a yellow sulphur pyramid on the far shore. Each component of the scene seemed to leap out at her like a 3-D image, but the view itself remained a blur.

Her reverie was broken as a group of Japanese tourists, chattering loudly and clicking cameras, moved into her line of vision. Philippa's professional eye was captivated by an enchanting and vivacious creature, a veritable Madam Butterfly in spite of her T-shirt and designer sunglasses, who was holding the hand of a doll-like child, as petite and charming as her mother. The bond between the two was palpable and touching. Sopranos routinely died for love, but Butterfly's sacrifice always struck Philippa as particularly poignant.

Meditating on the inconstancies of love and the cruelty of the Pinkertons of the world, Philippa continued her walk.

As she neared Brockton Point, a red tour bus overtook her on the road. She glanced at the back of the bus as it went by. Under the rear window was a colourful advertisement for the Butchart Gardens in Victoria.

It was covered with roses.

Abandoning the sea wall, Philippa bought a hamburger from the concession stand, and headed towards the rose garden. Thoughtfully, she strolled through the arbour and looked for a suitable spot to eat her last dinner of the season, finally settling on a bench near the ivy-covered stump that had given birth to the five small cedar trees. The weather was still clear, but the evenings were starting to give off a distinctly autumnal chill, and although she had chosen a bench in the sunlight, she found herself shivering. She pulled her sweater around her shoulders; then she suddenly realized that she was sitting on the same bench where Althea Cray had stopped on her walks through the park.

Philippa stared at the cedar stump, willing her eyes to see in it whatever had fascinated the Black Widow. It had once been a magnificent, stately tree, and judging by its size, probably one of the first-growth trees when Vancouver was born. Seeing it at closer range, she realized that the gnarled effect was caused by the tree roots snaking down the outside of the stump and twisting round the clumps of ivy.

She was about to unwrap her burger when she noticed a familiar figure coming along the path. Martha Trimble's resemblance to her sister was startling, and for a moment Philippa could have sworn she was seeing the same figure that had passed through the arbour three weeks earlier. However, this lady was not alone. She was pushing a stroller, and beside her walked a young Philippino woman, who was loaded down with a blanket over one arm and a large canvas bag under the other.

Trimble paused and spoke to her companion. The young woman nodded, and as Trimble moved ahead with the stroller, she sat on a bench by the trellis and piled her belongings beside her. Philippa returned her burger to the bag and crossed to the other bench.

"It's a lovely evening, isn't it?" she said. "Getting cold though. Time to start bundling the baby up again."

The young woman acknowledged Philippa with a friendly smile.

"She's already wrapped up warm. She's a well-cared-for baby. Her mother adores her."

"Isn't that Althea Cray's sister?" asked Philippa innocently. "I used to see Mrs. Cray walking through here regularly…before the tragedy. The resemblance is amazing."

"Yes. They were identical twins."

Philippa glanced towards the arbour where Martha Trimble was gently rocking the stroller back and forth. Her appearance was identical to that of her sister, but Philippa suddenly realized that her manner was totally different. Althea Cray had moved like a figure from a Greek tragedy. Her sister was relaxed, focused on the baby, and oblivious to the surrounding gardens.

"Do you work for the family?"

"I'm the nanny. Mrs. Cray hired me when her sister moved here with the baby."

"Are you going to stay in the job?"

"I think so. Mrs. Trimble is a lot more reserved than her sister. She doesn't talk to me much, but she hasn't said anything about me leaving, so I assume she's keeping me on."

"She must be grieving for her sister. Losing a twin must be awful."

The nanny nodded. "They were very close. It was so much fun when I first got the job. They were such lively ladies. They used to wear the same hairstyles and swap clothes back and forth. And whenever her sister admired anything she bought, Mrs. Cray would go out and buy a duplicate so they could have the same outfit."

"How could you tell them apart?"

"By their wedding rings…except at night, because they took their rings off at bedtime. But then it was easy because they had different housecoats. Mr. Cray always knew which was which though. They never fooled him." The nanny sighed. "It was such a happy household until he died. Then everything changed."

"It must have been a comfort for Mrs. Cray to have her sister there after she lost her husband."

The nanny looked puzzled.

"It should have been…but Mrs. Trimble was so distressed herself. Mrs. Cray was upset that her sister didn't show more concern for her. There wasn't a very nice atmosphere."

"Mrs. Trimble must feel guilty about her sister's suicide. How sad…to quarrel like that, and then for one of them to die."

"Oh, no. They made up. It didn't last long. They were on good terms again in no time. It's just that Mrs. Cray was so dreadfully depressed about losing her husband. She did try to snap out of it. The week before she died, she bought a blue silk nightgown with lace down the front and appliqué all over the skirt. It was so beautiful. And her sister loved it. She admired it…made such a fuss of it…it was just like before…and of course, Mrs. Cray went out and bought an identical one…everyone knew she would. But she was just trying to convince herself that she was coping. Underneath, she was so unhappy."

The nanny's voice trembled and her eyes suddenly looked moist. Philippa felt guilty, but before she could utter any condolences, a sharp voice broke into the conversation.

"We're ready to go back now. I assume you're coming."

Philippa had not heard Martha Trimble return. She looked up to see her standing in front of the bench.

Trimble's face was not visible, but Philippa could sense hostility behind the veil. The nanny hastily gathered her bag and blanket and stood up to join her employer.

Philippa shivered as she watched the two of them move away down the path.

*   *   *   *

Awards night took place three weeks after closing night. The cast and crew of *Oklahoma* and *Pajama Game* assembled in the Pavilion, along with guests, councillors, commissioners, and the volunteers who had worked on the summer shows. Philippa's parents and nieces were present, though they had arrived separately as Adam had borrowed his father's Mercedes to drive Philippa to the event. Adam had shaved off his beard and was resplendent in a brand new tuxedo, bought with his earnings from a recent concert. He was looking extremely handsome, singularly unlike Jud Fry, and as Edwina commented, resembled a modern-day Howard Keel—high praise indeed from the Beary matriarch, who was often heard to complain that they never made films like *Lovely To Look At* any more.

As the Pavilion became noisier and more crowded, Edwina lost Beary to the bar and Ado Annie, but she barely noticed his defection as she was watching their grandchildren. Laura and Jennifer were toying with the fruit punch they had been served and eyeing the pop machines in the hall. Only the gimlet eye of their grandmother prevented them from making a foray in that direction. Philippa watched with amusement as her father detached himself from Ado Annie, directed Edwina to a photographic display in the foyer, and slipped some change for the pop machines to Laura and Jennifer. He saw Philippa watching him and lumbered over to join her. He lowered his large form into the chair opposite hers.

"You're going to see the duplicate Black Widow tonight," he announced. "She's presenting the Warden scholarship. The board decided it would be appropriate to ask her."

"Did they indeed?" said Philippa, her attention caught immediately. "Do you think you could introduce me, Dad?"

Adam returned from the bar with a glass of wine for Philippa. He sat beside her and plopped his own drink on the table.

"Don't you dare," he ordered Beary. "This is a cast party. We're supposed to be having fun. You should be out there dancing, not encouraging your daughter to play detective."

Beary looked incredulous.

"You're not serious," he said, looking at the dance floor where the cast members had formed a line and were performing a series of synchronized acrobatic convulsions that suggested they had been rehearsing for months. "What are they doing?" he added, genuinely curious. "Fine-tuning the numbers for next summer's musical?"

"They're just improvising, Dad," said Philippa. "Having fun. Anyone can join in."

"Not me," Beary said firmly. "Or your mother," he added.

"Don't worry," said Adam. "The band will take pity on the civilians later on. They'll play some ballroom-dance numbers after the ceremonies. Now let's stop talking about the Crays and concentrate on having a good time."

Andrew Bishop materialized at Philippa's elbow.

"Did you say Cray?" he cooed. "I bet you haven't heard the latest. She had a twin sister," he announced breathlessly. "It wasn't a ghost. It was a look-alike."

"No!" said Beary.

Philippa gave her father a warning glare.

"We did hear that, Andrew," she said. "The sister's name was Martha Trimble."

"I know," said Andrew. "She was engaged to George Cray before he married Althea, and the buzz is that Martha's marriage broke up because she was still in love with George Cray."

Philippa's jaw dropped.

"How on earth did you know that?" she asked.

"Althea's hair stylist just started working at Clippers," said Andrew. "That's where I go," he added, patting his chiselled curls. "According to Gerard, Martha always resented her sister taking Cray away from her, and later, when he was in Ottawa on business, she had an affair with him."

"Good Lord," said Beary. "Did her sister know?"

"Not at the time. But Gerard says after George's death, Althea became suspicious because her sister was in such a state, and finally Martha admitted the affair."

"Andrew, you're brilliant," said Philippa.

"That's an about-face," grunted Adam.

"Oh, that's not all," said Andrew, relishing being the center of attention. "The really juicy bit is what came out later. Rumour has it that Martha's baby was George Cray's child and that's why Althea killed herself. She'd been used and betrayed by the two people she loved most. It's positively Shakespearean, isn't it?"

Andrew sailed off in the direction of the bar, and Beary and Philippa shook their heads in disbelief.

"What do you know?" said Beary finally. "The bloody hairdresser knew more than any of us. This rather changes the dimension of things. I wonder if Trimble ever forgave her sister for stealing her fiancé from her."

"I doubt it," said Philippa. "And once Althea Cray discovered the affair, she would have ceased to trust her sister. I would say from that moment on, the relationship between them ceased to be a loving one. Althea Cray may have put on a big show of conciliation, but underneath, both of them must have known things would never be the same again."

"Yes," nodded Beary. "Trimble would have known she wasn't going to have a free ride any more."

Adam, now as intrigued as the rest of them, leaned forward and joined the discussion.

"I wonder if she decided to get rid of her sister before she could change her will," he chimed in. "If that's the case, Philippa was right. It *was* murder…murder for gain."

Philippa did not respond. She was lost in thought. The noise of the party faded, and in her mind's eye, superimposed on the whirling dancers in the pavilion, the image of Althea Cray materialized—the Black Widow, immobile as a statue, in the midst of the rose gardens, staring at the twisted roots of the nurse stump.

"Good Lord," she said suddenly. "That's exactly what it was."

"Speak of the devil," hissed Adam. "There she is."

He nodded towards the foyer where Martha Trimble had just arrived. She was resplendent in a black gown that sparkled with sequins from neck to hem, and she was escorted by the Chairman of the Parks Commission who bowed and smiled with all the obsequiousness her millions demanded.

"Excuse me," said Philippa, and got to her feet. She hurried towards the entrance hall, where Martha Trimble was admiring the photographic display while her escort delivered her full-length mink coat to the hatcheck girl. Trimble's back was turned.

Philippa paused in the doorway and steeled herself, fully aware that the next few seconds could result in her being placed on a permanent theatrical blacklist. Then she cried out sharply.

"Mrs. Cray! Watch out! Behind you."

The Chairman of the Parks Commission watched in amazement as the woman he knew as Martha Trimble whirled round, then froze rooted to the spot as the alarm on her face slowly altered to a look of icy rage.

*   *   *   *

"Why didn't she bluff it out?" Adam asked Philippa much later as he whirled her around the dance floor. In addition to his singing talents, Adam prided himself on his prowess at ballroom dancing. One never knew, as he was fond of saying, when one would get a crack at the lead in *Die Fledermaus.*

"Because the police reminded her they could prove identity since her sister had borne a child and she had not. Once they pointed that out, she broke down and confessed."

"So Althea Cray murdered her sister? But why?"

"Don't you see?" Philippa explained. "She was all twisted up inside. To be denied a child all those years, and then to find, not only had her husband cheated on her with her own sister, but the baby she had been denied had been borne by Martha Trimble."

"I should say she decided to kill her sister then and there," wheezed Beary, as he steered Edwina past their portside in a stately foxtrot. "All those hours in the rose garden must have been spent working out how she would do it. She had to ensure that when she assumed the identity of Martha Trimble, she would hold onto her fortune and properties, and that she wouldn't be accused of murdering her sister for money. Sorry, dear," he added to Edwina.

"If you're determined to talk about this wretched murder," snapped Edwina, rubbing her ankle, "do it off the dance floor."

"How did she pull off the fake suicide?" Adam asked as they returned to their table.

"It was quite clever, actually," said Philippa. "On the night of the murder, Althea Cray and her sister were wearing duplicate nightgowns, although Trimble had a robe over hers. They always took off their rings, so the robe was the only way the nanny could tell them apart. When the nanny was in the child's room, Cray began to create a scene. Once the nanny came out and had registered what was happening, Cray ordered her to leave. Then she ran out to the roof garden, knowing that Trimble would follow. The nanny could hear them on the terrace. Cray's voice became calmer, the crying became softer…but she heard her keep repeating how cold she was…"

"I get it," said Adam. "Trimble would have given her the robe."

"Exactly," Beary interjected. "Then once Cray put it on, she resumed the hysterics and rushed to the edge of the roof. Trimble followed thinking she was holding her sister back from going over the railing, then at the last split second,

Cray grabbed her and pushed her over. Trimble would have been caught completely off-guard."

"And," Philippa concluded, "when the nanny rushed onto the terrace, she saw a woman in Martha Trimble's robe standing shocked and distraught by the balcony rail."

Adam looked appalled.

"What a devilishly wicked plan."

"So you see," said Philippa, "the smile I saw *was* a smile of triumph."

"Yes," said Beary. "The triumph of a woman about to commit the perfect murder."

Adam suddenly became galvanized again.

"Hey. Just a minute. If she wanted revenge on her sister, why pick such a complicated scheme? I realize the sister was a less likely candidate for suicide than Althea Cray, but it wouldn't have been hard to stage an accident. And another thing. You said it was murder for gain. How can that be when Cray had all the assets?"

"Come on, young Adam," boomed Beary. "Think."

Adam paused and reflected a moment. Beary watched him, sipping his Scotch and nodding encouragement.

"Remember the one thing Trimble had that Cray wanted," prodded Philippa.

"The child, of course," said Adam.

"Exactly," said Beary, downing his Scotch.

The band struck up a tango. Beary lumbered to his feet and gave Edwina a hearty whack on the back. "Come on, old other-half," he said, pulling her to her feet. "This takes two."

As Beary steered Edwina back onto the dance floor, Adam turned to Philippa. "But how would that..."

"Think whose baby it was," she prompted him. "Come on, why don't we try this one."

"You don't have to tango in *Die Fledermaus*," said Adam stubbornly, "and you still haven't answered my question."

"That's all right, I'll teach you. Now go on...who were the baby's parents?"

"We've already gone through that. Martha Trimble and George Cray."

"Not in the eyes of the law."

Suddenly the light dawned. Adam produced his own smile of triumph.

"Of course," he cried. "The custody suit!"

"You've got it," said Beary, manoeuvring Edwina toward them with the grace of a Dreadnaught under full power. "An aunt would have no claim when there was a legal father."

Philippa and Adam performed a neat chassé and allowed them to pass. Like twin pilot boats, Laura and Jennifer giggled past and danced off in the wake of their grandparents. Philippa looked after them fondly.

"Yes," she said. "That was the motive. Althea Cray wanted the child."

978-0-595-34409-3
0-595-34409-7

Printed in the United States
33462LVS00006B/1-78